A TASTE FOR INTENSITY

DOMINIQUE PERREGAUX

A TASTE FOR INTENSITY

Bronco

PUBLISHING

NEW YORK

2013

Published by Bronco Publishing, New York, New York.

www.broncopublishing.com

Bronco Publishing and the colophon are registered trademarks of Hellweg & Prinz AG.

Book design by Creative Spring Ltd.

Library of Congress Control Number: 2012936564

ISBN 978-0-9852634-1-6

Manufactured in the United States of America

First Edition

A TASTE FOR INTENSITY

PRELUDE

But I must tell you the story; shall you turn it into a book which no one will believe, though it may be interesting to write.

Alexandre Dumas fils, *The Lady of the Camellias*

Friday, December 12, 7:47 am: I am resting comfortably in a leather chair in the office of my contemporary art gallery in Central Hong Kong. My white leather shoes are casually balanced on the corner of a designer aluminum desk, beside piles of papers, open art books, and magazines. I am wearing my black cashmere coat, as I am trying to keep warm, the temperature having lately dropped unexpectedly. My mind drifts from memories, to ideas, and to unrelated thoughts that will nourish and shape the novel that I am about to write. The blank page on the screen of my laptop has been waiting for me to begin my work at the keyboard for quite some time.

Half awake, tired from a late-night party with my newlywed friends Laure and Neil, I am mechanically sipping hot coffee with a splash of Baileys to try to rouse myself when I rotate slightly on my chair and catch sight, through the large double windows, of two Nepalese cleaners in rough blue overalls scrubbing the deserted pedestrian street. These other human presences with their frantic, yet coordinated movements bring me slightly out of my lethargy.

Suddenly a young couple enters my vision as well. They are climbing the street steps hand in hand, avoiding the hose soaking the stairs, and they giggle as they hop. I wonder, now almost completely focused, how they live their relationship, how it all started, and of what their common reality is made. Observing them reaching the top of the street and stopping at the corner with Hollywood Road, kissing each other with a passionate embrace, provokes profound emotions to resurface. A cold shiver runs through my entire body. Taking a deep breath to lighten my heart, I calmly let reminiscences and sensations unravel through my mind. A familiar train of thought rapidly prevails over other random considerations. I can feel the inspiration for my book slowly emerging from the innermost depths of my healing soul.

I HAVE ALWAYS BEEN fascinated by observing how people can live in the same world, be a part of the same community, belong to the same generation, have seemingly similar cultural values, and yet, unwillingly or consciously, drift apart from one another's sense of reality. When such a situation occurs between two romantically involved people, the reality drift can have traumatic emotional consequences.

During the observation of such disconnections, I am always curious about the things that triggered them, and I am impressed by the resilient way some people survive the subsequent distress. I am, indeed, always touched and moved by the ability that some people have to overcome traumatic events, and even to create marvelous things out of them. French neuropsychologist Boris Cyrulnik wrote, "Only one event can provoke death, a little is needed. But when we come back to life, when we are born a second time and that the hidden area of memories emerges, the fatal event becomes holy as it personifies the instance of the metamorphosis, the magic wand, that shows us that there was a before and there will be an after." Finding our own resilient response after being deeply wounded by the actions of another is fundamental to becoming the heroes of our own lives. When we return to the living, our story becomes a myth that we can share with others.

I was forced to search for such resources within myself a year and a half ago, when I became one of the main characters in a traumatic sentimental story that saw me, because of the actions of a woman of whom I thought the world, nearly capsize into eternal insanity. Thankfully, this did not quite happen, and I can contemplate these dramatic events serenely now, although with some remaining regrets and disappointments. I can still clearly remember the differing ways in which this woman and I coped with our emotional turmoil, and how we finally integrated our different perceptions into our respective and now separate realities.

The capacity of resilience not only allows one to recover one's reason, but, most interestingly, also provokes sublimation. It provides a way out of distress that is utterly gratifying, thus giving positive symbolism to the trauma. After a year of endless mind dwelling, I finally came to understand that my salvation would take the form of the novel you have just begun.

Waiting for my staff to arrive, as they will in about an hour, I am enjoying this time by myself in the gallery. Surrounded by paintings and books, I nostalgically touch my healed right ear—another former source of much distress—and reflect on the intense story that led, slightly more than a year ago, to a dual drift from reality. Vivid, sentimental memories are like scars paving life's journey, upon which we can reflect and through which we can grow. Indeed, I sometimes like to remember the episodes they evoke, as they became part of the constitution of the man I am today.

Finally moving my fingers over the keyboard and feeling the stimulating inspiration now boiling through the pathways of my brain, I would like to share with you this adventure and thus make you a witness—and perhaps even an accomplice—to my preference for disorder above injustice.

FOUNDATIONAL ACTS

This time could be what
We've both been searching for
Our whole lives waking up
And coming back for more

New Order, "Jetstream"

The Central and Mid-Levels districts of Hong Kong Island, where many expatriates live, are geographically confined. As people meet frequently at private parties, bars, and restaurants, the potential to meet someone again by chance is high, as groups intersect a great deal in this summer camp for adults. The story I am about to relate started in September, three and a half years ago, during one of these frequent outings, at the birthday party of an acquaintance, David Van P., a journalist and editor for a weekly local publication, at the 1/5 Bar on Star Street.

WHEN I ARRIVED AT the party around 11pm, the resident DJ was loudly playing Bomfunk MC's' "Freestyler", and I instantly felt energized. At first, I did not take much notice of the woman standing next to the entrance, as the place was dark, densely packed, and smoky. I remember thinking to myself "she must be German" while passing beside her, as she had a kind of ageless European look. She had uncombed blonde hair, curled mid-length, and was wearing a white blouse tucked into a pair of blue jeans. Yet that was it, and I did not think anything more about her, as I believe I did not even see her face at that time, maybe just her profile.

Much later, well past midnight, I was talking to Milos, a middle-aged man living across from my gallery, when the *German* woman, who I had not seen since my first furtive impression of her, slowly approached from the other side of the bar. A tanned and bleached blonde girlfriend accompanied her. She seemed determined and, throwing sparks, looked straight into my eyes. When she reached us, she slid her hand over my arm without hesitation, touching my soft brown leather jacket and stroking its right sleeve sensually and provocatively.

The incendiary woman then slowly walked away, still staring fiercely at me. I quickly put an end to my conversation and, recovering from the shock of her bluntness, I ran after her.

I searched frantically in every dark corner of the bar and then rushed outside for a last chance to catch her before she left for good. Alexandre Dumas fils' words echoed my quest, "The memory of this vision—for, truly, a vision she was—did not fade from my mind like many others I had already seen, and I searched everywhere for this woman in white, so regal in her beauty." Alas, like Cinderella, she was already gone, yet she hadn't left a glass slipper by which to trace her. I cannot remember precisely what I thought then, standing in the blue darkness feeling the dampness of a light rain, as I was by then a bit tipsy, but I already sensed, despite the brief nature of this encounter, that this woman represented something special and that we would meet again. Whether her inviting gesture had been driven by a genuine interest in me or by the voluptuousness of too much alcohol, that night our destinies irrevocably converged.

ABOUT A WEEK AFTER this late night apparition, I was invited to a party at the Kee Club on Wellington Street. The Kee is a private club, with a distinctive and posh atmosphere, daringly mixing Tibetan religious artifacts, European royal symbols, and vintage designer furniture. I was exceedingly familiar with this place, as, aside from being a member myself, I sometimes organized VIP events there for the international artists I represented, in conjunction with their exhibition openings at my gallery.

That evening I wore the same soft brown leather jacket I had worn at David's birthday and was talking with Christian, the Austrian owner of the club, when, to my utter and delighted surprise, the 1/5 Bar incendiary woman reappeared. Unfazed, she walked around the black grand piano and stopped just a few meters away from me. At this hour of the evening, the club was dark, yet still somewhat lighter than 1/5, so I could see her much more clearly than I had seen her the other night. She was tall and slender, and the features of her face were strong yet refined. They were enhanced by a delicate and mischievous nose, illuminated by alert and attentive blue eyes, and completed by an affirmative, yet delicate carriage that promised a strong personality. She looked like a dream morphing between Tea Leoni, Naomi Watts, and Penelope Ann Miller. There was not a moment to lose this time, and, quickly reconnecting with last week's memories and fearing that she might evaporate again without warning, I looked straight into her eyes and, smiling impishly said, "Hi again. What a surprise!"

She smiled back at me and replied instantly, "Hi. Why is it a surprise?"

"Because you disappeared the other night at 1/5. I wanted to thank you for your gesture but you were already gone."

"What gesture? What do you mean? I'm sorry, but I still don't understand."

"You were at David Van P.'s birthday party last week at 1/5, weren't you?"

"Yes I was..." She seemed intrigued.

"You don't remember that you felt the sleeve of my leather jacket?" I demonstrated how she had done it.

"No. I actually don't remember doing that, no ..."

I was surprised that she didn't recall her foundational act, as I would call it much later. Had she remembered it, she might have been slightly embarrassed—perhaps she wasn't usually daring enough to approach men in that way, or at all. Maybe she had been even shamelessly drunk then. After talking for a while and despite her continued insistence that she could not remember our previous meeting, she nevertheless gave me her business card and I discovered her name for the first time—Elizabeth Bennet. She was an award-winning American financial analyst in her late thirties working for an independent Wall Street firm, and she was also a published author.

I looked at her card attentively, then back at her, and said,

"Well, Elizabeth, it's very nice to meet you. I am Hector." Smiling, I handed her my business card, the Asian way, with two hands.

THE TWO YEARS PRECEDING this first encounter with Elizabeth had been especially tough in my life. I had moved to Hong Kong when I was thirty-two without knowing many people in this city and I had opened a contemporary art gallery at a time when I was almost broke. Up until a few weeks before I moved to Asia from Switzerland, being an ex-stockbroker, I was still heavily trading for my own account on the international equity and commodity markets, using high leverages. I was making large sums of money in a short period of time, but also sometimes losing as much, and more, in the blink of an eye. It was obvious that I was actually using this gambling flaw to hurt myself—it can be difficult to get rid of self-inflicted masochism—and it worked.

So with moving to a city in which I was a complete stranger and opening a gallery to promote well-known international contemporary artists at a time when people were buying almost exclusively Vietnamese and Chinese art for purely decorative purposes; setting up a new business from scratch and without any prior knowledge, except for a genuine love and understanding of art; and being almost broke, I was at my limits, emotionally. All of these things were too new and overwhelming for me to even consider starting a serious emotional relationship, even two years after settling down in Hong Kong. Thus, despite the immediate attraction I felt for Elizabeth, I preferred to wait for the right time, taking the foolish risk of potentially never starting anything romantic with her at all, rather than pursue her knowing full well that just then I would be unable—either mentally or financially—to sustain a steady relationship. I therefore kept her precious card, and resigned and frustrated, decided to wait.

At that time, I was in fact occasionally and casually seeing a Chinese architect and interior designer. Olivia was tall and athletic with a sensual, curvy, and extremely reactive body. It was a friendship with carnal benefits, and nothing more. On a Sunday afternoon, a little less than one month after the Kee Club encounter, following a healthy brunch on the rooftop of the Life Café in Soho, I was walking with Olivia on Queen's Road Central when, to my surprise, I ran into Elizabeth, who was shopping with a young boy. When mentioning this timely encounter to a mutual friend later and expressing my surprise at seeing her with a child, I learned that she had just gone through a painful divorce and that the boy was her six-year-old son Alexander.

We looked at each other, smiled, happily surprised, and simply exchanged some polite and appropriate greetings. As I was with Olivia, I couldn't take this opportunity to chat with Elizabeth. Meeting each other by chance this way yet unable to develop any kind of relationship was the destiny that awaited us for the next two years. Our paths crossed regularly, yet we never managed to say more than a few words to each other. She told me much later that she did not understand why I hadn't contacted her sooner, especially since she admitted that she too felt a strong attraction each time we met. I was simply not ready; I could not go up to her then and say, "You know, Elizabeth, I am attracted to you, even though we don't know each other, but I am simply not ready to develop a serious relationship yet. And with a woman like you, that is the only kind of relationship I want to have."

It would have been too awkward, and anyway, would not have led to anything significant. Therefore, each time I had the delicious yet frustrating pleasure of seeing this woman, I would always greet her with a mix of resignation and sympathy.

THE CASUAL RELATIONSHIP WITH Olivia gently faded and

about six months later, I met Su-yeon at the opening of Fludi, a new club in Central. She was an alluring, smart, and bubbly Korean woman, working as a hedge fund manager for a Swiss financial company. She gave me her phone number before leaving the party and, a few days later, I called her. Following some long-awaited professional successes, my mind was finally free, and I took this opportunity to see if I was ready to develop a steady relationship. After several weeks of courting, we left together in May for Seoul to visit the Korean International Art Fair and join Andy Wauman, a promising Belgian artist I represented, whose solo show was opening at the Sook Mi Art Center. Andy had made a strong impression several months before when my gallery hosted his new series of unique black-and-white paintings on canvas sporting abstract shapes and cryptic phrases like "Robbed from Free Foreigner," "No go Body," or "Nothing Saved for the Next Pitch." His coded work, which criticizes our passive acceptance of self-imposed standardized lives, while also questioning our perception of reality, had been met with praise from collectors, especially bankers and lawyers, who understood the masochistic irony of owning such anti-system pieces.

It was during the first day of this trip, after a fun night at J.J. Mahoney's, that, back in our hotel room, Su-yeon and I sensually sealed our relationship. As I was at that time living spartanly on the first floor of my gallery, she invited me, after the trip, to move into her bright and spacious apartment in Pok Fu Lam, overlooking the South China Sea. We quickly developed our relationship into that of a classic couple: meeting at home after work, cooking for each other, and talking about our respective days while sipping wine on the balcony. Sex was good at first, as Su-yeon was spontaneous and playful. Yet for some reason, these sensual times eventually became unfulfilling. Furthermore, her overly maternal attitude and her subconscious attempt to meld our two individualities into one put me under too much pressure. I grew distant and she felt hurt, not understanding what had gone wrong. I was equally incapable then of fully comprehending why I was losing interest.

It was in this state of mind, and at this stage in our relationship, that I held an exhibition preview at the Kee Club for the Japanese cult anime artist Yoshitaka Amano in September of that year. Su-yeon looked stunning in black satin pants, a bolero jacket, and a black leather cap that set off her dazzling eyes. The party was a monumental success, with more than two hundred people in attendance. Most of the guests ended up lining up, in a queue that stretched across the different rooms of the club, to get a personalized sketch from the *Sensei*.

I had also organized an after-party dinner at the restaurant on the first floor. By 9:15pm, the collectors I had invited were already sitting around the artist, chatting, drinking Champagne, and ready to order.

I was still on the ground floor, saying goodbye to some friends and collecting business cards dropped in the lucky draw box. I was quite chic that evening, wearing a new tailor-made black-on-black pinstriped suit with an open-necked white shirt and a red handkerchief tucked into the jacket pocket. As I walked toward the stairs to join the dinner party, I felt an electrifying presence moving toward me from the back of the lobby. I turned around to see who was so intensely stimulating my instinct and saw Elizabeth gracefully emerging from the shadows. Instantly attracted, our eyes met, and I felt an intense longing mixed with deep regret; I was finally ready to get to know her better, perhaps even ask her for a date, yet I was still with Su-yeon. Even though our relationship was already nearly done, I was not willing to start a new one before the finality of our situation was totally clear, out of respect for and honesty to both women. I knew that night, though, that this American woman had taken my emotions hostage and that they had gone quite willingly. Indeed, what I felt that evening was so powerful that I could not ignore that we had a strong and unique attraction. I was eager to test this overwhelming impression. From then on, the divine vision of Elizabeth breaking through the darkness of the Kee Club relentlessly haunted my nights. My heart could not forget the magnitude of the suppressed emotions I felt that evening.

My relationship with Su-yeon ended before Christmas though we remained dear friends. At the same time, the gallery was becoming more and more successful. I was feeling more comfortable, which professionally translated the following year into a much-improved exhibition program. Established or upcoming international artists such as AES+F, Stephan Balkenhol, Dale Frank, Yuichi Sugai, and Troels Wörsel were joining the ranks of the renowned artists I already represented. I was gaining international credibility and I had a midterm vision instead of a month-to-month one for the first time since coming to Hong Kong. This recovered sense of confidence was also because international private collectors had started to give me significant mandates to source modern artworks for them. I therefore finally had the means to move this project, and thus my life, forward. Yet despite these achievements, I did not contact Elizabeth, as I could not find any context in which I could easily link all of our past chance encounters.

BY THE FOLLOWING SEPTEMBER, I realized that the episodic discomfort I had been experiencing for some time in my right ear—itching, pressure, hearing problems—was persisting and had become quite annoying and disconcerting. After consulting an ear, nose, and throat specialist at the Matilda Hospital, I was referred to the best neurosurgeon in Hong Kong, Doctor Stephen Liu and quickly made an appointment with him.

The waiting room of his practice on the ninth floor of Hutchison House, between Central and Admiralty, was simple and cozy. On the left side of the entrance was a glassed reception area where two nurses were prettily giggling, and on the other side stood a small green leather L-shaped sofa. An overly made up Chinese lady probably in her late sixties, incongruously wearing a classic yellow Chanel suit and a pair of pink beach sandals, was waiting there. Framed diplomas and associate professorship credentials engraved on wood or metal tablets decorated the walls. I announced myself, sat on the sofa beside the *Tai Tai* and took a lifestyle magazine from among a pile of monthlies lying on a white marble coffee table. A few minutes later Doctor Liu appeared and showed me into the examination room.

After looking into my right ear with his surgical microscope and running several tests, the diagnosis came as a total surprise and shock. It seemed that I had borne the pain and the hearing nuisance for too long and had visited him too late. I would have to have a CT scan and an MRI exam back at the hospital to confirm his first impression, but he feared the worst.

The extra tests done a few days later confirmed that a benign, yet still potentially deadly tumor had spread from my middle ear into my skull probably in an attempt to reach the brain. An antibiotic treatment would have to be administrated swiftly to prevent the growth from expanding further, but a last chance, high-risk surgery was probably unavoidable, as the drug therapy did not have the capacity to kill the tumor. He added that postoperative complications were also frequent and that I had three months of grace—at best—before facing the alien trying to kill me for the ultimate showdown.

Strangely, though, a few days into the understandable distress and questioning that this sudden potentially shortened lifespan provoked, a veil was lifted from my sight and I could clearly see the truth, where I was heading, what I genuinely wanted in life, and what my priorities were. After spending time putting my life in perspective, I began to think again about Elizabeth. I realized that it had been a year since the Yoshitaka Amano event at the Kee Club and that we had seen each other only a few times since then, and never in a context where I could express anything meaningful. Yet I knew I was finally ready. No further obstacles were blocking my way and Doctor Liu's dramatic news had in fact energized me. Being of a highly optimistic nature, I was convinced that I would eventually win this battle against the tumor.

ALAS, I STILL COULD not contact Elizabeth out of the blue, as I did not know her state of mind then toward me. Luckily, providence manifested itself. A friend of mine, Werner K., a Swiss financial journalist who knew Elizabeth and sometimes saw her at the Hong Kong Club told me that the American Club had invited her to talk about her new book—about the global consequences of the Chinese economic boom—two weeks later. This was the opportunity to make a move that I had been waiting for; the first tangible notes of a long-anticipated and hopefully uplifting symphony could finally be written. I was doomed, yet potentially soon to be blessed.

During these two weeks, I was also preparing, with Su-yeon—who was going to accompany me—my first trip back to Europe after a three-year absence. When I was in a relationship with her, we had planned to go on such a trip but I eventually had to abandon the idea, as my financial situation did not permit it. I was now in a much better position, and as she had been initially very much looking forward to this trip, we planned together a two-week platonic journey that was going to bring us to London, Paris, Rome, Florence, and Venice.

THE DAY OF ELIZABETH'S conference I was like a child on Christmas night, gaping in front of the shimmering presents below the fragrant tree. I was feverish with excitement, as this day could potentially become a cornerstone in a future relationship. Our past zigzags were like stardust sprinkled on each other's lives, but too discrete, volatile, and impalpable yet to be of any true significance. We had no real past together, only a feeling of joint attraction and, therefore, hopefully a joint future. It was a lunch presentation and I arrived a few minutes early at Exchange Square, where I took the elevator to the forty-ninth floor. I was dressed in my *Miami Vice* summer style, a pink-and-white pinstriped open-necked shirt, gray pants with sheen, and white loafers. I was trying to locate my name on the table plan at the reception desk when Elizabeth walked past a few meters from me; I turned my head and my heart started to drum Ravel's *Bolero*. This woman already had an incredible and almost hypnotic effect on me! Bringing my attention back to the plan, I realized that I had been lucky enough to be placed at the best table, right in front of the podium, only a few meters from where the speech would be delivered. I was going to be strategically seated to listen attentively and to occasionally meet her eyes.

I walked toward the corner where Werner K. was conversing with Devorah—Elizabeth's best friend in Hong Kong—and her husband, Lazlo. I knew them both a little, as they had come to some of my exhibition openings, and we exchanged a few words. They were both surprised to see me there, as they had never put me in the same picture with Elizabeth. This made sense, as at that time we never truly had been. Devorah commented that I looked good and different. Not knowing what she meant, but nevertheless flattered, I nodded and savored the fulfilling feeling of being in a place where a potentially crucial act would be played out. The fifty-seven guests and the organizers were like extras in a movie in which the two main protagonists were ready to move onto the set and to play roles that only they could understand. How exciting!

We sat at our designated tables and at once were served some California white wine and the entrée. On the podium, Elizabeth was sitting behind a long table covered with a dark green felt cloth on which the acronym of the club appeared in gold. Next to her were Werner K. and an American journalist who looked ridiculously proud in an ill-fitting black jacket. The latter was in charge of introducing the speaker and did it in the most vulgar, rude, and sexist way possible, calling the thirty-eight-year-old Elizabeth an "Oklahoma girl" and ending his introduction by reading from her book an imaginary signature referring to a fictional night they had spent together. I was stunned that nobody reacted or objected to his uncouth manner.

After the introduction, Elizabeth stood up and moved behind the stand. Majestic in her pose yet looking slightly tense, she was wearing a plain dark gray suit with a satin burgundy blouse, and her wavy blonde hair was slightly ruffled, as usual. She did not seem to be overly comfortable, despite being a regular speaker at international seminars and conferences. It was then that I thought for the first time that she might have been in a pattern of seeking recognition for most of her adult life. Her success as a renowned financial analyst and praised author and the solicitation for public speeches were probably ways for Elizabeth to sublimate herself and prove to the world that she was actually worth something. Being a stunning beauty, she seemed to try most of the time to hide her magnificence under plain haircuts and strict clothes, reinforcing the feeling that some sort of trauma must have affected her self-esteem and that she was probably conducting an ongoing battle against this lowered self-confidence. From this suspected childhood flaw, she had bravely succeeded in amassing the strength and resources to become successful professionally and, once upon a time, even to create a balanced and happy family. Being quite intuitive and having always been interested in psychology (and having myself undergone psychoanalysis), I have the habit of analyzing the people who I meet. Yet not knowing anything about her background at that time, I admit that I may have been totally wrong about my perception of Elizabeth and that coming from

America's Midwest could be unusual and exotic enough to confuse my European judgment and nineteenth-century romantic references. Her unassuming stance and austere clothing were after all maybe only the signs of her Oklahoma origins and not the traces of a personal trauma.

DURING HER TALK, SHE looked straight at me from time to time, as if she were seeking in my approving nods some reassurance or appeasement. As the speech went on, I held her book tightly in my hand. It was full of annotations and had dog-eared pages. I had read it thoroughly, as the economist that I once was found genuine interest in the subjects it covered. I was also preparing and rehearsing in my head the most prominent line, yet to come, of our play. Indeed, to break the status quo that had prevailed between us for so long, and thus to create a second foundational act that would hopefully lead us to our first date, I had to intervene and ask her a question, and not just sit passively in the audience.

She ended her presentation and opened the Q&A session. After some financial analysts and journalists asked a few questions, I raised my hand. My heart started to throb so intensely that I wondered if the people around me would notice the uncontrollable groundswell in my chest, under my shirt. She looked at me, waiting to hear my voice intelligibly for the first time in a few years. Only she knows what she felt then, when this known—yet unknown—man stood up. Holding the microphone tightly, I asked her if she thought China would go back into some kind of isolationism, relative or radical, as the world was unmistakably sliding into its worst economic depression ever.

My intervention was actually longer and more elaborate than that, as I wanted to show her that I had read her book. Yet some information may have been lost in translation, as she looked at me in bewilderment and could not come up with an answer. Instead, she abruptly told me that she did not understand my question. I found it quite ironic and comical that our first exchange after so long had led to incomprehension. Yet it did not matter, really, as the whole point of the question was to create a new and tangible spark that I hoped would start a fire in our respective souls.

After Elizabeth answered one last question, the lunch was over and the guests were encouraged to move to the podium to have their books signed. This was obviously the second phase of the plan, and I rushed up to the stage to then truly meet Elizabeth. I had to wait until an old French journalist had finished chatting her up clumsily (I could not possibly blame him for trying!) to exchange a few words about her book.

To be suddenly so close to her, to see her charming blue eyes, see her inviting and gentle smile, and finally have the opportunity to talk at length was such a blessing that I could hardly handle it. I tried to explain my question again, but she embarrassingly still could not seem to understand it. As many people were starting to become impatient in the line behind me, I presented her with my copy of the book for her signature. She wrote a plain, standard message first but then quickly added an almost-too-small-to-read *until later* that opened a whole horizon of hope:

Dear Hector,

I am glad my book has raised so many questions! Until later, enjoy the read.

Elizabeth

I thanked her sincerely and we agreed that we should get together soon. Proudly leaving the stage, I rushed out of the room, ran down the stairs four at a time, and reached the elevator in a state of ecstasy. It took ages to reach the ground floor. I needed to get some air quickly to relish this day and express my jubilation in the open. Reaching the ground floor, I hurried out of the elevator and ran outside. I then stopped, looked up at the sky, stretched my arms to their widest expanse, closed my fists, and let out a shout that sounded like a stag's bellow, scaring a few bankers, accountants, and lawyers who were walking by in pantomimic hurry. It was such a sweet, yet powerful victory that I spent the whole day with a smile on my face—like someone touched by Grace. This excitement would have to wait, though, before being consummated; a week later, I was leaving for Europe.

THE FOLLOWING FRIDAY I waited for Su-yeon at the Hong Kong International Airport, watching, through the large glass windows, the planes taking off and landing on this dark late September night. I was a bit nervous, as this was the first time I would be back to Europe after a long absence, and I felt somehow disconnected, not knowing if I would find my place back in the Old Continent. I had left it in such a strange spirit, washed out after losing a lot on the stock market and anxious about starting a new endeavor in a foreign place, that I somehow had the impression as I returned that Europe as a whole was still in the same tense mood. I therefore imagined that I was flying toward countries with aggressive and gloomy people and that this reminiscent trip would be a constant struggle. Yet I was keen to go back after so long to places full of memories and past symbolism, and of course to see my family again after such a long time away.

We landed a little after 6am at Heathrow Airport, and it took more than an hour by *Tube*, going through the flat and foggy suburban English scenery, to reach Knightsbridge Station, where I had booked a room at the Millennium Hotel. We checked into the same double room and decided, after having taken a regenerating shower, to go for a stroll through the city.

Su-yeon had been in London before, and even though I had also been there often, my most vivid memories of that city dated from four years earlier. At that time, I was going back and forth between the City and Canary Wharf with my friend and business partner, Valentino S., to set up the Trimalchio Capital Investment hedge fund. This venture eventually did not work out, as we could not raise enough capital to make it self-sustaining from the launch. It was in fact in Hong Kong that we had to acknowledge that the tens of millions that our Chinese investors had promised us would not arrive any time soon. The alternative for me was to go into art dealing, and the city I was in when I came to make this key decision somehow imposed itself.

We walked past Buckingham Palace and cut through St. James' Park to reach Piccadilly before finally having a late lunch at Covent Garden, taking a well-needed break from our stroll. After another day ambling at the Tate Modern, contemplating part of the Union Bank of Switzerland Art Collection, and shopping in the Notting Hill boutiques and market, we spent a last evening attending *Les Miserables* before heading off early the next morning to Paris.

AFTER LANDING IN FRANCE, we took a bus from the airport and my friend Nicolas B. picked us up in front of the Opera Garnier and drove us straight to his apartment, situated directly behind the Louvre. His bachelor pad was a place I knew well, as I had stayed there many times over the years when I visited, as an art collector, the Foire Internationale d'Art Contemporain and Paris Photo and then later, when I was setting up the program of my future gallery and was visiting artists such as Pascal Lièvre, Fabien Verschaere, or the late Philippe Bradshaw. I had always liked this small apartment, in this classic block built at the beginning of the nineteenth century, now owned by Nicolas' family and hosting Christian Louboutin's atelier on the ground floor. Even though I was quite familiar with London, it was really when I stepped into this apartment in Paris that I fully reconnected with Europe and with my continental roots. I was feeling more and more serene and relaxed. Sitting comfortably on the sofa in front of the empty fireplace while Nicolas prepared some hot chocolate and Su-yeon took a nap in the tiny guest room, a lot of memories began to unravel. Paris became suddenly the pretext to a flow of nostalgia and of unexpected remembrances.

IN THE EARLY MORNING of September 4, 1973—I was then almost two years old—the French police frantically knocked at the door of our apartment situated in a tall industrial building in Marseilles' Boulevard des Dames, and ordered my parents to open up. They were after my father, who had, a few days before, while supporting a strike of shipbuilders in Fos-sur-Mer, physically barred the city mayor and a group of police officers in anti-riot gear from entering the shipyard. The French official could not accept the affront of a Swiss citizen encouraging social unrest, which was quite extensive and broad-based at that time.

Thus, a few days after this incident our apartment was swiftly invaded, and police officers swarmed everywhere, checking loudly in every corner, in every drawer, and in every cupboard. The situation was extremely chaotic. I am sure I could hear the noises and the voices, feel the tension, and see their frantic shadows through the blurred glass walls that separated the children's room from the corridor. I could also probably see the silhouette of my mother in front of our door, stretching out her arms and banning entry to anyone, and dramatically feel her anguish. She must have felt a panic, fearing that her children might be affected by this excess of violence and by seeing their father being handcuffed and forcefully taken away by the police, not knowing when they would see him again. I am positive that my sister and I fully experienced this extreme tension and distress and that we assimilated those strong feelings and made them ours.

We were eventually reunited with my father in our home country of Switzerland, six months later, in Geneva, where we finally settled down. I refused to see him at first, though, screaming every morning for the next few months at the sight of him, as I mistakenly thought that he had abandoned us. These early childhood traumatic experiences followed and haunted me for an exceedingly long time.

SU-YEON AND I SPENT the following days visiting the Invalides, the Louvre, and Beaubourg, meeting some of the artists I represented for lunch or a drink, and lounging around the city. After a last dinner with Nicolas at the refined and exquisite restaurant Petrelle, we took a late plane to Rome.

THE ARRIVAL IN ITALY was quite chaotic, with a long journey from the airport in a timeworn coach through the dark countryside followed by a lengthy holdup in a noisy traffic jam at the entrance to the city. The next morning, after a long and regenerating sleep, all of these hassles were forgotten once we walked up to the flowery terrace of the Marcella Royal Hotel to have a copious Italian breakfast. I was now jubilant to be in this place blessed by a thousand myths.

I was not new to the poetry of this city, as I had visited Rome many times as a child and again later, as a teenager, during the summers, when I was improving my Italian at the *Università per Stranieri di Perugia*. It was actually there, in the medieval capital of Umbria, that I had experienced for the first time the addictive and fulfilling sensation of total freedom that utterly changed my perception of life. To renew this unique experience became a quest for the next twenty years, until I moved to Hong

Kong and became my own boss. I therefore feel fortunate today to live out this dream. It was indeed in Perugia that for the first time I experienced the freedom to do whatever I wanted, whenever I wanted. I could make that choice each day, for one full month in August, for two years in a row. I was registered at the university and obviously had to attend classes, yet I quickly realized that the other foreign students, whom I would meet at the Corso Vannucci in the evening, had other agendas. I soon befriended a group of Swedish and Norwegian students with whom I would plot, on the forecourt of the Palazzo Dei Priori, every morning before classes, where our escapes would lead us. It was therefore with Elke, Annika, Gina, Daniel, and Swen that I discovered the wonders of Assisi, Gubbio, Spoleto, Orvietto, Florence, and of course Rome. The company of these fellow students, the beauty and authenticity of Italy, and the freedom to go wherever I liked, was blissful for a Swiss teenager like me. I remember restraining tears when I had to separate at the end of August from my Scandinavian friends, especially from the fresh and pretty Elke.

AFTER BREAKFAST, SU-YEON AND I took a taxi to the Piazza del Popolo. It was there, sitting at the bottom of the Obelisk while sipping a Crodino that I truly started to notice the couples walking hand in hand through the antique streets and monuments. Suddenly, images of Elizabeth appeared in my mind, and from then on, they accompanied me for the rest of this European trip. Looking at these countless lovebirds walking in the Eternal City made me realize how much I was drawn to this woman. I also realized that this almost messianic attraction was a bit crazy, as I knew almost nothing about who Elizabeth truly was. Yet the powerful emotions I felt each time I saw her motivated me to jump blindly, intensely, and passionately into a story I already imagined magnificent. I didn't see any other woman during the rest of our trip who was as bewitching as Elizabeth was. Having high expectations and approaching the first exchanges with enthusiasm made the waiting time and the first spats more thrilling and challenging.

It was a beautiful morning to discover further the city and lounge through its antic streets, keepers of so many myths and wonders. Our stroll led us by chance to the church of St. Peter in Chains and I decided to enter. Following a habit developed during my Perugia years, I lit a candle and knelt in front of the reliquary. In Perugia, I would thank any saint available for having passed my high school years, and now, in Rome, I closed my eyes and pleaded for the upcoming relationship with Elizabeth to be a splendid and lasting success.

After one more day visiting some of Italy's most spectacular Roman and Renaissance heritage, we left Rome by train. After a day in Florence, we finally reached Venice. The plan was to stay together in the City of the Doges until my family joined me a few days later. Su-yeon would then leave for London alone and later return to Hong Kong by herself. As we had only two days together in Venice, we decided, after checking in at the Locanda Ca'Gottardi, to head right away to the Giardini, where the Art Biennale was being held.

We were quite far away, but walking allowed us to inhale the atmosphere and better sense the pulse of this fantastic city. We had fun getting lost in the small interlocking lanes and were thrilled to imagine the sensuality of the Venice of the fourteenth, fifteenth, and sixteenth centuries, when the masqueraders would, in heat, chase their prey in this labyrinth of a city.

We crossed the Rialto Bridge and stopped at the terrace of a small restaurant overlooking the canal, behind the old market, bathed by a late September sun. Once again, sitting by this water, overwhelmed by the osmosis with our romantic environment and the light feeling of contentment and happiness, I thought about Elizabeth and how much I would have liked to share this moment with her. After nibbling some typical Venetian snacks with a soft Bardolino wine, we waited for a gondola to cross the Canal Grande instead of passing by the Rialto again, and then made our way to St. Mark's Square.

Before reaching the square, I entered, as I had in Rome and Florence, a small church hidden in a dark lane, followed by an intrigued Su-yeon, wanting to perpetuate my candle-lighting tradition. I recognized the church's heavy and blackened wooden door, as I had visited it four years before, when I spent my last holidays in Venice with my family before leaving for Hong Kong. That autumn, I was too broke to carry out my rite and to spend even one Euro to seek divine support for success in my new art endeavor. Every evening after dinner I would anxiously check how my highly leveraged positions in the markets of pork bellies, frozen orange juice, gold, currencies, or stocks and indices were behaving. Most of the time they would go against me, as I was then at the peak of a self-sabotaging dynamic. Whatever the enormous sums of money I would win, I would make sure to lose them quickly—and much more—over the following days. This instability and mental torture was obviously making me feel miserable and furious at the same time; I was under extreme pressure, yet I was not willing to permanently become the victim of my demons. But now I had some coins to offer and could, thus, follow my tradition.

When we came out of the church, the sun was high and bright and we decided to leave the visit to St. Mark's Basilica for the following day. We crossed St. Mark's Square to the rhythm of the Radetsky March played by a pianist perched on the podium of the Caffè Florian and we arrived at the gate of the Biennale within twenty minutes, with a bit more than two hours before closing. This was all the time that was needed as Su-yeon felt that she could not take in too many pieces of art and as for myself, I would anyway return a few days later with my family. I was therefore quite keen to have only a quick overview that day.

After visiting the more promising national pavilions, we left the park at sunset.

The following day, our last in Europe together, we rested and talked about our journey while brunching at the terrace of the Club del Doge restaurant overlooking the Canal Grande. We then spent the evening in the best fashion possible in Venice, watching an unforgettable performance of *La Traviata* as directed by Lorin Maazel at La Fenice.

WE WOKE UP EARLY the next morning with Verdi's music still resonating in our ears and I accompanied Su-yeon to the bus terminal and led her onto the coach that would take her to the airport for an early flight to London. I left my Korean friend with mixed feelings, as I had been wondering all along about her expectations; we had innocently shared the same bed for two weeks and she perhaps thought that this trip would trigger a fresh start to our relationship.

It was close to 8:30am; the air was fresh and scented, the sky a comforting cobalt hue. I took the vaporetto and headed back to the hotel. Because my father had aerophobia and, thus, wished to avoid traveling by plane as much as possible, my parents and my sister were arriving later that day by train from Geneva. As I had not mentioned to them that I was making this trip with Su-yeon, I planned to check out swiftly from Ca' Gottardi and to wait for them with my luggage at the Metropole, the hotel that they had booked and in which we would stay together for the next three days.

I was sitting on a wooden bench outside, at the stern of the boat, and despite wearing a light collarless purple-and-white pinstriped shirt, white cargo Bermuda shorts, and brown Docksiders, I did not feel cold at all on this refreshing and sunny morning. Lost in my thoughts and somehow isolated wearing sunglasses, I did not at first notice the three people who sat among the other passengers in front of me. They were also not immediately aware of my presence, but suddenly, as if an instinctive fire alarm had rung in sync in our burning brains, we looked at each other in common surprise. Suddenly recognizing these familiar faces, I was left speechless and bewildered for a few seconds. To my astonishment, as well as that of my parents and my sister, the family P. was reunited on this Venetian vaporetto after a three-year absence. The palpable emotion was strong when we hugged and kissed each other. What an unexpected and thoughtful gift from destiny! I love it when fate becomes playfully proactive in our lives. As Leon Bloy wrote, "Chance is the modern word for Holy Spirit."

I had actually seen my mother the year before in Hong Kong, as she had stopped for a few days on her way back from a conference on plurilingualism in Tokyo, but this was the first time in three years that I had seen Marie and my father. My sister had not changed much—still hiding behind long bangs and thick-framed glasses—except that she seemed taller than I remembered. It was my parents who looked the most different. With my father at seventy-three years old and my mother at sixty-five, I realized that even though I still considered myself a *young man* when I was with my parents—their son, which sounds more like the description of a child than an adult— they now belonged to the category of *old*. My awareness of the shortness of our lifespan on earth deepened further. We had little time then to talk and recollect, as the boat had already reached Ca'd'Oro and, changing my plan slightly, I had to check out of my hotel and collect my luggage before joining my family at the Metropole.

THEIR HOTEL WAS STRATEGICALLY situated right on the lagoon, between St. Mark's Square and the Giardini, looking straight out over San Giorgio Island and its Benedictine monastery, its imposing campanile standing at attention. When I arrived, my parents were already installed in their suite of this sixteenth-century hotel and were preparing themselves—waiting for me to deposit my baggage into the room I would share with my sister—to step out of the hotel and formally begin our holiday together.

Making us share a room is a long habit that my parents have that brings my sister and I, involuntarily—or maybe not—back to the role of children. I sometimes had difficulty in positioning myself back into the status that I had tried so hard to escape from. I had built my own reality and had worked hard to construct myself without being handicapped by guilt, doubts, and fears that actually originated with my parents. Although nothing traumatic happened directly to me during my childhood, I was nevertheless hypersensitive to the energies flowing in my close environment when I was a baby and a child. I assimilated damaging emotions felt by my parents during challenging periods of their lives, made them mine, and let them develop and invade my subconscious—which eventually turned those emotions against me. Therefore, being in contact with these stigmas of the past, with reactions and behaviors that I so much tried to escape from, at some point always made these reunions painful. Even though I could now look into the eyes of that reality, which was no longer mine, its simple recollection was sometimes oppressive. However, the unease I felt at being brought back temporarily into this world was quickly replaced by the joy of seeing these people who were so dear to me.

What happened in Marseilles when my father was deported echoed a similar experience that my parents had endured a few years before, when living in Neuchâtel, a city in Switzerland's northwest. My father, Alfred, was then a Protestant pastor and was about thirty-four years old. He had a girlfriend and things were no more serious than that until he inadvertently got her pregnant. As he belonged to a powerful family from the local aristocracy that would not tolerate a scandal, he was firmly advised to marry and he quickly did so, being a man of principle, faith, and duty. He was not in love with her then, but even so, he still believed in the power of this ravaging emotion. When his wife was six months into her pregnancy, my father met by chance Nelly L., the woman who would become my mother, and they fell madly in love. With understandable hesitation, and maybe also with a sense of defiance, they started to date, despite stepping into a situation that seemed doomed and sure to bring dramas and disasters. It did not take long for this relationship to come out into the open and for it to receive, as expected, violent disapproval. For my father's family, a potential future scandal—should this situation become public—seemed unbearable and much worse than the crisis they had barely escaped from just six months before.

The Protestant synod also stepped in, as they could not tolerate that one of their own, a representative of the highest morals and an example for all, could potentially bring such discredit on their institution. Pressure intensified, with Nelly being depicted and disparaged as an evil woman ready to use all her spells to corrupt my father. He was brought almost by force to a religious retreat near the lake of Morat, to be reminded of the conduct expected of him, or in a certain way, as some thought, exorcized. But it was written that love would prevail. When its ravaging power strikes, indeed, there is nothing strong enough to forbid it to express its splendor. Despite the intolerable pressures from all sides, my parents decided that their destiny would be together. Yet, to be able to live their lives in peace and to prevent a scandal from staining the family's honor and the church's reputation, they agreed to go into exile, far away from Neuchâtel. My father therefore divorced just a couple of months before his first wife gave birth, remarried, and left with my mother for the South of France, to Marseilles. All of these tensions and an acute feeling of guilt never left them. Those emotions were still strongly present a few years later, when my sister, and then I, came into this world.

WE STEPPED OUT OF the hotel together and without wasting any time, we walked along Riva degli Schiavoni, toward the Biennale site. Another peculiar habit that I had developed within my family dynamic and that I thought, somewhere deep inside, was expected as I was still a child to my parents, maybe forever, was almost never to talk about my girlfriends. As a result, I had seldom brought any of them home. It was therefore routine for me to hide that I had spent the past two weeks in Europe with Su-yeon and to pretend that I had been in Venice alone—and only from the day before. I often question myself, as an adult now, why I do not simply tell them what actually happens in my life. I believe that I don't because of reserve and laziness, as I do not want to change our traditional balance. I therefore prefer to stay in a certain comfort zone, even though that involves keeping a few secrets from them. It was therefore with faked surprise that I entered, with my family, the Giardini, supposedly for the first time. I was not totally pretending, as I had spent only a few brief hours there two days before, rushing through the pavilions at an exceptionally fast pace. Yet having to cover up slightly did not make me feel completely comfortable—even though I was accustomed to it in such circumstances.

ART HAS ALWAYS BEEN a passion for me, and before I learned to walk, I was already constantly scribbling on walls, on clothes, or on any pieces of paper that I could put my chubby hands on. At kindergarten and primary school, I filled up my homework notebooks with penned imaginary battles between hundreds of tiny stick figures and caricatures of my teachers and classmates in the margins and on the blank pages of my exercise books. I had drawing in my blood, and used this gift to create fantasy worlds and universes to which I could escape and transcend myself. I later started to paint and do collages as a natural progression, following the urge to express my creativity.

For as small as Switzerland is, the country is home to countless public museums, cultural institutions, and around a thousand private cultural foundations. To our common enjoyment, my parents would therefore often drive us on weekends to Bern's Kunsthalle, to the Beyeler Foundation or the Kunstmuseum in Basel, to modern art galleries, the Migros Museum and the Kunsthaus in Zurich, to Le Museé de l'Art Brut in Lausanne, La Fondation Gianadda in Martigny, or the Tinguely Museum in Fribourg.

We would also often tour Geneva's galleries and visit art dealer friends and artist's studios throughout Europe. All of these experiences were eye-openers to me, coloring and fueling my youthful imagination and creativity. Going back by car to Marseilles every Easter, despite my father's official ban from France, and stopping on the way at the wonderful Maeght Foundation at Saint-Paul-de-Vence, was also a tradition that I cherished. Over those years, I developed acute and empirical knowledge about classic and modern art. At nineteen years of age, I received from my mother an illustrated book consisting of recollections of exchanges between the French collector and movie producer Claude Berri and the iconic New York gallerist Leo Castelli. New horizons subsequently opened up when I discovered in more depth the works of Robert Rauschenberg, James Rosenquist, Ellsworth Kelly, Cy Twombly, and Richard Serra. The high interest I had in these artists encouraged me to develop my own tastes and to move away from my parents' guidance in matters of art. I started to go to contemporary art gallery openings and to travel to Art Basel and to other art fairs in Europe and in the United States. From there, and driven by a primal need to possess and accumulate, it did not take long before I logically started my own art collection.

Beyond the historical knowledge I can glean about periods, trends, and artists, I have a sensitive and intuitive perception about art and I react to it at different levels. As a collector, I choose artworks because I connect emotionally to them—analyzing these emotions can be extremely enlightening—or because I like the intellectual concept behind them and they make sense in the logic of a multilayered collection. As a gallery owner and art dealer, my understanding is more contextual. I position the art I see within a constellation of other works and ideas, to extract a subjective and substantive multifaceted opinion of each piece. In this process, my interest tends toward artists who give me the impression that I have never seen before what I am exposed to in their artwork and who display a strong mastery and maturity in the realization of their art.

Among the national pavilions of the Biennale, even though many featured challenging artists, my interests were especially drawn to two countries. The renowned Russian collective AES+F was presenting its already iconic and extremely sophisticated video installation *The Last Riot 2*. I was proud that they had been selected to co-represent their country because I was going to exhibit them in Hong Kong a few weeks after this trip. *The Last Riot 2* film and photographs series actually became one of the biggest sensations of the Biennale. They portrayed bare-chested androgynous kids and teenagers who, wearing camouflage fatigues within a hyper-sophisticated videogame environment, killed each other virtually using Samurai swords, plastic M16 rifles, or golf clubs. In these works, AES+F was exploring the limits of and paradoxes between our addiction to and our victimization by advertising, technology, and fashion, using mythological, religious, and literary references. Through these hyperaesthetic artworks—visually appealing yet effectively disturbing—the artists also confronted us with our attraction to and contradictions toward violence and sex.

The French pavilion was also positively phenomenal. Through her installation entitled *Take Care of Yourself*, Sophie Calle, through different media and 107 interpretations commissioned to female friends, linguists, actors, philosophers, psychoanalysts, and so on, cleverly and brilliantly explored an e-mail sent to her by an ex-lover, ending their relationship. Her wit, manipulative sincerity, sophistication, lack of prudishness, and mastery in the way she treated this personal, traumatic, and intimate subject was one of the finest examples of visual art as an act of resilience.

IT WAS SLIGHTLY AFTER 6pm when we left the Biennale. Even though we were a bit tired, we decided, before taking a regenerating rest, to do a quick family pilgrimage to Harry's Bar for some well-deserved Bellinis. These light cocktails and the refined canapés that accompanied them were perfect before an hour's nap.

The dinner that followed at the Antico Martini, beside the Fenice, was deliciously pleasant. Sitting on the patio, we finally had time to go through our impressions of the past three years in length. The family's dynamic rekindled as though we had never gone our own ways: the affectionate skirmishes between my sister and me, my complicity with my mother seasoned with blunt truths, and my father's attempts to find balance and consensus within these relationships, were all there. It was at the end of this family dinner, when we were content with the luscious meal and the spicy and powerful Amarone, that I mentioned the tumor. I did not want to alarm them and I therefore played down the diagnosis. I explained convincingly that the growth had been spotted early enough and that the treatment should easily take care of it. They were of course concerned, a bit shaken, yet reassured, and they indicated their full support in case I needed anything. I assured them that everything was under control and told them that I had anyway made an appointment with Professor P. in Geneva a few days later to get a second opinion.

I was actually quite worried ahead of this meeting, because I was hoping that the pertinence and the efficacy of the treatment and surgery would be confirmed. To the contrary of what I had told my parents, I was technically not well at all, as the tumor had spread extensively. However, just then I did not want to look beyond the prospect of the possible failure of the surgery. I did not tell my parents the truth because I felt the need to keep some crucial parts of my life to myself and to act alone on them, this time, as I perceived it, like an adult. I also did not want to seek any pity for my current sufferings, and I therefore maintained by masochism and stubbornness the idea that I had to go through this ordeal—and through life in general—alone. Not lonely, but alone, as we live and shape our own lives, not someone else's.

After spending two more days enjoying almost *ad nauseam* the magnificence that Venice offers, we had to leave the enchanting lagoon. The train back to Geneva was departing at noon, and we took advantage of the last sunrays that we could capture to enjoy a long and lazy breakfast in the garden of the Metropole. Following my frantic trip through Europe, I wanted to take a break and decided to stay for a few days with my parents at our family estate of Valrolz, situated in the middle of an impenetrable forest, overlooking Neuchâtel's lake, where a lot of colorful and emotional childhood memories remained.

THE FOLLOWING DAY I woke up in a total silence only slightly perturbed by the noise of the wind in the lime trees and of the horses neighing. My room looked as if it were frozen in the nineteenth century, with its white-painted wood-paneled walls, botanical etchings, lacy curtains, and imposing turquoise-tiled heater in the corner. Looking around me and feeling at peace was a priceless and rejuvenating contrast to the rather busy week I had just spent. Walking out in the corridor to the rhythm of the clock's loud beat, I could smell the bread toasting in the kitchen downstairs and I heard the murmurs of a conversation between my parents. I looked around; nothing had changed. It could have been twenty or thirty years back. I was back in time, yet I had changed. How to behave? My parents heard me and invited me to join them for breakfast, but before accepting their invitation, I felt the urge to walk through the house to recollect my past and, thus, feel the evolution from it and be convinced that we were indeed in the twenty-first century.

On the second floor was the room in which I used to stay during holidays from the age of eleven. The attic had been unoccupied for a while and was now furnished with two empty narrow wooden bedframes and a small cabinet on which an empty enamel basin was lying, covered by a lace doily. The sketch of Minka, the horse on which I had my first ride, when I was about six years old, was still pinned on the wall, frameless. Leaning through the window, I admired the vast forest and the calm and glittering lake. I was, though unaware of it, looking for some emotional clues.

Attentive and receptive to each detail of my past, I suddenly saw myself in reverse through this window, back in the summer of 1984, at the beginning of the holidays. I was twelve and felt for the first time, during an outing with friends to a public swimming pool in Geneva, a strong emotion for a girl three years older than me. Her name was Michèle, and I remember having to dive into the pool to calm down my excitement when she first brushed my blond hair and innocently kissed me. A brand new and electric emotion had just shaken my mind and body; I was indeed struck by a sweet pre-teenage love! At that age, children naturally do not have much control over their day-to-day planning, and a few weeks later, I had to follow my parents to Valrolz for a long weekend. I was devastated and I still remembered standing in this same room on that Saturday afternoon, after the hour's drive from Geneva, looking at the sky through the open window and missing Michèle so much. We had been seeing each other almost every day since that first poolside kiss. Thinking about this juvenile and emotional moment, the image of Elizabeth suddenly appeared as a hologram in the azure sky. I wished then that I could kiss and embrace this mirage. I did not know her yet and could therefore not miss her—but just as in the summer of '84 with Michèle, I hoped I could be with her.

THE TIME TO GO back to reality and to fly to Hong Kong was approaching fast. I had a few friends to see in Geneva and I therefore decided to go there on my last morning, before taking a night flight home. My anxiety level was especially high, because that afternoon I had a meeting with Professor P. at the Hôpital Cantonal de Genève to discuss the tumor. I had informed Doctor Liu about this visit and he was fully supportive of it. He had already been in contact with the professor and had sent him a copy of my medical file. The consultation went as well as it possibly could, and Professor P. confirmed the diagnosis as well as the pertinence of the treatment I was following. Being professional and realistic, though, he told me, with the aplomb of someone who has looked death in the eye many times, that I should fully accept the fact that surgery would have to be scheduled. He probably believed there was some denial in my optimistic pose. The drug treatment was maybe giving me the illusion of borrowing time, but it was only a means to prepare my body for the surgery; it was keeping the alien at bay as much as possible, but it did not have the capacity to destroy it. I had therefore better start getting used to the idea of the operation, despite the tremendously high level of risk. I was not too pleased by this wakeup call, of course, as I had tried as much as I could to avoid thinking about this potential and serious outcome. Taking pills and having my skull opened were two very different things.

Before taking the plane back to Hong Kong I had just enough time to have a last coffee with my sister who wanted to get some feedback on my visit to the hospital and to introduce me to her boyfriend, Stephane. My mother then drove me to the airport and hesitantly asked how my romantic life was.

I replied briefly, "I am working on it. I may actually have a surprise soon."

WHILE I WAS IN EUROPE I had virtually followed the affairs of my gallery, and I was in daily e-mail contact with my assistants, who were holding down the fort there. I was therefore coming back knowing that everything was under control. I was exhausted yet contented by these two nomadic and intense weeks and looking forward to finally focusing my attention on Elizabeth, although I had to keep my health under constant watch. I must say, though, that since I had been diagnosed with the tumor, a kind of weight had been lifted off me and I was feeling more and more euphoric. Realizing that I had an alien trying to kill me from within, instead of depressing me, had actually provided invaluable insights about life—and I even felt galvanized by it. Even though the outcome was uncertain, as the surgery was going to be delicate and life threatening, this unfortunate fate was giving me wings and many projects and prospects suddenly seemed within reach. It made sense to me that closeness to the end actually brought lightness; instead of causing stress and worry, it freed me from a lot of hang-ups as, after all, once we are gone, we are gone. I did not then feel any fear of dying, as I could not possibly be afraid of something I didn't know.

I returned to Hong Kong at the end of the first week of October, regenerated and full of resolutions, hopes, and commitments. Even though my priority was to contact Elizabeth, I first had to monitor the upcoming exhibition of AES+F, the opening of which was scheduled for slightly over a week after my return. Because the video *The Last Riot 2* had become a hit in Venice, these artists were extremely sought-after internationally. Having them in Hong Kong was therefore important to me, and for the reputation and credibility of the gallery. Their video and photographs had been installed at the end of the week and the vernissage invitations had been sent out. On the one addressed to Elizabeth I wrote:

Dear Elizabeth,

I am finally back from two weeks in Europe and will call you on Tuesday to see when you are free to finally meet properly. I would be happy, though, to see you before at the opening if you can; these artists are truly remarkable.

Hector

I ONCE EMBRACED THE PRAIRIES WHERE THE LILACS GROW

How very beautiful the meadow seems today!
I have come upon magic flowers Which sickly
twined about me to my head; Yet ne'er have
I seen such soft and tender Stalks, blossoms,
flowers, Nor has anything smelled so childlike
sweet Or spoken so dearly to me

Richard Wagner, *Parsifal*

On the fateful Tuesday, October 22, I was feeling well yet I became agitated and rather nervous late in the afternoon. A little after 7pm, I opened a chilled Kirin beer to calm me down before I contacted Elizabeth. It was an easy phone call to make, yet suddenly many questions resurfaced. Elizabeth had been on my mind for a long time, and there was an undeniable mutual attraction each time we bumped into each other. She had suggested that we should get together and talk more after her conference, and she had written the winking *until later* in her book. Yet it suddenly seemed that I needed a higher reason to call her. What would I say? My heart was beating quickly and I opened another beer to relax myself further and try to stop these inner jitters. I was quite annoyed with myself actually for masochistically trying to find pretexts to postpone this call when the only thing I genuinely wanted at that instant was to hear Elizabeth's voice and imagine her, pleasantly surprised, hopefully smiling, at the other end of the line. I finally took her business card, picked up the phone, and dialed her number, damning myself for the early hesitations. After three ring tones, a soft voice answered.

"Hello?"

"Hello, could I speak to Elizabeth please?"

"Speaking..."

"Hi, this is Hector."

"Oh?" A brief silence followed. "Hi ... Hector."

"How are you?"

"I am well, thank you." Her voice was hesitant.

"I am calling you to see when you could be free to ... to discuss what we talked about just after your conference at the American Club."

"Ah, right, I see. You mean at my book presentation?"

"Yes, we agreed then that we should finally get together soon ..."

"Hmm ... I am not quite sure I remember, actually I ..."

After a few seconds of intuitive reflection, I continued, "You don't seem to know who is calling. You don't remember who I am, do you?" I was surprised yet amused by my own question, as I was confident that she knew perfectly well who I was, yet she seemed to have momentarily forgotten.

"I ...Yes. I mean, no. I am sorry. I don't know who you are, I ..."

Unfazed by her amnesia, I moved on seamlessly and said, with an impish tone, "It's Hector, Elizabeth! Don't you recognize my voice? Don't you remember my lilting accent?"

"Oh, right! You are the Swiss art dealer, aren't you?"

I feigned offense and disappointment but continued with a pert intonation, "Of course it's me! I am THE Hector. How could you not recognize me?"

"Sorry again. I am a bit off today. I just came back from India this afternoon and I am still jet-lagged."

"It's fine, don't worry. As long as you know now who I am and you don't hang up ..." I giggled. "So, would you have time for us to finally meet properly?"

Elizabeth's voice had recovered full confidence by then. "Yes, of course. I would like to."

"Are you free this week?"

"Yes I am. What about tomorrow evening? There is a German short film festival at the Fringe Club. We could go together ..."

"Sure, that's a very good idea. What time does the screening start?"

"Let me see." She paused for ten seconds while looking for the program and finally replied, "It starts at eight o'clock. Is that too late for you?"

"No. Not at all. It actually leaves us some time to have a drink first. What do you think? Shall we meet at the Fringe at seven thirty?"

"Seven thirty sounds good. I am looking forward to seeing you tomorrow, Hector."

I smiled and replied impishly, "I hope you will recognize me then."

She giggled and answered instantly, "Of course I will."

I hung up and, euphoric, I shouted a resounding "Yes ... Yes ... Yes" in my office with eruptive vigor. I was ecstatic, literally jumping around, punching the air, an immense smile shining on my face. Recollecting the quick talk we had just had, I interpreted the fact that she had suggested that we meet the following day as a sign of her own anticipation and desire to finally meet this man of mystery. I felt strong and I sat in my leather chair to cool down and fully appreciate this moment. I replayed her voice in my head again and again, like a sweet symphony.

THE PREVIOUS YEAR, AFTER the smooth break-up with Su-yeon, I had moved into a studio on Hollywood Road, as I finally had the means to rent an apartment. A large and bright balcony with bay windows and a rooftop overlooking Central's skyscrapers compensated for the smallness of the space. The only inconvenience (as I guess is the case, by definition, for all studios) was that I had to choose to make the space either a bedroom—and therefore be unable to really have guests—or a living room. Choosing the latter option, I purchased a large L-shaped herringbone beige sofa that took up almost three-quarters of the space but was so large that I could also sleep on it. The walls and ceiling were painted light gray, and the floor was made of clear wood parquet. The kitchen and bathroom were in two separate rooms and there was just enough space left for a large black teakwood classic Chinese cabinet and a ceramic black coffee table. The walls were adorned with an oversized plasma television, a large black-and-white portrait by Dutch contemporary photographer Erwin Olaf, and an abstract landscape painting by David Godbold entitled *The Journey is the Destination*.

That evening, sitting on the wide sofa, alone, looking at the big city's bright lights, anticipating the following day's date and recollecting again Elizabeth's bewitching voice and our past ephemeral encounters, I felt transcendent and blessed. This was already in itself a battle won against the deadly tumor. I was feeling strong and invincible as never before.

ON WEDNESDAY AFTERNOON, THE heartbeat I had felt in my chest since that morning was pure dopamine coursing ecstatically through my system. I have always enjoyed the fulfilling feeling of success, and I felt transported. I was looking forward so much to spending this first precious time with Elizabeth, just the two of us. This anticipated pleasure was prevailing over everything else I could have in my mind and I went home at a little after 6pm to shower and change. Wanting to symbolically link Elizabeth's original foundational act with that night's date, I decided to dress the same way as I had, almost two years before, at the 1/5 Bar; I wore my soft brown leather jacket, an open-necked dark brown cotton shirt, dark blue jeans, and black leather ankle boots. While changing, I drank a Kirin as a precaution, this time not to cool my agitation down but rather to tame, a bit, my excitement in order to prevent any overflow. I was literally euphoric, yet I knew I also had to perform and that this first date was crucial, as nothing could be taken for granted. Not now, not yet. Never, actually. The door of our relationship was ajar at most. Everything still remained to be built from tonight onward to open wide the gate of her heart.

I HAD JUST ARRIVED at the Fringe Club's bar on the ground floor and was listening to the lyrics of "My Girl" by the Temptations playing in the background when, like the vision of Don Quixote's Dulcinea del Tobosco, Elizabeth appeared. She was radiant in her unassuming black top and blue jeans. And what a smile! In observing her, I could not help but think of Cervantes' words, "Her rank must be at least that of a princess, since she is my queen and lady, and her beauty superhuman, since all the impossible and fanciful attributes of beauty which the poets apply to their ladies are verified in her; for her hairs are gold, her forehead Elysian fields, her eyebrows rainbows, her eyes suns, her cheeks roses, her lips coral, her teeth pearls, her neck alabaster, her bosom marble, her hands ivory, her fairness snow, and what modesty conceals from sight such, I think and imagine, as rational reflection can only extol, not compare."

Converted long ago and now already melting, I opened my arms and greeted her tenderly. I felt for the first time her silky skin against mine, and the exhilaration of her scent when I kissed her cheeks. There was nothing much to add right then, so I just declared an Archimedic, "Finally!" with a renewed and wide smile.

We sat around a high wood table, near the window, in a quiet corner; I ordered a glass of Sauvignon Blanc for her and a draft beer for me. We started to talk with an ease and complicity that seemed to confirm her pleasure to be here with me, and the unique attraction I had felt for this woman each time our paths had crossed. Elizabeth was feminine, intelligent, and tremendously sensual; I was confident, witty, and considerate. The soft and warm tone of her voice, the determined way she moved her head closer to talk, and her sometimes staccato phrasing were charming. I realized quickly that she did not know much about me—I did not know much about her, either, but I was a bit more informed, thanks to Werner K.—and I believe that she was therefore happily surprised when I told her that I had once been a banker. Our common understanding of economics and finance was an element that would bring me closer to her own professional field of expertise, and her expressed love for art would likewise bring her closer to mine.

At about 8:30pm we forced ourselves to stop our conversation and left the bar for the rooftop to see some of the films. We sat tight beside each other, at the back, as we were late and among the last to arrive. The films were quite short, around five minutes each, and our complicit and pert comments were pretexts to get closer to each other in spirit. At some point earlier, she had briefly touched my arm at the bar downstairs and she slightly brushed my shoulder once on the rooftop, as if she needed some physical proof that we were indeed finally together.

At some point Elizabeth turned toward me and asked in a calm voice, "Tell me Hector, why did it actually take you so long before contacting me? I mean, I felt that we had an attraction each time we met, so I never understood why you never called or talked to me."

"Because life is complicated," was my mysterious and supposedly witty answer. She nodded and did not ask me to elaborate. With that evasive comment, though, I was already starting here, at this early stage of the relationship, to answer by ricochet or riddle.

The quality of the films being quite uneven, and Elizabeth becoming slightly chilled because of a light late autumn breeze, we decided to leave for a much-anticipated intimate dinner after less than an hour on the rooftop. Walking away, we bumped into Helmut M., the director of the festival. Knowing him well, I cordially shook his hand and pertly commented about the high quality of the short films. Standing back slightly, observing me interacting with other people, Elizabeth smiled.

Thinking of a place to go to eat, she mentioned to my surprise—as I would never think of bringing a date to these kinds of restaurants—that she was open to anything except a steakhouse, because she was a vegetarian. As Werner K. had once mentioned that she came from a small city located in the middle of the vast Oklahoma prairies, I wondered if her choice for this specific diet—common in Asia but unlikely in the land of the Sooners—was one more way of marking some distance from her origins. Right beside the Fringe Club, opposite the Foreign Correspondent Club, was one of the most enthralling culinary experiences I had in Hong Kong, and I therefore suggested dining at Chez Quis.

We thought first to dine inside the kitchen space and to watch the cooks prepare our delicacies, yet the wind coming from the air conditioner was too chilly and we eventually decided, instead, to retreat into the main room. Sitting at an asymmetric black marble table by the bay window overlooking Ice House Street, we both ordered the tasting menu—with a vegetarian twist for Elizabeth—and a bottle of Pouilly Fuissé. Cy Coleman's classic piano jazz standards were playing in the background, providing a perfect soundtrack to our date.

FOLLOWING UP ON OUR colorful conversation at the Fringe Club, we continued to discover each other and the beginning of the dinner sailed smoothly along with humor, erudition, and a lot of fond smiles. One of the important subjects to tackle and clarify, of course, was the reason for the two-year gap between the 1/5 foundational act and the present. I had been more than evasive at the Fringe Club, and it was time to start being more explicit.

"You know, Elizabeth, since coming to Hong Kong, this is probably the first time I have actually felt truly ready to start a relationship. Setting up the gallery and my art dealing business was exceedingly tough and brought a lot of pressure. That's why for a long time I have been unable to truly commit to anyone. But now my projects are working well, so I can finally envision getting involved with someone special."

"I understand what you mean," answered Elizabeth sympathetically. "I have myself been working really hard for the past few years. Writing my last book took so much time and energy that I could not develop a relationship, either. For some reason I felt I needed to drown myself in my work, and I agreed to participate in too many symposiums. Now that the book is finished, I can finally think about myself. I plan to reduce my workload and the pace of my travel and to participate in only one conference per month. So my priority now will be to take time for the persons who matter the most to me."

I understood her well when she said that her book had taken so much time that she had no space for any romantic adventure during its writing. What she did not mention, maybe because it was too early in our relationship for her to be so candid, was that her ex-husband was creating many difficulties and was nastily interfering in the joint custody of their son, as I was to learn later. Writing books and working too much were obviously ways for her to feel strong about herself, but they were also a method of distracting her mind as much as possible from the still painful and present reminders of her divorce. Our timing seemed in sync as I explained to my evening muse the difficulties I had gone through in setting up an art business about which I had no prior experience—except the empirical knowledge of art that a passionate collector has—and parachuting myself into a city where I knew almost nobody. We realized we were further in tune when I told her that the times we had bumped into each other without being able to elaborate or to follow up had been like stardust in space forming a distinctive milky way—our own cosmology. She smiled at this image and, looking deeply into my eyes with her electric blue gaze, embraced the allegory.

We naturally remembered and discussed the first time we had met, and to my surprise she once again did not recall, or was afraid to admit, her foundational act at 1/5. The memory of the leather jacket was very much present in her mind, but came from the Kee Club, when we met for the second time as I was wearing it then as well. At that point, she shivered again and, considerate and attentive to each of her movements, I offered to let her wear the much-talked-about jacket, to keep her warm. She appreciated this thoughtful gesture and I provokingly said, smiling widely, "So you finally succeeded in getting what you wanted. You didn't actually want to meet me, but what you were actually looking for was to feel the jacket again, weren't you?"

She smiled, and the only thing I desired then was to immerse myself in her magnificence, so much was I feeling whole and fulfilled with her that evening. Our first real time together was working perfectly. I continued our conversation, "I don't see why relationships have to be complicated and be sources of stress and frustration. I think relationships should be easy, smooth, and fulfilling. I don't think that the fundamental differences between men and women are what make so many romantic adventures fail. I believe that it is unsolved personal issues echoing original fears that are actually the main reasons for breakups. I don't buy John Grey's stigmatization of our differences in his book *Men Are from Mars, Women Are from Venus*." I then paused, smiled widely, and added, "Having said that, though, some women actually believe that men are even further out than that."

Elizabeth smiled back, looked at me with a lot of tenderness, and murmured, "I hope that we are indeed not that far away from each other." Being both keen readers, we shared some views about books we discovered we both had read. At some point she enquired, "Have you also read Tarun Tejpal's novel *The Alchemy of Desire?*"

"No. I have actually never heard of it," I replied. "What is it about?"

"It is a story about two Indian lovers who retreat from their busy city life into an isolated house in the forest. The man discovers then the incredible story of the last owner. It is a very heartfelt book. I truly liked it."

She did not elaborate much more about the essence of the book, but as I felt that she was touched by it, I kept its title in mind and made a mental note to read it soon.

OUR PLEASURE AT BEING together was filling the restaurant with a comfortable mellowness. Bringing up one of my favorite topics of discussion, the notion of human limitations—having only five senses—I told her how this subject was fascinatingly addressed in Clifford Simak's book *City*, in which a scientist and his dog, Towser, mutate to acclimate to life on Jupiter. I explained how this transformation blessed them with thousands of senses, and it changed the perception of the scientist's own humanity. Switching subject again, answering a question, I explained that when I was nineteen years old, I went to Sydney to study for two years but that I actually spent more time surfing—as I was living right on Bondi Beach—than attending Camden Business College. Talking again about myself, I said, "You know, I felt quite strange when I called you yesterday. I had been waiting to contact you for a long time, but then I suddenly did not know what to say on the phone to prompt you to accept to meet."

"You did not need to say anything. I was actually thrilled when you called. I really wanted to see you too."

"Were you waiting for my call? I mean, I wrote in the AES+F opening invitation card that I would call you on Tuesday. I was wondering if you had been waiting for it that day."

"No, I had just come back from India and did not know you were going to call me, actually."

"Really? You didn't see my note on the invitation?"

"Yes, I noticed that you had written something but I couldn't manage to read it."

She added, to my mild astonishment that, unable to read my scribble, she had thrown the card away. Such radicalism and bluntness amused me and I told her jokingly, "I see. So you first denied the foundational act with the jacket at 1/5, but you remember me wearing it at the Kee Club. During your conference, you bashed me in public but you invited me later to contact you. And tonight you embraced the cosmology imagery and you confirmed the attraction we felt for each other but you threw away the invitation card. You like to wield the carrot and the stick, don't you?"

She smiled mischievously, looked at the baby zucchini stuffed with morels and goat cheese on her plate, and brushed my assertion away lightly, as she understood it was a joke, though it probably touched on hidden valid points. I then complimented her book. I genuinely thought her analysis of the situation in China was intensely interesting and pertinent, as I felt—like her—that a Pandora's box had been opened. I also told her how appalled I had been when the sexist man introduced her so greasily to the American Club audience.

"I am really glad you liked my book," she replied, genuinely flattered, "but you know, I did not pay attention to the behavior of that journalist. I am used to these kinds of comments, as I have to deal mostly with men in my job. I have learned not to care about such chauvinistic attitudes."

I then clarified the question I had asked about China during her conference. She understood it this time, yet she surprisingly still could not come up with much insight, and I therefore gave her my own answer, "I actually believe that the economic depression the world is sliding into could force China to eventually close its borders. My hypothesis is that the economic slowdown will be so severe that unrest will increase substantially, triggered by angry and desperate unemployed people, and by expropriated farmers. China's totalitarian and reactionary regime is, by definition, paranoiac. Feeling that this extreme domestic vulnerability may give destabilizing forces within and outside of the country the awaited opportunity potentially to topple the regime, the Communist government could close like a frightened and protective oyster. If that happens, it would certainly need to deal with these crucial issues without being threatened by external factors. When a dictatorial government feels under threat, it takes drastic measures, and these measures may not always be rational." She listened and agreed with me that this might be a possibility, even though my analysis seemed a bit far-fetched.

A waiter dressed in black and sporting an odd and spiky hairdo approached our table to fill our glasses with more Pouilly Fuissé. I jokingly asked him if the people working in the restaurant were sponsored by a hair salon, as I had noticed that most of the staff had either original cuts or blue hair. The waiter smiled and Elizabeth giggled.

Then, after talking about Switzerland but without elaborating much further about my background, I asked her about her own origins. I had read Steinbeck's *The Grapes of Wrath* and Josephine W. Johnson's *Now in November*, as well as history and economics books about the Great Depression, the devastating droughts, and the subsequent Dust Bowl that sent hundreds of thousands of people into poverty throughout the Midwest during the 1930s. I was therefore interested in understanding how these dramatic events might have affected her story, as I believe that each generation passes some of its stigmas to the next.

"You are right," Elizabeth said in an almost solemn tone, "I come from Oklahoma, and that part of the United States still has the echo of these dramatic events pulsing in its veins. The people who came to the Midwest were quite poor, and they took the opportunity to own vast prairies and become farmers during the late nineteenth century. The majority of them actually were strong Christians and thought that these prairies were their Promised Land despite having high wind, strong sun, few rivers, and little rain. They had almost no farming experience and limited education, but they believed that they were guided. They unfortunately neglected the land they had managed to acquire after so much suffering and they developed poor land-use and farming practices. The Great Depression and the worst drought in our history wiped out the efforts of two generations and broke them down." Elizabeth paused, and then continued. The tone of her voice had become quite emotional. "I remember my grandma Belle telling me stories of that time, like when she would hold my baby aunt in her arms for hours while standing in endless breadlines, day after day, as food was then in short supply. She always had a witty twist or a happy ending to her tales and often finished with a smile but I knew they went through hell. Yet I never heard her or anyone else in my family complaining about these times. They were already hard-boiled people you know, but these traumatic experiences toughened them up even further. If you go to the Great Plains states of Oklahoma, Kansas, or Iowa and meet the people, you will still feel today that we are survivors. We still have our ancestors' survival instinct deeply rooted in us."

Listening attentively to her heartfelt story and picturing these admirable people, I could hear in the background of her recollection Virgil Thomson's dramatic music from the documentary *The Plow that Broke the Plains*. I had seen the film in high school and still remembered the off-camera voice solemnly proclaiming, talking about these brave men and women, "Backed out, blown out, and broke."

Elizabeth was still examining her roots, moved by her own story, "Having said that, though, and without refuting my background, I felt a strong need to discover the rest of my country. So, I went to a university on the East Coast. That was not an obvious decision to make, though, as where I come from people don't really travel outside of their state. And much later, when I told my family that I was moving to Hong Kong, they thought I was going to the moon." She smiled and I could see melancholy passing through her eyes. "This city is far from anything I have experienced before, but I wanted to live overseas, to discover a totally different culture, and meet people from many different parts of the world. I must admit, however, that I sometimes miss Oklahoma, especially when Hong Kong's overcrowding weighs in. It sometimes happens. Don't you feel the same?" I nodded and she continued, "And when it does, I then wish I could simply escape with my horse, as I did at home, and ride for hours in the prairies. That, I really miss."

Filled with nostalgia after this mental trip to the prairies where the lilacs grow, she looked at me, her smile enlightened by emotions.

Linking her recollection and her Asian escape to the rootlessness of the people settling down in Hong Kong—but also in most transit cities, where there is a strong and disconnected expatriate community—she asked me if I felt I belonged anywhere, as I had not said much about myself before, when talking about Switzerland. Failing to talk about my origins, or to explain the pride I felt in belonging to an old and illustrious European lineage—as the contrast between a privileged European man and images of dusty farmers in rags lining up for food seemed too strong, almost unreal—I said only that my family owned the estate of Valrolz and that therefore there was a place in this world where I would always be able to return, and that belonged to me. I actually later regretted not having found ways to elaborate on my background that evening, omitting to bring up my relative Jean-Frédéric P., who was Napoleon's banker, a generous and enlightened patron of the arts and who created the Banque de France in 1800. I also wanted to talk to Elizabeth about Edouard de P., Comte and grandson of Jean-Frédéric, who married Alphonsine "Marie" Duplessy in 1845, thus being both central and real-life characters in *The Lady of the Camellias* by Alexandre Dumas fils and, subsequently, of Verdi's *La Traviata*. Talking about the book and the opera would have put a certain romantic perspective on our inaugural date and what would follow.

IT WAS JUST SLIGHTLY before midnight, I think, when we had to burst the bubble of mental lust in which we were bathed and leave the by then empty restaurant. I walked her slowly to the taxi stand beside the Fringe Club, trying to prolong this first celebration and the pleasure of her presence as much as possible. We stopped in front of a cab waiting to be transformed into a pumpkin. I gently put my hand on her shoulder, she touched my elbow, and we blew each other chaste kisses.

Radiant and smiling, I looked at her and said, "Thank you for this exceptional evening. I am so pleased to have added a twinkling star to our cosmology."

Staring back into my eyes, she replied in a murmur, "Yes, me too. Thank you for this wonderful evening."

"I hope we will have the opportunity to see each other again soon."

"I would love that."

We looked at each other, stunned and happy. In a split second, she disappeared, swept away by her taxi.

WHAT A FIRST EVENING! I was overjoyed, as I knew it was a bright start and that we could bind ourselves together emotionally, and with brilliance. Walking back home on Wyndham Street, my happiness elevated me so much that I almost crashed into Jean-Loup A., a French friend who was impeccably dressed in a dark blue pinstriped suit and flashing a three-day beard. His neglected chin was actually similar to mine, as out of laziness and complacency, and because it gave me a roguish look, I had decided not to shave for our first date. I told him that I had just spent the most delightful evening with *the future Mrs. P.*, expressing through this pert pirouette and my sheer ecstasy the high importance I was giving to Elizabeth. He seemed pleased for me, even though he had just ended his ten-year marriage a few weeks before. I was obviously serious about making the relationship with this American woman work, and I was anticipating a bright future together, as this night had been the first confirmation that our initial physical attraction, years before, could very likely lead to profound and intense feelings.

That night, lying on my sofa, looking beyond the balcony to the myriad city lights, I felt paradoxically agitated, yet serene and proud, as I knew that we were both on the same latitude, at last! Falling slowly asleep, I remembered her mesmerizing voice saying, "Now I can and will take time to develop a relationship. Each time we bumped into each other I felt there was an attraction between us and I therefore did not understand why you never contacted me. I thought that maybe you were after all not interested." Closing my eyes, I further indulged myself in remembering her soft and sensual touch and the embrace of our special cosmology. With that in mind, and in the certitude that we were starting something strong, I abandoned myself totally in the arms of Morpheus.

THE FOLLOWING DAY I was ecstatic. Early in the morning, I went to my fitness club for a forty-minute treadmill session and to pump some iron. After more than an hour of exercise I spent some time in the sauna, recovering. I was sporting a pious half smile on my face and I felt that all of these physical efforts were no longer for my own vanity alone but that I was now working out also to look my best for a special person. I shaved as I had by then started to look more like a bum than an urban adventurer, and at 10am, walking on Hollywood Road toward the gallery, I received a text message from Elizabeth on my mobile phone:

It was a lovely night! Thank you. Hope to see you again soon. Elizabeth.

I was kept quite busy that day, shipping some AES+F photographs purchased the week before to a Taiwanese foundation and outsourcing a portrait by Picasso of Dora Maar and an Odalisque painting by Matisse for a prominent English collector. In the evening, I had to deliver and personally hang one of Erwin Olaf's *Separation* series photographs for my collector friend Amandine.

THIS FRENCH FASHION DESIGNER lived in a high apartment tower on Conduit Road, not far from the gallery. At just after 8pm I was at her door in my khaki cargo Bermudas, a collarless, open-necked pink-and-white-striped shirt, and navy blue suede loafers, holding a toolbox in one hand and the drill in the other. Amandine had cleaned up her living room, moved aside an imposing teak desk, a Japanese cabinet, and her collection of colorful and smiling Chinese social realism ceramics. She had reserved, on the main white wall, opposite to her *Le Corbusier* black leather sofa, a vast empty space. Erwin Olaf's photograph, portraying a mother offering a birthday gift to her young son, both dressed in black vinyl S&M outfits, was mounted on aluminum and acrylic and was quite heavy. Nevertheless, after I had measured the center of the wall and drilled and screwed several fittings, Amandine helped me hang the artwork. Its black and dark turquoise blue tones and glossy feel matched perfectly with the overall atmosphere of this trendy apartment.

Interestingly, the inner message of this provocative photograph is actually quite touching. The artist is expressing the sensation that we can sometimes have of being disconnected, lost, and foreign while being in a familiar and comfortable place—hence the title *Separation*. The conceptual and esthetic paradox of this artwork contrasted interestingly with the Chinese propaganda ceramic on her floor portraying Mao with smiling children living in hell.

At a little before 9pm, to celebrate this purchase and thank the handyman, Amandine opened a bottle of chilled Mâcon Villages that she had put aside for the occasion. She had forgotten to provide any snacks and so with empty stomachs the exhilarating effect of the white wine hit us rather swiftly, bringing into our conversation some lively topics. I, of course, mentioned my date the day before, and Amandine told me that she had met Elizabeth a few times at the Kee Club and that she thought she was a charming woman. The bottle was already half empty when my mobile phone blipped twice announcing a new text message. It was from my cosmology fairy:

Hi! I had a fantastic time with you last night. Thank you again for a wonderful evening. By chance, will you be at the SportAsia party at 1/5 later? It would be great to see you. I will be there around 9:30pm Can you? Elizabeth.

In courtesy to Amandine, as we were then chatting, I did not answer Elizabeth's message right away. However at some later point and because the bottle was almost empty, I gently interrupted my hostess and suggested that we go to this party together. She actually had some friends going there as well, and agreed to accompany me to my apartment first so that I could change. I finally sent a text message back thanking Elizabeth also for the amazing evening and confirming that I was coming, as soon as I could, to 1/5.

AT MY STUDIO, AFTER a seven-minute stroll downhill followed by walking up the five flights of stairs, I served Amandine the icy gin and tonic she was craving and I went to the bathroom to change. I traded my Bermudas for a pair of dark gray pants with a sheen and put on an open-necked pastel pink shirt with two breast pockets and a pair of black suede loafers. At a little before 10pm we arrived at the 1/5 restaurant, situated one floor below the eponymous bar. The party seemed to be already over, or nobody ever joined it in the first place, as the venue was almost empty. Amandine's friends were grouped strategically around a table at the back, giggling, eating canapés, and monopolizing the bottles of Moët & Chandon. Elizabeth was standing in the middle of the room, radiant and alluring despite wearing a black dress that seemed more fit for a square dance than for an after-work cocktail. She was talking with the owner of the bar and restaurant, the publisher of SportAsia magazine, and Devorah, Werner K.'s friend. The latter was also awkwardly groomed, with a coarse black dress that could hardly hide her plumpness.

I moved straight to Elizabeth and, delicately brushing her bare left shoulder, I advanced my lips and kissed her cheeks. I was instantly exhilarated by her delicate scent. She softly ran her fingers over my chin in a movement of approbation, having just sensed the difference between my smooth-face kisses and the itchy ones the night before. We were happy to meet again, and she seemed relieved to be rescued from a failed party and conversations that were shouting boredom. I was lightly tipsy, my stomach irremediably empty. I nevertheless accepted a flute of Champagne before we all sat at a table where some Italian hors-d'oeuvres were waiting to be devoured.

I sat beside Elizabeth and Devorah sat opposite us, together with the publisher. In a suspicious attempt to play the Don Juan, the Indonesian owner of SportAsia—who tried to give himself some gravitas and seemed not to admit his homosexuality to himself—clumsily praised Elizabeth's perfume and mid-length wavy haircut. Half surprised, and touched by her reserved and embarrassed reaction, I observed how she shyly and unassumingly brushed away the comments. I could feel how annoying it must be for such a beautiful person to so often receive empty compliments from phony men. We sat tightly against each other like two magnets, our hips touching, and she stretched her arm out on her right leg under the table, her palm wide open in an invitation for me to seize it. I felt the tension running through her body and I sensed right away what this offering meant. I wanted, however, to be the one playing the stick and carrot this time, so I decided to slightly frustrate her, and myself, and to wait until sometime later that evening to take her hand. The party never recovered from its poor start and as there was nothing more to drink, we decided, together with Amandine and her friends, to move to Hallo, a posh new club on Stanley Street.

As soon as we arrived, Elizabeth and I sat down on a wide velvet sofa, our bodies sensually touching. The mood was light and we continued our playful conversation while Devorah explained her wallpaper business to the publisher, who was tightly hugging a bottle of vodka. After toasting with some Cristal Rosé to this second and impromptu date, Elizabeth mentioned again, how much she had enjoyed the night before, and then added, "I feel so comfortable with you, Hector. I am so glad that you came tonight."

"Of course I came," I answered, overjoyed. "I am so happy to be here with you."

"I really wanted to see you again. You know that I am still promoting my book and often have to travel overseas for it. I will actually have to leave tomorrow for Saudi Arabia and I will not be back until Sunday. I am so excited, as I have never been to the Middle East before."

Though I was disappointed to learn that I would be unable to see Elizabeth as often as I wished in the short term, I nevertheless did not let this slight setback affect my elated mood and I therefore followed up on her announcement, "It sounds like it will be intriguing to visit this petro-monarchy to talk about China. But is the subject of your book not far from their preoccupations? I mean, they have their own economic boom in the region, in Dubai, Abu Dhabi, and Doha, and they are culturally far away from China, aren't they?"

"Well, actually China is a big oil importer and the emirs are closely following its expansion and growing demand for commodities."

"Ah, I understand. I hope then to see you soon after you come back to continue adding sparkling stars to our bright cosmology."

"Yes, me too," she answered, smiling. "We could actually

meet on Sunday evening if you are free, as I will be arriving back late that afternoon."

"I would love that. It will be great to see you then and to hear your fresh impressions of the desert."

AT MIDNIGHT, WE LEFT the group and took our time walking, followed by Devorah, through the almost deserted Lan Kwai Fong bar district. At this point, I, for the first time, gently took Elizabeth's hand in mine. She had a soft, feminine, yet slightly cold hand and she automatically squeezed mine lightly, as if she needed reassurance that this first sealing was happening for real. Finding her suddenly so fragile was tremendously moving. We looked at each other and we both felt fourteen years old. Peony-colored by the emotion and the Champagne, we were thrown suddenly into a new realm, disconnected from the reality surrounding us, savoring the inner upheavals provoked by this first physical binding. Stars were shooting in our minds and flesh, and we slowly capsized into an emotional dimension that I had for some time been longing for.

Arriving at the junction of Wyndham Street and Arbuthnot Road, Devorah wished us goodnight and walked alone the few meters to the entrance to Ivy House, her apartment tower. Elizabeth's flat was located on Kennedy Road and, consumed by the ongoing desire to be with her forever, I hailed a taxi in which we were both swiftly engulfed. In the backseat, snuggled against this wonderful woman, feeling her bare legs against my pants, I was like an adolescent on my first date. I was so proud of being with her. I was savoring every second of this precious time, and hand in hand we let the emotions flow until they submerged us. Six minutes later, the taxi stopped in front of St. Paul's. Our eyes met and we gently kissed each other's lips goodbye for the first time. Observing her walking away in the darkness, I knew that she was becoming mine; our souls were ready to erupt and create a glorious new world. I was also ready to give myself entirely to her. As soon as I arrived home, I sent her a text message, saying how enchanted I had been at seeing her again and having felt the silkiness of her lips for the first time. She replied after a few minutes:

Me too! It was great seeing you and feeling you tonight.

The following morning I was awoken by the blip of my mobile phone, announcing an incoming message. It was Elizabeth:

Hi! I had a great time last night. I'm looking forward to seeing you Sunday, and I just saw that my flight lands at 7:20pm. Sorry it's a bit late! I'll call you from the airport after I land and we can sort out where to meet. Have a terrific weekend. E.

Our cosmology was slowly getting brighter and more palpable, as we had finally left the fantasy world to land on a real, yet magical, territory. I felt blessed to have the chance to start a relationship wth this wonderful woman despite my health ordeal, and a new competitive spirit was emerging in my fight against the tumor. The vertiginous emotions I had felt while holding her hand for the first time and after the innocent first kiss in the taxi were new confirmations that the visual attraction we had felt for each other throughout the years was a sign of intense feelings deeply sown that were ready to grow, blossom, and explode as this love affair evolved.

IT WAS LATE OCTOBER and business at that time was favorable, yet slow. I had found from different collectors in Europe three rare portraits of Dora Maar by Picasso and one colorful Odalisque by Matisse to propose to my English client. One of the Picassos was especially appealing to me, as it had similarities to the painting *La Dame au Coq*. From one of the regular trips to museums with my parents when I was a child, I kept a print reproduction of this painting by the Spanish master. For some reason, this austere portrait of a woman holding a chicken mesmerized me as a five-year-old. We had the poster framed and it hung in my room until I left for Australia fourteen years later. I must still have that print in a tube somewhere in my office in Hong Kong. The similarities between the Dora Maar portrait and *La Dame au Coq* lay in their common languid pose and sad eyes, yet the shades of the Dora Maar were much more vivid. The cobalt blue and the bright yellow gave the impression that light was coming from the painting itself, giving a holy beauty to the melancholic portrait.

The brightness and precise contemporary color scheme used by Picasso, but also by artists like Van Gogh, is quite remarkable. Seeing the paintings of these two artists up close in museums or at the homes of collectors is always an immense pleasure, as they still look fresh after so many decades. It is fascinating to know that the colors chosen were meant to convey moods and emotions, rather than reality. Van Gogh actually said once, in a spurt of lucidity between two glasses of absinthe, "Instead of trying to reproduce exactly what I see before me, I make more arbitrary use of color to express myself more forcefully." Totally relating to this concept, I could have used similar terms to describe myself as being a Romanesque, as the French would say, as I was also painting and molding my life with bright colors, using my imagination and sensitivity as brushes.

During that period, my priorities were Elizabeth and checking the pulse of the alien trying to kill me. I had no other concerns on my mind. That night, following another of my goodnight messages—*See you in my dreams*—I received a short new missive from the Middle East:

Here I am, about to slip off to sleep, and maybe I'll see you in dreamland! I have just experienced 'Saudi Champagne' which involves apple juice, not alcohol! More in person soon. E.

These exchanges were pure indulgence and I was savoring their lightness and sweetness as well as what was left unsaid. She was not only responding but actually also initiating the different phases of our game of common emotional fulfillment.

On Friday night before going to bed, I sent a text message to Elizabeth about our cosmology getting brighter and my wish to be with her in the dunes. She almost instantly replied:

I think I will see a lot of stars in the desert, and can't wait to tell you all about it. I wish you could be here too, so next time you can pretend to be my brother! They'll never believe that!

The idea of traveling incognito with her to Saudi Arabia, booking a room in the same hotel, and risking our lives meeting my Scheherazade discretely and sinfully at midnight sounded exciting and Romanesque indeed.

I HAD AN APPOINTMENT with Doctor Lui earlier that day to check my health condition and to receive the results of tests done one week before. I saw him at 3pm at his Hutchison House practice. Despite his friendly, "Good afternoon Mister P.," his smile was contorted and he could hardly hide his concern under his thick glasses. To his surprise, the tumor seemed to have actually accelerated its growth, instead of having been confined by the antibiotics. This had to be analyzed and confirmed swiftly and I therefore had to go later that day to the Matilda Hospital to undergo a new MRI.

Despite a certain sense of defiance sprinkled with a bit of denial, and thus somehow minimizing what was happening inside my head, the intensity and perversion of the tumor's attack was actually worrying me enormously. In these vulnerable times, I chose not to disclose the health battle I was going through to my friends. Seeing life as a lonesome cowboy odyssey, I was not used to sharing my emotional hurdles with anyone, and I had developed a natural propensity to keep key battles to myself and to mention only the outcome to the world. I also specifically kept this dire and crucial information unknown to Elizabeth, as at no time did I want the tumor to become a pressuring factor or a burden on our budding relationship. I planned, of course, to reveal this secret once I had vanquished it, or before, if the dilemma of keeping this crucial information from Elizabeth became too difficult, too immoral. Whatever the options, this was a hard decision to make—a selfish one, by all means—but I felt then that I had no choice, as I wanted this woman so dearly. Thinking of her was a priceless source of hope.

A few days later, I received the following text message:

Hi from Jeddah airport, finally! I wish you were here; I'd love to see you. Today was long, but interesting. My presentation went well. Remind me to tell you about the goat heads! Sorry, I just realized that is not very romantic. I'll make it up to you soon. E.

ELIZABETH'S PLANE WAS SCHEDULED to land early on Sunday evening, and I decided to surprise her by picking her up at the airport. We had spoken over the phone before she boarded and she told me that she would call once she arrived in Hong Kong, to see what plans we could make together for the evening. A positive tension was mounting, because of the surprise and my exultation and anticipation of seeing and feeling her again.

At 7:43pm, twenty-three minutes after her plane's scheduled arrival time, I started to feel a little nervous, as she had not yet appeared. At 7:55pm, I was still without news from Elizabeth, but I could not call her without revealing my plan. I was becoming concerned when my phone rang. It was her, calling from a taxi speeding away from the airport! When she learned where I was, she was happy but sorry that we had missed each other. She must have exited from another gate. Her taxi was already on the expressway and could not turn back. She needed to rest a bit anyway, take a shower, and freshen up, and she therefore suggested coming to my place at 9:30pm with a bottle of Champagne to celebrate the success of her Middle East trip. I was pleased by her forwardness in inviting herself to my place, as this was a moving sign of a proactive and independent woman, and I liked that a lot.

After the twenty-five-minute express train ride from the airport, I walked straight up to my apartment through the pedestrian overpasses connecting the different parts of Central, and went directly to my rooftop to prepare a romantic setting. The brown square-shaped garden furniture and cream-colored pillows gave a clean and trendy feel to the open setting, which was surrounded by low white brick walls. I added some candles here and there to sanctify the space. The view was splendid, with the day fading and lights breaking through the office skyline on one side and the Mid-Level District's regiments of apartment blocks on the other.

AT 9:20PM, I HAD changed and was wearing a pair of dark blue cargo Bermudas, an open-necked yellow shirt, and gray suede loafers when Elizabeth called to ask for directions, as her taxi had dropped her off in Soho. Hearing again her soft, yet breezy voice increased my anticipation of welcoming her on my rooftop. I was foreseeing her intentions and was pleased by them. Yet I wanted each step in this relationship to be memorable and perfect. Having dreamed of it for so long, and putting Elizabeth above all adorable things, I did not want our first night together—if I had read my muse's mind correctly—to be spent exploring each other's sensualities like wild waves smashing against cliffs, on the large sofa, in the small studio. The candlelight under the stars was romantic; throwing pillows off the sofa to increase the space, to make love there for the first time, was not. I had obviously entertained women there before, but the context and the stakes were totally different this time. I wanted each pivotal moment in the building of our relationship to be magical and memorable, and for all the right reasons. I should probably have shared these perfectionist concerns with her at the right time, instead of potentially looking indecisive, but there is never a perfect guidebook to follow when emotions and feelings are involved.

At 9:30pm, Elizabeth called again, still lost. She was now not far from my apartment and I told her to wait and I would meet her. Two minutes later, outside, seeing her graceful gait, so recognizable from far away, my heart started to race and I could hardly hide the torrent of sublime bliss invading my being. When she finally saw me approaching, her visage illuminated like fireworks on a national day and she met my gaze at once. She was gorgeous, with her wavy hair just dried, wearing a light cotton white top with delicate embroidery, tight blue jeans, and a pair of elegant flat shoes, home of her noble feet. She was natural, chic, and wonderful. I felt proud to see that she was comfortable enough with me to wear clothes that enhanced her beauty and natural sensuality, instead of hiding her feminine wonders as I had often seen her doing before.

When we reunited, the earth could have opened up and swallowed the city surrounding us; we would not have noticed! Overwhelmed by the cavalcade of emotions, I kissed her offered lips probably a bit too quickly for her expectations. She seemed surprised by this peck and may have expected, instead, a languorous embrace. Yet she appreciated my gallantry. I took the bag containing the Champagne bottle and held her hand to walk together through the deserted Sunday evening streets toward our magic escape. I do not know what her impressions were, walking up the stained and dusty staircase of my neglected block, leading to the rooftop, yet I am sure she did not expect to see such a romantic setting under the illuminated night. She was surprised and thrilled when she sat on the outdoor sofa, surrounded by candles and thousands of household lights dancing around us that celebrated our growing cosmological metaphor.

I SAT BESIDE ELIZABETH, kissed her lips gently, took the bottle, and, targeting the luminescent moon hovering over us, I popped the cork high over the rooftop. A few seconds later, we heard it land noisily on the trunk of a car parked on the street below. Elizabeth smiled; we cheered and enjoyed the warmth of one another's emotions. Feeling so well, yet suddenly submerged by an overflow of joy, I had to create a diversion from this overly emotional moment, fearing I would otherwise disappear in an inner whirlwind of blessedness.

Repositioning myself, sitting straight on the sofa, I invited her to talk about her trip to the desert, about her conference, about the goat head, and about the Saudi Champagne. I thought she was going to mention drinking jeroboams of Chanel No.5! After she filled me in on the details of her trip, we talked about our present and common adventure, and about building our relationship carefully, to give it a solid foundation. Elizabeth then asked me, with a cautious approach, looking at me intensely to catch my innermost reaction, "Do you know that I have a son?"

"Yes, of course I know. His name is Alexander, isn't it?"

"Yes, Alexander. How do you know? Ah, maybe Devorah told you about him? Or Werner K.?"

"No. Don't you remember? We actually bumped into each other, about two years ago, I think. It was on Queen's Road Central and you were shopping with your son. That's when I saw him for the first time."

"Oh yes, that's right. And you were accompanied by a Chinese woman, right?"

She remembered that moment and recollected that I was with Olivia. I interpreted this last precision as one more proof that all those times we had briefly met in the past were still vivid in her memory, as they were also in mine. However, lacking focus and responsiveness—Elizabeth's presence taking my whole psychic space—I kept quiet, instead asking her to elaborate on the most precious being in her life. In my innermost, I wanted to know everything about Alexander, every detail his mother would want to share with me that night. I also wanted to sense beyond this romantic time together the kindhearted, touching, and protective emotions communicated by a mother while talking about her son, and feel the strength in her love for him.

Yet I did not succeed in finding the resources to react and encourage her to talk about Alexander. I was utterly disappointed by myself and especially mad at my lack of response, as I fully knew, understood, and accepted—since I had decided finally to contact Elizabeth—that Alexander would become an important part of my life, and I of his. I looked forward to it, despite the pressure I could also feel, understanding the challenge it is for a young boy to be willing to share his mother with another man.

I had actually surprised myself while thinking about Elizabeth and her son, a few days before this evening, when I had realized that prior to meeting her, I had never actually considered getting emotionally involved with the mother of a child. Until I met her, I was indeed convinced that I had a strong sense of heritage and filiation, given my family lineage. I had therefore always imagined that I would have children of my own, continuing and passing on the tradition of the P. Yet, since I had made the decision to get involved with Elizabeth and had started to date her, these considerations had evaporated and I naturally and totally accepted my future responsibilities toward Alexander. I was very much looking forward to becoming part of this young man's development and to witnessing him growing up. I was actually delighted about it, as my commitment to his mother was unconditional.

Alas, despite my strong desire to know everything about

her son, the beatific emotional state I was in and the crucial subject that Alexander was made me brush Elizabeth's maternal evocation to the sidelines for later. Therefore, instead of elaborating on this central part of her life and, thus, of our future relationship, I tried to hide my frustration, retreating into neutral topics. I actually convinced myself that saying I knew about the existence of her son was enough to reassure her about my intentions for them both. After a while, Elizabeth thankfully interrupted my aimless circumvolutions and said, "Hector, I will have to leave Hong Kong again soon. I am obviously not pleased about this, as I really want to spend as much time with you as possible. But next Thursday I will have to go for slightly more than a week to Mainland China."

"Really?" I was disappointed to learn that she had to leave again so soon. "It is again a trip related to your book?"

"Yes, for my book and also for my job. I will go first to Tianjin to meet Admiral Yeh, the president of China Trans Shipping. I want to get some insights about the international expansion of his company. I will then go to Beijing for a presentation of my book during an economic forum. I am quite excited, actually, as I have tried to meet the Admiral several times before but he has never agreed to meet until now. He is a secretive man. I have heard that his company is planning to take over a major American shipping company and I will try to get some confirmation about this deal. I want to report this information to our clients before anyone else. I hope to get a scoop." She smiled. "But even though these trips are very interesting, I am getting quite tired of them. After China, and until the end of the year, I will try to travel less. I want to have much more time for myself, and for us to be together." Her smile widened. I answered it by holding her hand.

STARS WERE SPARKLING IN the dazzling sky and the time for talk seemed to have elapsed. I sensed that Elizabeth wanted to get into a position in which our two auras would move closer in passionate cuddling, hugging, and kissing. I was also hoping for that to happen. She knew what she wanted and my lack of reaction toward her son thankfully did not erase the attraction she had developed for me over our first two dates. She slid closer to me and rubbing her hips against mine, she offered me her lips. Happily surprised by her forwardness, I gently took her delicate and willing chin in my hands. Feeling her soft skin in my palms, her golden curls caressing my face, our mellow lips pressed together, and her mischievous tongue flirting with mine almost blew my heart out. Our first deep kiss tasted like the Silk Road! We were sealed in lust and I savored this moment like none before. I caressed the nape of her neck and slowly pressed her blonde hair, wrapped my arm around her waist, and brought her even closer to me, interlacing her fingers. Her breathing was fast, lifting her chest against mine. I could feel the tension spreading through her body. We could not stop and kissed in ecstasy. We were in an emotional kaleidoscope, indulging ourselves in the eye of the multicolor thunderstorm booming in our rapture. After a while, she slowly withdrew, recovering, and laid over me, her head on my thighs and her legs across the sofa. She murmured, "I have been waiting for this moment for so long."

I caressed her hair and forehead and then responded, flattered and touched, "Me too. I feel so whole with you."

We stayed like that, intertwined, our hands entangled, feeling alone in the universe, blessed by thousands of lights surrounding us and by the brightness of the stars piercing the thick Hong Kong atmosphere. We kissed again and after a while—which felt like a blessed eternity—probably foreseeing that I was not going to move forward and propose anything further to her that night, she whispered, "I wish I could lie longer and more comfortably with you, but I feel that if I do, I would eventually fall asleep in your arms. I would love to, but I have a presentation tomorrow morning at nine at the British Chamber of Commerce."

After some more intense, lengthy, and sensual cuddling and kissing, like two teenagers prolonging a first flirtation as much as possible, I finally accompanied Elizabeth downstairs to Hollywood Road at nearly 1am. A taxi stopped, and Elizabeth looked at me, more radiant than ever. Giving me a last and luscious kiss, she entered the cab and rode away into the promising night.

Back in my studio, my mind enlightened by shimmering thoughts, I sent my naiad a text message telling her how exultant and speechless I was with the gratifying and sensual evening I had just spent with her. I went to bed with the exhilarating taste of her lips on mine, her hypnotic scent all over me, her delicate and electrifying touch and the soft and addictive texture of her skin marked indelibly in my senses. Early the next morning I received her answer:

It was delightful to be with you last night! I will miss you while I'm in Tianjin, but I will be in work-hard mode then. Let's play when I come back on Thursday 8. E.

ELIZABETH WAS STILL IN Hong Kong for several more days, as she was not leaving until November 1. She was quite busy, though, and we could not meet until her return from Mainland China, so we kept in daily touch by phone, despite it being my least favored means of communication.

During these days, so close, yet so far away, I was thinking a lot, as questions began to appear and to interfere with my peace of mind. Beside the strong feelings growing fast within me for this ravishing woman, sporadic waves of doubt and slight sensations of panic were washing ashore. The tumor was hiding in the dark and damp shadows of a too-early end. The killer within was particularly present in my mind, provoking an intense perception of detachment toward our world, and a fear of not being part of it anymore. To my perplexed astonishment, I was starting to lose my sense of judgment. I was drifting slowly into an overly emotional realm, made up of luminescent and ruddy corners, but also of dark and frightening ones.

I am not unfamiliar with doubts, but I have never been through so many and so varied and powerful ones as during this courting period with Elizabeth. Believing in my singularity and in my capacity to develop a compelling, meaningful, challenging, and colorful life, I had always dated women who were, for me, the incarnation of charm and beauty, intelligence, and success and whom I could hence admire, be proud of, and of course love. Despite being a sensitive man, I was still not quite used to these kind of disorienting doubts and states of confusion while building a relationship. Coping with so many of them was new, especially as they were being triggered by different and opposite sources, including death. I had never before felt such a confusing vertigo, even when I dated the niece of the Thai king's brother (and almost married her, as she proposed three times) and spent holy days and birthday parties at her aunt's palace on the outskirts of Bangkok. I also had never feared losing my sanity, or free falling into an abyss of doubts, with my last girlfriend in Switzerland, Stefanie von H., child psychiatrist and daughter of an influential Austrian philosopher.

I was truly sinking into an unknown phenomenon, an emotional black hole, filled with paradoxes that were provoking a big bang within my mind and soul. Feeling uneasy about keeping my health ordeal to myself, I was also thinking that losing Elizabeth—given the possibility of my life's journey coming to an abrupt end—would not only be terrible, it would also be totally immoral to get her involved, without full knowledge, in this dramatic story in the first place.

I took this degradation seriously, as I perceived right away the erosive danger that these emerging confusing thoughts and emotional shockwaves could have on the future of our relationship. I had therefore to find, quickly, ways to curse the darkness and tame the dragon to regain the strength to be in control (as much as I could) to be the champion of her heart that Elizabeth and I were expecting.

ON TUESDAY, I DELIVERED a couple of large black monochrome paintings by the Australian artist Dale Frank to the house of Yam-kuen T. This bulimic local collector was a conceited gay Chinese man in his mid-fifties living surrounded by seven fox terriers in a big house on the heights of Happy Valley. He would usually welcome me in his living room on the first floor or in his private showroom on the basement, pushed by his Filipino helper on an old dented wheelchair, despite being able to prance like a calf, dressed in black army pants, black plastic sandals, and what seemed to always be the same black t-shirt covered with dog hair. The paintings from Dale Frank he had selected were perfect examples of the concept that this artist has been developing for the past thirty years. Using varnish and resins on massive canvases that create thick yet glossy and reflective pieces, this renowned painter explored the concept of metamorphosis. Immersed by the size of the works, we see the reality surrounding us through the distorted reflection emanating from them. Through this new prism, our mind morphs and enters into a new dimension.

On my way back to Central in the taxi, my phone rang and Elizabeth's name flashed on the screen. I picked up and jovially answered, "Hi, Elizabeth. How are you?"

"Hi," she replied with an exhausted yet bright voice. "I am fine, thank you. Well, actually, I am quite tired but I am so happy to hear you. The preparation for my Chinese trip is driving me crazy, as I have had to reschedule several meetings in Tianjin and Beijing several times. I really need to be distracted from work and I wish I could find time to be with you before I leave."

"Me too," I replied instantly. "You know that I am here for you, anywhere, anytime. I miss your touch and your kisses."

"Oh, me too. I need them ..."

In the evening, I had dinner at an outdoor Malaysian/Thai restaurant on Wing Wah Lane, off Lan Kwai Fong, with my then blue-haired friend Andy M. This German photographer living in the Philippines was still struggling to decide between his commercial assignments and the desire to become a contemporary artist. Between two rounds of beers and some friendly arguments about Andy's wobbly situation—being bankrupt had become almost as much a part of his character as the color of his hair—I sent a text message to Elizabeth that showed that she was always on my mind. After a few minutes, she replied:

Hi! Your day sounds intriguing. I wish I were there with you after a very long day, juggling the different facets of my life. I am leaving in the morning. I'd love to see you but tomorrow, like today, I need to be back at work by 7am. Ouch!

ON THURSDAY, NOVEMBER 1, understanding that her flight to Tianjin was scheduled for the late morning, I skipped my gym session and decided to surprise Elizabeth by faxing a thoughtful and tangible note to her office, as I knew she would be there early. I arrived at the gallery around 7am, planning to send Elizabeth some encouraging and thoughtful words that would accompany her to Mainland China. We never exchanged e-mails, as I did not want to flood her with virtual messages or make her feel that I was overly present. I also wanted to keep as much as possible for our real exchanges. Aside from the basic plan to send her a fax, I had not thought about what I was going to include in my missive. Looking for a while around my desk and at the numerous art books, biographies, and novels I had on the shelves surrounding the office space, my intuition eventually guided me toward Paul Claudel's play *The Tidings Brought to Mary*, as the phrasing of this French Catholic author is transcendent and his lyricism is quite contagious and inspirational. Going through the play swiftly, I found—guided perhaps?—the perfect page and made a photocopy. I then wrote by hand on top of the printed text, as clear as possible to prevent any premature disposal:

"Dear Elizabeth,

To keep you company in China and as I can't whisper them to you until your return, here are few words by Paul Claudel that I would like to share with you:

Jacques Hury: I love you!

Violaine: And that I am your wife and your only love.

Jacques Hury: My wife and only love.

Violaine: Then learn of the fire that consumes me! Know this flesh, which you have loved so much! Come nearer to me. (He comes nearer) Nearer! Nearer still! Close against my side.

I wish you a wonderful trip and will be thinking of you all along.

Kisses,

Hector"

The text expressed love and it was the first time I had included such intensity in any of our conversations or written messages. I knew I was taking a risk in using such wording, especially as I would have hesitated to do it in person. I was ready to give myself totally to Elizabeth and fall madly in love with her, yet, even though I was on the verge of welcoming her into the depths of my heart, I had not quite capsized yet. I knew that we were both riding fast on the same expectations and that we were not very far away from sharing such overwhelming emotions for real. Yet, even though the published passage was unequivocal and was used to express my attraction for this woman and my unmistakable romanticism, what followed in the book, unbeknownst to her, after the last sentence, was dramatically close to my own reality; Violaine takes a knife and incises a hole, under the left breast, near her heart, in the linen of her gown. Appearing underneath were the first spots of leprosy ...

My mobile phone rang at 7:40am. It was Elizabeth, "Good morning, Elizabeth. How are you so early?"

"Hi. I am well, thank you. And you?" Her voice was soft, as usual, yet with a mix of pleased surprise and slight embarrassment. She was probably wondering—rightly so—how exactly to take my message.

"I am very rested," I answered, letting her continue.

"I just came into my office a few minutes ago and saw your fax."

"Ah yes, my fax." I was confident of the wittiness and pertinence of my message, yet I could not hide a little apprehension.

She quickly reassured me though, when she continued, with a lighthearted yet slightly subdued tone, "Thank you so much Hector, it was certainly unexpected. What a surprise! It is so romantic."

I played it modestly, defusing the pressure, saying that it was natural for me to make such statements and it was a way to be with her in China. Changing topics, we talked a bit about my ancestors on my mother's side who went to Tianjin 150 years ago to trade Swiss watches and other goods and stayed there, and in Shanghai, for four generations, finally coming back to Switzerland at the beginning of the Cultural Revolution. I encouraged her to visit the foreign concessions, with the remains of colonial houses with their typical and distinctive nineteenth-century European architectures.

In the following days, and over the length of her China trip, we kept in regular contact through text messages and phone calls. Everything was going well; Elizabeth was moving forward, facing her personal and professional challenges, and I was free falling into a chasm of fundamental questioning and trying to keep my sanity together.

On Friday late in the afternoon, I received a message on my mobile phone:

Hi! My meeting with Admiral Yeh was today and I am writing part of my report tonight. So all is well. Your ancestors must have been extremely tough! It is freezing here. We will be warmer together for sure. E.

AS I MISSED ELIZABETH at the airport when she returned from the Middle East, I warned her this time that a surprise would await her again at Chek Lap Kok. She knew she could therefore expect anything when she landed back in Hong Kong in less than a week. My idea of a surprise was to rent a Rolls-Royce with a chauffeur and to pick her up in pomp and circumstance. I spent several days seeking the right car rental company, as most of them had only bulky Mercedes Benzes, instead of the iconic British brand. I finally found a wedding planning firm in Kowloon offering this service. As I had to choose the car and pay a few days in advance in cash, I went all the way across the harbor, to a derelict office tower in Mongkok—on the dark side of Hong Kong, as frightened expatriates would say—to find this company in the basement, tucked between a noisy pet shop and a steamy dry cleaner. I could not wait to see Elizabeth's beautiful and enlightened face when she discovered what these mysteries were all about.

ON SATURDAY, AROUND 7:30PM I called my dulcinea, hiding my excitement, "Hi, Elizabeth. How are you?"

"Hi, Hector, I am fine but terribly exhausted. It is still freezing cold here. How are you?"

"Very well, and even better now that I hear your voice."

"Yes, me too. I wish you could be here to cheer and warm me up."

"So you were satisfied with the interview of the admiral yesterday?" I asked, interested.

"Yes. I really wanted to understand his international expansion plans and see if I should advise our clients to invest more in the company."

"So did you get your scoop in the end?"

"Somehow yes, actually." She sounded proud of her findings. "It is always tricky to get key information through a translator, as the interview is often scattered and Admiral Yeh was not particularly forthcoming when talking about his firm. But I think I got the confirmations I needed. I will tell you all about it when I come back."

"I look forward to it. I have dinner soon with a few friends, but I really wish I could take the first flight to Tianjin to join you instead. We could then celebrate the success of your interview," I said, sincere yet joking.

"That would be lovely. But I will fly to Beijing tomorrow and I would not have much time there for us, unfortunately. I wish I could feel you beside me now, though, as it is still freezing ..."

ON SUNDAY EARLY EVENING, I met my friend Philippe G. and one of his relatives who was visiting Hong Kong. He invited us to the Peak to have dinner at the cozy restaurant The Peak Lookout, located at the former sedan carriers resting area, from the early colonial times. It was a mild evening for the season, and we sat in the open garden, amid the lush growth, and ordered some Indian tandoori, which are, surprisingly for this European-looking place, their trademark. Of course, my main topic of discussion was Elizabeth and the surprises I was fomenting.

I could sense in Philippe's expression that he probably thought I was getting out of control in my romantic descriptions of Elizabeth and in my courting, but I could not hide my natural exultation. I totally assume and assert my Romanesque urge to create a certain atmosphere, maybe slightly disconnected with our everyday realities, when building a relationship with a woman who could potentially be *the one*. To me, it is not really worth getting involved at all, if there is from the beginning no such fulfilling prospect in sight. I obviously take the risk that my intentions will be misunderstood. If such a situation arises, then I am usually able to reach out and to clarify or explain myself. I will, however, never renounce taking this risk, because choosing the option of blandness would mean capitulating to dull mediocrity. Yet, I was no longer on familiar ground, now counting the tumor into the equation of my love affair with Elizabeth. I was, therefore, doubling the risks, walking on an emotional tightrope that could swing and break at any time.

Philippe likes to quote his infamous French friend Jean-Marie B. when describing his job, "He is a *bancario*, not a *banchiere*." Yet sometimes, expanding with his usual optimism when talking about Hong Kong, he seems to work instead for the Tourism Board—as he surprisingly feels in his element in this overly polluted and provincial world city. We therefore had a friendly argument about the lack of accessible green sites in Hong Kong—he thought they were in abundance and well landscaped; I was complaining that people were forbidden to stretch out on lawns in public parks and that a lot of hiking trails in the countryside were made of asphalt. We were prolonging this conversation while walking around the Peak on the tar-paved Lugard Road, this bucolic stroll illuminated by bright spotlights, when my phone vibrated, announcing a message from Elizabeth, who was answering a text message I had sent to her earlier:

Hi from Beijing! It is sunset here, but not terribly romantic, unlike the Peak, with you. Hope you had a great weekend.

IN THE COURTING PHASE, or even fully into a relationship, it is essential, as in chess, to always be alert, focused, forward-looking, and receptive. As the Rolls-Royce surprise was already arranged, I was now thinking of the next plan. I had thought for a long time about purchasing a car, and I therefore started to look for the same type of Audi cabriolet that I had driven in Geneva, before moving to Hong Kong. I am not terribly interested in mechanics or technology, but I certainly like the look and reliable German qualities of this convertible, and I was looking forward to driving it here. This new toy would give me a lot of satisfaction and more flexibility. I was already picturing myself driving on weekends along Sai Kung's shoreline, with Elizabeth by my side and Alexander in the backseat, the three of us with our blond hair flowing freely in the wind, large contented smiles on our faces, singing in unison some 80's summer song. It was a perfect picture that I could not wait to see materialize.

After searching at length, I finally found a metallic black Audi at a car dealer in Tin Hau and went on Monday to inspect it with Andy M. The car looked almost mint. Opening the hood, we realized that the compact V6 horsepower engine was quite dirty, but that could easily be fixed. I liked the convertible a lot and I went for a test drive with Chee-Hwa, the owner of the shop. I had not driven a car for more than three years and I was a bit rusty and cautious at first, especially as the driving in Hong Kong is on the left side of the road. I soon felt comfortable behind the steering wheel, though, and indulged in the sensation of sheer liberty one can sense in a cabriolet. Some of the electronic components were not functioning, however, and there was a problem with the opening of the trunk. Chee-Hwa would therefore have to fix these problems before responding to my counteroffer.

ON TUESDAY MORNING, WALKING down Shelley Street after a long and exhausting workout session at the gym, I received a call from Elizabeth, "Hi there." Her voice was cheerful. "I tried to call you before, but it may have been too early. How are you?"

"Hi Elizabeth. I've just finished exercising. I am so glad to hear from you."

"Me too. This trip is thankfully ending soon. It was way too long and I so much look forward to being with you again soon. I have to tell you something though, regarding our Thursday plans."

"Yes..." I suddenly felt uneasy.

"I received a call from my boss in New York yesterday. He is asking me to write an update on a company in India by early Thursday evening. I will therefore need to go to my office for a few hours and I won't be able to be with you the whole time after I land. I had hoped I could be, but I can't. But don't worry. I can manage to write this report quickly and we can see each other once I have finished. I am sorry if this disrupts your plans ..."

Reassured, as nothing dramatic had come up, I replied, "Sure, that's fine. Of course I was looking forward to being with you the whole time, from as soon as you landed, but I understand the imperatives of your business." I then added, pertly, "Having said that, though, you have to know that even if I am a Zen type of guy, you can tell your boss that this time I forgive him, but if he interferes again with our relationship, I will fly to New York and kick his ass!"

"Really?" Elizabeth giggled. "I've actually never seen you angry. I always see you cool and calm ..."

"That's because I've never had any reason to be angry or

upset in your presence. But you should not underestimate Swiss volcanoes. When they erupt, they create havoc!" I laughed.

She laughed back. The tone of her voice had the distinctive mark of someone emotionally capsizing, and this made me feel suddenly strong and pleased.

THE CATHAY PACIFIC FLIGHT from Beijing was scheduled to arrive in Hong Kong at 4:05pm on Thursday, November 8, and I was to meet the chauffeur of the Rolls-Royce at the East Wing parking lot of the airport, beside arrival Gate A.

When this D-Day came, I dressed sharply in a dark blue jacket with a white handkerchief looming out of my breast pocket, and an open-necked blue shirt, white pants, and a pair of dark grey suede loafers. I also had brought with me two Champagne flutes and two piccolo of Bellini to savor during the ride. My mind was overflowing with expectation, excitement, and emotion.

The Rolls-Royce was a dark brown 1989 Silver Spirit with beige leather interior. Not as fancy as Curly McClain's Surrey with the Fringe on Top, but enough to achieve the effect I wanted, as, aside from the romantic attention, this surprise was meant to be taken with a wink, a wide smile, and a big kiss. I sent the chauffeur to the gate alone with a sign on which Elizabeth's name was printed and I waited in the car, in delightful anticipation of seeing her again after almost two weeks, and impatient to see her reaction. It was a pleasant and hot day, with the sun striking steadily on the Rolls-Royce's roof. Not wanting to roast inside, I got out of the boiling car and joined some chauffeurs in livery, waiting for their passengers.

The plane having been slightly delayed, my driver arrived about twenty minutes later in a rushed stride. He had met Elizabeth and she was waiting inside, close to the parking entrance, keeping cool and out of this unusual November heat. I could not see her because the glass doors behind which she was standing were tinted, but instinctively sensing her presence, my heart started to pound. The chauffeur drove the Silver Spirit to the entrance and the doors opened on Elizabeth when he entered the building to take her luggage and the laptop case reposing at her feet. Seeing her now for real, although from a distance, after so many days of anticipation, was like seeing a holy vision. She was stunning, as usual, with her characteristic and attractive gait, her delicate nose gauging the air, and her hair ruffled after a four-hour flight. I could not wait to rush to her, so contagious was her presence, and to take her in my arms. When she saw me coming, her pensive face lightened up at once and after a first expression of surprise, an ardent and emotional smile shone in its entire splendor for me. She apparently did not expect me to be there to pick her up as well. Acknowledging that, I realized that she might not have been used to such romantic expressions of tenderness by men and that my European ways might seem quite exotic to her.

I took her tightly in my arms, smelling her intoxicating scent at the base of her neck, and then I gave her a gentle peck on the lips. She looked at me, smiled, and said, "Hi Hector, it is so good to see you again. I am so happy." She then paused and added, "I really missed your blue eyes."

"They are all yours now. I also missed you very much, Elizabeth."

She took my hand and, nodding toward the Rolls, said, "I would never have expected this! This is wonderful."

She was wearing a pair of blue jeans and an elegant azure silk jacket with colorful embroidery, probably Thai—or maybe ethnic Chinese. We walked a few meters to the Rolls-Royce, embracing and looking at each other as if it were the last time, and I could feel her high emotions through the rapid movements running through her slender body. The chauffer opened the right door and we swiftly jumped into the car. Elizabeth sat on the left side, lying sideways, her back slightly against the window, stretching one leg over mine. I took her hands and blended our fingers in a sensual imbroglio. The car started up and she continued to express her excitement, "You can't imagine how relieved I am to finally be back. And I am so glad to feel you again. Holding our hands like this reminds me of the first time you took my hand in Lan Kwai Fong. I was so thrilled that you did it. You know, my body was electrified." She smiled, almost embarrassed by this admission, but she continued, "The emotion that I felt then was so strong, so overwhelming, that I could hardly breathe. Just like now." She looked at me with a sweet and almost imploring expression.

Flattered by her admittance, I replied, equally touched by that remembrance, "Me too. It was such a magic moment."

Moving fast along the highway, passing the high-rise and monotone apartment blocks of Tung Chung, the emotion in the cabin soon reached its paroxysm. Had we been alone we would probably have lost all control and indulged ourselves by kissing passionately and further exploring each other's sensuality in a blissful choreography. I broke a brief virginal and emotive silence by twisting open the Bellini's cap and poured the peach nectar into the crystal flutes. We toasted each other and when I asked her if the spirit of my ancestors had taken proper care of her in Tianjin, she replied, "Yes, they certainly did, thank you. I thought a few times that I would actually freeze and break on the spot, as it was so cold up there. I wanted to tour the city, but I ended up staying in the hotel most of the time. The weather was too tough for me. I honestly don't like cold weather."

As she had informed me about her professional deadline, I had rescheduled the other surprises that were planned for this romantic day. Tightly embracing, we bravely sliced through the thick emotional steam emanating from our burning souls. After some more talk about her trip, I turned our conversation to tackle the stakes that building a relationship involved and said, "You know how much I want our relationship to succeed. But we should be extremely cautious while building it. We should make sure that each brick becomes the strong groundwork for our future."

"What? What did you say? I do not understand." Elizabeth seemed suddenly agitated, and her voice sounded worried. She then asked nervously, "You want to put some brakes on the relationship?"

Surprised by her reaction, I did not understand at first and mumbled, "Huh? Brakes? What?" Then I got it and, instantly smiling, burst out laughing. "No, not brakes!" I shouted. "I meant bricks." I lightly touched her knee to reassure her. "What I meant is that while we move forward, we have to make sure that each brick of the fundament of our relationship is super strong."

"Oh, I see." Relieved, she laughed at her own fear. "You scared me! I thought you wanted to slow down."

"Slow down? Of course not. Not at all!"

We exchanged a light kiss of understanding, so happy to move forward, fast and steady. Our legs and hands were continually entwined; the glow of her body excited my senses.

As Elizabeth had mentioned *The Alchemy of Desire* a few times, I had purchased the novel right after our first date. I had just finished reading the last of the 528 pages the day before. I had told her once over the phone that I had been touched by one of the heartbreaking stories in the novel, and I was therefore looking forward to sharing our impressions of it in a romantic situation. A moving car, even a Rolls-Royce, did not seem to fit such a desired setting, yet Elizabeth spontaneously initiated the recollection, and I was not going to postpone this conversation for futile contextual reasons. I had actually been especially moved by the heartfelt and lonesome story of the character Catherine, with whom I could identify on many levels, as she was also a free spirit living her life in a Romanesque way. I told her that I thoroughly sympathized with the heroine and was not sure I had fully recovered yet from this reading. She seemed pleased and somehow proud that I had become so emotional about a book that she cherished. She confessed a few minutes later that she also connected with—and felt deeply for—Catherine's character, depicted as an independent and adventurous American woman. We exchanged another kiss while the driver kept a suspicious eye on us in the rearview mirror.

AFTER EMERGING FROM THE West Tunnel connecting Kowloon to Hong Kong Island, the Rolls-Royce entered Central at a slow pace, because of the heavy traffic. As Elizabeth needed to get some documents from her apartment prior to heading to her office to meet her deadline, I asked the chauffeur to park the Silver Spirit in front of Tang King Po College and to wait for us. Together with her Filipino maid, who had been waiting outside the apartment block, we walked up the five flights of stairs to her flat.

She was living in a cozy place, with oversized windows that let the sunny day in to brighten the living room. Several green plants were aligned along the wall, on the right side of the entrance, beside a sculpture of steel bamboos by Korean artist Seo Jung-Guk. The ochre tile floor gave a kind of Mediterranean feel to the apartment, and an alcove led off to her bedroom. On the opposite side from the entrance, a small Chinese chi wood bed, converted into a sofa and covered with colorful pillows, faced two cute blue, almost monochrome canvases hanging on the white wall, probably from an Indian or Southeast Asian painter.

Elizabeth escorted me to her bedroom. The red lampshades above and beside her bed gave an incandescent tone to the entire space, giving it a boudoir atmosphere. I was like a bull stimulated by the sanguine color that was firing the room; I wanted to take Elizabeth in my arms, kiss her languorously, and finally seal our two ardent bodies together. However, she had to hurry, her deadline looming, and anyway her maid was waiting in the living room. We therefore quickly headed back to the Rolls-Royce and drove toward the Bank of America Tower. Stopping right in front of her office building, the chauffeur opened the trunk, handed her the leather briefcase, and got back into the car. I was left on the sidewalk with Elizabeth; the world had stopped once more.

"Well," I said, smiling, looking her in the eyes. "Here we are ..."

Slightly blushing, she answered softly, "Yes."

I then clarified our program, "Let's meet for the second part of the surprise at 8:20pm at Pier 9. You know, it is just beside the Star Ferry jetty."

"Fabulous! That leaves me plenty of time to finish my report and to prepare myself for our evening. Thank you for being so thoughtful, Hector."

"It's my pleasure." I softly brushed her cheek with my palm, held her right hand with the other, brought my lips to hers, and gave her a goodbye kiss. She seemed surprised, probably taken aback a bit, as she was in front of her office tower, somehow exposed. Yet she quickly recovered and smiled at this impromptu and demonstrative sign of affection. I believe she realized then that she was, of course, free to formalize a relationship in Hong Kong, and so a weight may have dropped off her chest, enhancing her feelings of lightness. No longer was anything forcing her to impose an emotional reclusiveness on herself. Even though this acknowledgement may have been a refreshing surprise to her, it may also have seemed dangerous, as I think she started to feel emotionally vulnerable.

She hesitantly walked away. I re-entered the Silver Spirit and, while turning to the rear of the car to take the two Champagne flutes and put them into a small bag, I perceived, almost subliminally, that Elizabeth's face was turned tenderly toward me. Despite the doubts, the inner struggles, and the emotional freefalling, the simple sight of this stunning woman turning around to have a last glance at me was another touching proof that we were both moving forward, with growing feelings and a lot of emotions and expectations. I was relieved, touched, and elated by this symbolic gesture.

The chauffeur drove me back to the gallery, as it was only 5:40pm. I had a few art deals to work on, among which was the price negotiation for my favorite of the three Picassos that the English collector had selected. I was pleased that he had chosen to purchase the bright and colorful *Dora Maar*, as that would give me the opportunity to see this radiant painting up close. To travel the globe and see, during a presale check at a discrete and secure viewing room or still hanging on a collector's wall, masterpieces just purchased through me or offered for sale at my discretion is one of the finest privileges and pleasures of dealing art.

Elizabeth called a while later, asking what the dress code was for the evening and wondering if she should wear the same black dress that she had at the 1/5 restaurant cocktail party. I shivered at this thought as the dress did not fit her well, and her beauty deserved a much nicer and nobler jewel case than this pious gown. I said that she did not need to be that formal and that being dressed in a chic and smart casual style would make it easier for us to enjoy each other's company. As the weather was decent and mild for the season, I myself opted for a light khaki open-necked shirt, white pants, and my pair of gray suede loafers.

AT A LITTLE BEFORE 8:20pm, I was at Pier 9. Five minutes later Elizabeth emerged from a taxi, more splendid and glamorous than I had ever seen her; she was a stunning and fresh beauty in a long cream-and-blue Indian tunic with embroidery around the chest, worn over white pants, her feet groomed by a pair of delicate evening shoes. She was unbelievably attractive in her simplicity and was showing, in comparison to the 1/5 *square dance* dress, full control and awareness of her grace and femininity. She had made a real effort and I was proud that she felt comfortable enough to open her sensuality to me so much again. I actually felt underdressed in the face of her splendor. Taking her hand gently, I led her to the pier. She thought I had booked a table at the new restaurant on top of the Star Ferry wharf and had therefore no idea what was actually awaiting her. This prompted more inner excitement on my end. Like a naughty child, proud of his unfolding plot, I knew my surprise was much more original, romantic, and exciting than a simple restaurant booking.

Pier 9 was almost empty, and we leaned over the fence, looking at Victoria Harbor, toward the lights of Tsim Sha Tsui. We held hands tightly while a light breeze caressed us. The imposing sailboat *Aqualuna* was approaching on the opposite side of the jetty but Elizabeth, pensive, her eyes riveted to the horizon, had not the least idea of what was happening behind us. Having noticed the movement of the ship, I took her shoulders and turned her slowly around. Her eyes opened wide in surprise. The dark brown teakwood junk was majestic in the night, with its flamboyant red sails flapping in the wind. We walked toward the boat that was softly lighted by a myriad of lanterns. After being greeted by the crew, I casually guided my nymph over the gangway and up the stairs, leading her to a covered deck furnished with welcoming and comfortable velvet red ottomans, inviting us to rest.

I could feel how pleased and touched she was by these romantic surprises, and she gave me a kiss that I answered with another lengthy and passionate one. Emotionally chained to each other, we ordered two glasses of white wine. We were seated just opposite the captain's small cabin, and, saluting the jolly and chubby man who was going to sail us around the illuminated and fragrant harbor for an hour, I jokingly asked Elizabeth if he looked like China Trans Shipping's Admiral Yeh. We were not alone on the junk, but the small group of Korean businessmen on the aft area of the deck did not disturb us in the slightest, as we had slid into a bubble of careful and exclusive emotions. We felt so good holding hands, enchanting ourselves by diving into one another's burning feelings. The setting was just perfect for sharing this precious and charming time together.

"This is marvelous. I never knew that we could sail with such an amazing boat on the harbor," complimented Elizabeth, excited by the originality of this venue. "It is a wonderful surprise!"

"Yes, it is truly a unique experience, isn't it?"

Emerging from our soul readings, we moved into varied and colorful conversations, indulging ourselves in the common intellectual, cultural, and sensitive wavelength on which we were riding. Elizabeth may have been a bit more in control of herself than I was, yet she also had obviously not thoroughly mastered her emotions, as she brought up, at some point, unexpectedly and out of context, Katie Holmes, running the New York Marathon. It was odd to suddenly have a third person, coming from the popular press, a gossip character, intrude on our romantic date on this wonderful junk. I took this evocation as a visible sign of Elizabeth's unsteady emotions, maybe clumsily searching for topics, which touched me highly as I realized then that I was not the only one feeling fourteen years old and combating inner emotional overflows.

I had been struggling for several weeks now, trying to decide if I should mention the tumor to Elizabeth or not, as I did not think it was honest to conceal this crucial information from her. I eventually opted for the uneasy option of selfishly keeping my health issues to myself for the time being, because I did not want this alien to be openly part of the equation of this nascent relationship, potentially putting pressure on or confusing my naiad. Keeping this life struggle quiet was not an easy decision to make, as the neoplasm seemed committed to finding a breach to continue expanding through my skull, and to reach its deadly goal. I therefore decided to simply mention for the time being that I had a secret, which would be unveiled in due course. I do not specifically remember how I packaged and presented this opaque announcement, but I think she sensed that it was something important. Respecting my lack of elaboration, she did not ask me to explain myself or to develop this key subject.

The evening flowed gently by, and we were savoring each minute together when a deckhand announced that we had arrived back at Pier 9. It had been slightly more than an hour already, but we had been so merged into one another that we had not felt the passage of time around us. As the setting was truly breathtaking, and as we felt so complete together, we could have chosen to take another tour, but I suggested disembarking instead, as another surprise was still to come.

WE STEPPED OFF THE junk and caught a taxi. Despite giving only the name of the street to the driver, to keep the surprise secret as long as possible, Elizabeth, smart and canny as she was, nevertheless understood right away where we were heading. She was thrilled when she discovered that I had booked a table at Dehla—a chic, modern, and creative contemporary Indian vegetarian restaurant—as she told me it was actually her favorite restaurant. She gently squeezed my hand in appreciation, and then gave me a light kiss.

Dehla had been opened about three years before by Charmy K., a short and sharp Hindu businesswoman at whose house I once had the pleasure to dine, and to admire her collection of Indian contemporary art. She tried to bring sophisticated Indian cuisine to a city where most ethnic restaurants were serving overly traditional and expected dishes. Perhaps because of the restaurant's location, tucked slightly away from the main entertainment areas, she had, however, had difficulty keeping her place full. It was therefore no surprise to be welcomed by a single Nepalese waitress, and to see two men in suits finishing their business dinner at the only other occupied seats.

Our table was set in the middle of the restaurant, and the staff was bemused, I think, to see us honoring our booking at that late hour. It was close to 10pm by then. Even though we were doubling the number of guests that night, our presence also meant that they would have to stay on duty substantially longer, as lovebirds are usually not in a hurry to put an end to their romantic twitters. I let Elizabeth choose for both of us from what inspired her among the creative dishes listed on the menu, and I ordered a bottle of Chablis Saint-Martin to accompany our dinner.

The atmosphere at Dehla was cheerful and romantic, and the conversation was voluble, with many smiles from each side of the table. Fully connected, we felt we could stay like that forever. Time was flying fast again, though, and it was only when we saw the cook discretely leaving the restaurant that we realized that only the waitress was left to accommodate our desires. It was slightly past midnight when we burst our dazzling bubble and stepped out onto Arbuthnot Road. As the night was hospitably warm, and we had no reason or will to leave each other soon, we walked together toward Elizabeth's apartment, like two teenagers. We were embracing so closely that we were occasionally stepping on each other's shoes. Passing by the gate of the old Governor's House on Upper Albert Road, we stopped, turned toward one another, and in a passionate embrace exchanged a politically incorrect kiss under the approving moonlight.

Following up on one of her comments, I put an unexpected halt to our sweet misbehavior and mentioned that I would have lunch the following day with my old friend Harold C. This seventy-one-year-old British gentleman was a board member of several multinational firms and a worldwide expert in camellias.

He traveled the world giving speeches during botanical symposia and was now visiting me on his way to Shanghai. I told Elizabeth how dear in my heart this particular species of flower was, but that now I would have to make some space for another beautiful one as well. She smiled, confused, and asked me how I knew so many things about this mother of all flowers. I told her that I would explain my family connections with the camellias and my knowledge about this plant another time, because we had just then arrived at the door of her apartment block. As if the world would not see another day, we kissed in a passionate embrace. I then kissed the palm of her hand and she entered her building, pensive, leaving me outside on the steps, as she had to wake up early for another professional assignment. I did not ask for a nightcap. I probably should have, as it would have shown that despite my seeming lack of urgency I desired her like I never had desired any other woman before, but instead I walked away.

THE NEXT MORNING, ELIZABETH sent me this text message:

Thank you so much for a fantastic afternoon and evening! I had such a good time. E.

A few minutes later, still slightly sleepy, I received a call from my friend Harold, kindly asking me to book the China Club for lunch. He specified that our common friend and my former University of Geneva fellow-student Dragan S., who had recently become the new CEO of Croatia's main investment bank, would accompany him. I had not seen my Slavic friend for many years, and he wanted to surprise me by joining us unannounced, but Harold blew it!

As usual, the traditional Chinese dishes were delicious. Eating in this baroque surrounding daringly mixing the style of 1920s Shanghai and the best of the worst of Chinese contemporary art, was always a fun and a singular experience—

especially when shared with dear friends. The atmosphere was excellent, as we were ecstatic to be united again after not having seen each other for almost four years. We recollected, with a light spirit, funny common adventures and enquired about one another's current projects and relationships.

I, of course, mentioned Elizabeth and described our dates in detail, regretting that it was too early in our relationship to introduce her to these faraway yet close friends. I also realized that I had never mentioned the book *The Lady of the Camellias* to any of them, and with Harold's floral expertise, I could not stay quiet about the story of my relative any longer. I therefore explained to them that the character depicted, with undeniable jealousy, as a lightweight by Alexandre Dumas fils, impersonated by the Comte de N. in the book, was actually my ancestor Comte Edouard de P. He had been madly in love with a classy courtesan. When she fell ill with pneumonia and was crumbling under debts, as all her powerful and wealthy suitors disappeared almost overnight, he brought her to London, where he was living at that time, and they got married. They moved back to Paris, where Marie Duplessy slowly recovered some vigor and happiness. The marriage did not last, yet Edouard gave her enough money to pay off her debts. She also kept the proud gratification of signing her correspondence *Comtess Duplessy*. She died a few months later, and Edouard and Alexandre Dumas fils were the only two persons walking behind her hearse, accompanying the Lady of the Camellias to her grave. Acknowledging some similarities with Dumas' novel, I secretly hoped, however, that my sentimental journey with Elizabeth would not find such a tragic ending as that of Armand and Marguerite in the book, filled with misperceptions, unnecessary suffering, indifference, and, of course, death. I also felt the need to share my health worries with my friends for the first time.

While Dragan felt sorry to hear about the tumor and saluted my courage as well as my relative's story by lifting his Tsingtao beer in my direction, Harold—who at the age of sixty-six had come out of the closet and divorced his American wife, with whom he had two sons—was more interested in Elizabeth, despite his passion for the Camellias. After finishing a mouthful of tingling and spicy Tan Tan noodles, he started to talk, seemingly willing to give me some perspective, "It's fantastic that you finally found a woman you deeply care about. I am so happy for you Hector. I can feel when you talk about her how moved and passionate you are and it is great to sense this. I sincerely hope that she will become that special one for you. She seems to be worth all your intensity and anticipation."

"Yes, she is," I replied, pleased by his support. "I am so excited to have finally met someone like Elizabeth. I know that my courting may seem quite intense, but I honestly can't help it. I may take a risk but you know that I am a Romanesque. I like to create memorable and precious situations that make each time with her the most exciting possible. I know it may seem crazy, as I have not known her for very long, but I have never felt such magnetic attraction for someone before so I need to celebrate each moment we spend together."

"Do you think she fully understands what you are doing?" enquired Harold.

"What do you mean?"

"Where does she come from in the United States?"

"Oklahoma."

"Really? That's interesting. You know that Edna (his former wife) was also from Oklahoma."

"Huh, no. I actually didn't know that. I don't think you ever mentioned it."

"Well, she came from the same state as Elizabeth. I certainly do not want to bring any negative thoughts here, so don't take my comment in the wrong way, but hearing about the way you plan and organize your dates, and knowing a woman from this region of the United States, I just wonder how she is reacting to your intensity."

"Really? I know I am going full speed and that it may, maybe, look über-intense. I admit that. But so far she seems to have enjoyed my surprises. She also shares the same emotional expectations I do. I talked about building our relationship intensely yet cautiously, one brick at a time, and she is going along with it."

Harold was attentive to my comments and I could feel he was trying to tell me something. "I am certainly glad she responds that way Hector. I was just a bit concerned that you might scare her with your intensity." He smiled, and then continued, "I was just reflecting about Edna and about the way relationships work in general between men and women in America's Midwest and in the so-called Bible Belt."

"Oh, I see. But she doesn't seem to be overly religious, actually. Well, we have never talked about religion, but she is definitely not a bigot. I am the one holding us back from going too fast on the physical front, if you see what I mean. I desire her immensely but I can wait a bit more."

I then explained to my friends my unease about my tiny flat and my intention to find a perfect and romantic place for our first time, when Harold gently interrupted me, "I did not mean religion or sex. I meant that I was concerned that your nineteenth-century European references and way of courting may scare her, as she is probably not used to such demonstrations. You know, people in the Midwest are extremely pragmatic. They have been shaped by rough events, and not many have developed the luxury of exposing and expressing their feelings openly."

After a few seconds of reflection, I finally understood. "Ok, I get it now. I have read books about the Great Depression and the Dust Bowl. Elizabeth also told me about some dramatic situations that her family went through during this hellish period."

"Exactly! These people are pioneers. They are survivors.

Think Zola's *L'Assommoir* for some kind of European equivalent of what they went through. Also, people in that part of the United States are small-town people. They seldom travel outside of their state and few have therefore experienced the world outside of their region, let alone outside of the country. Their history and rural configuration implies that they have quite a practical approach to relationships. The Midwest is a land of farmers and cowboys. Do you understand? You come from Switzerland. Your country is one of the wealthiest in the world. You speak, what, three, four languages?

"Five actually," I replied, proudly, though I was not trying to show off.

"Ok, five. And London, Rome, Paris, Barcelona, and Berlin are less than two hours by plane from Geneva, and if you don't take the plane, you are still close to borders with France, Italy, Germany, and Austria. The central geographic situation of your country, its history, and its people are international by essence. Can you see the contrast?

"Sure, I do. But I am not sure I understand where you are heading."

"Well, What I am trying to explain—and really, again, don't take me wrong; I just want to give you some perspective, because I care about you, Hector—is that the place from which Elizabeth comes, the dramatic times her grandparents and maybe even her parents went through, have shaped the spirit of the whole region. The Baptists had also a huge influence."

Dragan seemed fascinated to hear about a part of the world and a people he could hardly imagine, so far away from his native Balkans. He was surprisingly keeping quiet, listing attentively to Harold. I must say that despite the few books I had read about Midwest history and the Great Depression, I did not have any empirical insight about the sociology of this part of the United States. Yet I could guess what Harold was getting at, using his own experience to be sure I understood all the cultural and emotional potholes that could potentially separate Elizabeth from a Continental European man like me. I had better be aware of these differences, given the intensity with which I was courting her.

Talking about the Midwest, Harold inevitably remembered his ex-wife. These unexpected emotional reminiscences moved him, after so many years kept buried, deep inside, and his voice became veiled with melancholy. This did not stop him, though, for he continued, as if driven by a sudden need to share part of his own story with people he could trust, "Well, when I decided several years ago to leave Edna, even though my sons were adults and had left home a long time before, it was obviously a heartbreaking decision for me to make. I still loved my wife dearly, but I simply could not live a life of lies any longer. This experience was obviously also extremely painful for her. Besides the somewhat embarrassing reasons for our separation, divorcing is considered shameful where she comes from. Yet she always kept her suffering to herself. We talked together a lot and in length about our situation. We spent nights talking. I could sense several times that she was quite tense and on the verge of breaking into tears, yet I never saw her crying, at least not in front of me. She stayed a rock throughout our ordeal, taking each blow in the guts without moving an inch. I was quite amazed, actually. It was unmistakably her survivor roots that allowed her to tap into such strength. Yet in what type of armor she protected herself or how she coped with all the pain inside, as she was also a caring and sensitive person, I will never know."

Now we were both, Dragan and myself, listening quietly, in communion with Harold's emotions. He continued, his voice quavering, "We had been living in our Gerrards Cross house for almost ten years before I disclosed my homosexuality. You remember, you visited us with your friend Valentino when you were in London, setting up your hedge fund, I think."

"Yes, that's right. I loved your place," I sympathetically

replied.

"It was indeed a lovely house. So, Edna and I had a lot of friends there. But when we separated and the papers were signed, it took her only a couple of weeks to turn around and head back to the United States, to her hometown of Broken Arrow in Oklahoma ... or was it Broken Bow? I always mistook them."

Harold looked at me with a pert gaze, signaling that he had emerged, with this final light twist, from the melancholy in which he had sunk a few minutes before. Yet his voice became grave when he concluded, "Our friends never heard of her again. And myself, I had only indirect news of her through our sons. She simply turned the page, disappearing from our lives. She could do it. She could bury all those torments. She had survival in her blood, and this was the only way she had learned to react in the face of adversity. As a privileged subject of her majesty, I myself never developed such bunkering skills. As the ancient Aesop said, 'in a strong wind the reed bends, but does not break.' It bends all right," added Harold, "but then it stands back, tall and proud."

I felt touched by my friend's story and thankful for his insights and perspectives. Yet I also felt sorry to see his sorrow and pain reemerging when, on my side, I was so jubilant to be starting a promising relationship with an outstanding woman.

THE LAST DATE WITH Elizabeth had been an unqualified success, and it confirmed if I still needed to be convinced, that we were dearly attracted to each other, and that our feelings were blossoming into a colorful ribbon of emotions. All the doubts haunting me, however, were worrying me sick—as the closer I got to Elizabeth, the more I thought about the perverse alien trying to put a premature end to my stay on earth and about its influence on my mental equilibrium. I was doomed and blessed at the same time. It seemed to be a paradox that had decided to take as strong a toll on my sanity as possible. My head was exploding!

Early that evening, at my desk at the gallery—having finally agreed on a price for Picasso's *Dora Maar* and having arranged for my client to view the painting in Geneva before closing the deal—I thought again about the irony of *The Lady of the Camellias'* story. Death, like a vulture circling above my head since September, was not only at the center of Alexandre Dumas fils' novel, but also in Paul Claudel's *The Tidings Brought to Mary*. I sent a text message to Elizabeth saying that I wanted to offer her a book, one of the most heartfelt love stories ever written, that would explain my camellia allusion. I told her that it would shed some more light on who Hector P. was, as I planned to use the book to finally talk about my own health ordeal. I could not stand this dilemma any more. She replied instantly:

Hector, how brilliant and thoughtful! I will shortly be meeting with a client from London, but I will call you tomorrow. Have a great night!

BECAUSE ELIZABETH HAD TO go to Beijing to visit some companies for two days the following week, we planned to meet the Sunday before her departure. We needed to be together, to keep the momentum of our burning desires as intense as possible. We also wanted to move the relationship to another level. It was therefore essential that we spend more time with each other, instead of just a few sporadic evenings. I had hoped that we could meet on a Saturday or Sunday to learn more about each other. We could have brunch and then go sailing or perhaps hiking along Hong Kong's scenic hills, and then share our much-awaited first night together.

On Saturday afternoon I was at the gallery, supervising the building of a crate made to ship a painting by French artist

Fabien Verschaere to a Korean collector, when Elizabeth called me on my mobile.

"Hi there," I said, jubilant at seeing her name flashing on my phone.

"Hi, Hector." I could feel her smiling on the other side of town. "How are you?"

"Fine, thank you. I am in the middle of some carpentry work, actually."

"Did I disturb you? Shall I call you later?"

"No, you never disturb me. How was your evening with your client?"

"It went quite well. But I later had a visit from an old girlfriend from Singapore who is going through a difficult time. She needed to be comforted, as she had just separated from her husband of three years. I stayed awake until 2am with her and I am knackered today."

"Until 2am? I am sorry to hear that! It is always tricky, isn't it, to know what to advise when friends go through such situations."

"Yes it is. I told her to take some time to reflect and not to rush into making any decisions she may later regret. I also advised her to share with her husband any doubts she might have, and to keep a communication channel open with him, as I believe they still have strong feelings for each other."

"I think you are so right. It is vital to keep a channel of communication open. To have a friend like you who can act as a bridge between the two if they have difficulties communicating directly is a powerful thing."

"Thank you. By the way," her voice became slightly hesitant, "I am sorry but I will have to spend tomorrow with Alexander, so I won't be able to be with you as we had planned. I truly wanted to, but sometimes it is too difficult for me to juggle the different facets of my life. I hope you can understand. I genuinely wanted to be with you, but I can't this time. I am sorry."

I could feel that she was apprehensive of my reaction but I totally understood her situation and would never pressure her to choose me before her son. I tried to reassure her and answered, considerately, "Don't worry, I know you need to spend time with Alexander. I totally understand that. Of course, I was looking forward to seeing you, but we will have plenty of other Sundays to spend together in the future. And soon, hopefully, you will not need to stretch yourself so much and we could all spend time together."

I was, of course, disappointed not to see her that Sunday, as beside wanting to be near her, I thought it was crucial to soon spend a whole day, and night, together. We needed to go through so many more subjects and emotions—to know so much more about each other and to experience further the power of our emerging love, feeling so good and so fulfilled with each other. I was also actually wondering—a bit crossly, I must admit—why she had not proposed spending this Sunday with both of us, taking this opportunity to introduce me to Alexander. My comment about "stretching" was obviously a reference about spending time—and our future—with her son as well. This first introduction was as important for her as it was for him and for me. I was, however, not going to ask her to initiate this crucial presentation, as I had no right to impose myself on them. I therefore decided to wait until she deemed the timing and circumstances were right.

I obviously wanted to spend more time with Elizabeth, but I was also extremely interested in finally meeting Alexander and moving, when the time was right, our duo into a holy trinity. I understood very well that Elizabeth was not whole without her son and that they were somehow the same being, indivisible. Embracing Elizabeth meant embracing Alexander. I had known this from the beginning, from the first time I had seen them together on Queen's Road Central several years before, and I fully accepted it. The apple of Elizabeth's eye was also one of the reasons why I had waited so long before contacting her, as I had wanted not only to feel ready for her (despite the dilemma that the tumor was causing) but also to feel ready to enter the reality of her young son, to take care of him and to participate in his personal progression, as a new element in his life. These responsibilities were not something I could consider lightly, and I thus had had to wait until now to be fully ready to take them on.

ON MONDAY, ELIZABETH HAD to leave for Mainland China, and as it was by then almost a tradition, the ring of my mobile phone announcing a new message woke me up around 8:30am. It was her, of course, texting me from the airport:

Morning! How about we get together on Thursday at 8:30pm? Friday I can't, I am with kiddo. Besides, I want to see you as soon as possible. Plane taking off ... must go.

Thursday, like any other day, was of course fine with me as freeing time for us was my absolute priority. I called the restaurant Gaia right away to reserve a table for two. Despite nesting on a piazza surrounded by skyscrapers, the terrace of this succulent Italian place was utterly romantic. The alfresco space with trees lit up by a myriad of electric fireflies would, thus, be perfect for two lovebirds like us. I had just hung up my mobile phone, satisfied, when the fixed line of the gallery rang loudly in a premonitory way. It was Doctor Liu's assistant. They had received the results of some new tests and the doctor wanted to see me to discuss them as soon as possible. He had some surgical appointments the following day at the Matilda Hospital and the nurse therefore suggested an appointment on Thursday morning at 10:30am at his practice.

The week before I had made a final offer for the Audi cabriolet to Chee-Hwa, the car dealer, and he had accepted it. I went by taxi to Tin Hau to pay for the car and to sign all the needed documents. After a last checkup there were, unsurprisingly, still some problems with the electronic system controlling the windows and the soft top. Chee-Hwa promised that everything would be fixed by Friday and that I could therefore come again that day, in the late afternoon, to collect it.

A few hours later, Elizabeth called to see if I was also available on Wednesday, late in the afternoon. She wanted to bring Alexander to my gallery, to see the current exhibition and, implicitly, to finally introduce us to one another. I loved and was flattered by the idea of showing her my space and by the indication that she wanted to see me, even before our dinner. I was also, of course, enthusiastic to meet her son, at last. As she was a friend of a woman who ran an art space opposite to my gallery and as there was an opening there that day, she thought it would be an excellent occasion for us to see each other prior to bringing Alexander along for the awaited introduction. She cautiously asked me, though, what the nature of AES+F's artwork was as she wanted to be sure that it would be suitable for Alexander. I then replied jokingly that, as an American, she should not be worried, as the video and photography exhibit did not feature any nudity per se, but instead featured a lot of violence! She laughed. I suddenly felt relieved and joyful to finally have the opportunity to meet Alexander. Indeed, I actually felt guilty at not having followed up when Elizabeth had mentioned her son in our conversations, despite having thought a lot about him.

ON TUESDAY EVENING, I spent some relaxing time drinking cocktails and eating a light dinner of sushi on the terrace of Dragon-i with my friend Laure and Pierre-André, her business partner and ex-husband. I had been keeping them informed about the progress of my relationship with Elizabeth all along, and actually proudly went to see them at their graphic design studio the day after our first date. While bringing a goose-liver futomaki to my mouth, I received a text message from my beloved, who had just landed in Hong Kong on her return from Beijing a few minutes before;

I am just back, exhausted and looking forward to seeing you tomorrow! Xoxo.

ON WEDNESDAY MORNING, I woke up like the Energizer Bunny, agitated, and jumping around at the thought of seeing Elizabeth again, after too many days apart. Seeing her in a different context—and especially in my gallery, on my territory— was a source of pride I could hardly contain. At my office, I confirmed with Chee-Hwa that I would pick up the Audi (running hopefully as new) on Friday. That was important, as Elizabeth had told me earlier over the phone, to my disappointment, that she would have to leave again the coming Saturday for a week in London, her last trip for the promotion of her book. I was upset but relieved at the same time, as I understood that she would thereafter be staying more steadily in Hong Kong, providing thus the awaited opportunites to spend much more time together and to further consolidate the foundations of our relationship. I planned to get used to driving on the left side of the road while she was away, so as to be ready to surprise her in picking her up in the cabriolet when she returned from the United Kingdom. I had, therefore, decided to keep the purchase of the car a secret— one more—until her return. Early in the afternoon, I sent a text message expressing my happiness and exultation at seeing her in person again very soon. At around 4pm, Elizabeth replied:

Hi! I am excited to see you too! Would it be ok if I came by myself at five for a private tour? I'll need to leave around six to pick Alexander up to go to the opening with him.

I was elated. I was of course looking forward to meeting

Alexander for the first time and teaching him a bit about contemporary art, observing his receptivity, and answering his questions. Yet having the opportunity to have Elizabeth all to myself for an hour at the gallery was also priceless. Thinking about seeing her made my heart race like crazy, and I was delighted to acknowledge the increasing feelings I was having for this woman.

At just after 5pm, the doorbell of the gallery rang. As usual, my assistant Kenix stood up and walked down the stairs to the exhibition space. He came back thirty seconds later and said that a woman was asking for me. Of course, I had anticipated that it was Elizabeth, but with his confirmation, my excitement increased tenfold. I walked down the steps with the fast pace of my heartbeat rippling my dark green polo shirt. She was in the first room, near the main entrance to the gallery, looking, a bit puzzled, at AES+F's *The Last Riot 2* video on a hefty flat-panel screen. When I reached her, a large smile further increased her beauty, and like two opposing magnets, we felt the strong flow of energy between us collide in a wonderful impulse of strong emotions and happiness. Her exhilaration quickly emboldened my senses. The urge we felt to cuddle, embrace, and kiss each other was so strong and spontaneous that I almost had tears streaming down my face. We kissed passionately and intensely, acknowledging the remarkable forces that were at play. Our emotions were so ravaging that, breathless, we could hardly articulate any words. I don't think I had ever experienced anything so intense with a woman before. In a dry voice, after what seemed to be an eternity and after having recovered somewhat, I told her that the magnetism we were touched by was blowing me into a million particles of joy.

She had come straight from her office and was wearing a beige tweed suit, a crew neck purple top, and black leather loafers. Once again, I interpreted her subdued appearance as a subconscious attempt to cover her sensual femininity and her natural beauty. I turned her around to face the plasma screen, clasping her from behind. She joined her hands with mine and I passionately kissed her neck. She closed her eyes, her body shivered, and she moaned slightly. I was almost overcome, as the vibrations and the energy emanating from our radiant bodies were like powerful tidal waves. As we needed an interlude to recover from this overflow of kisses and caresses, I told her cheekily that we should not get too frisky, as my assistant upstairs might have a heart attack if he was watching us through the closed-circuit television. She smiled at this light joke and I explained, my voice uneven with emotion, the concept behind the AES+F video and the photographs exhibited.

Yet the need to feel each other was too strong and more frolicking, hugging, and kissing interrupted my artistic descriptions, as the gallery visit was, after all, only a pretext to be reunited in passionate embraces.

The place was ablaze as our bodies were getting ready to fuse with each other. The elation of experiencing these delightful common feelings was wrapping us in a halo of energy. Face-to-face, my fingers in her blonde and wavy hair, her head bent slightly backward, I was kissing her sensual lips, her soft cheeks, her delicate chin, and going back to her lips when a young couple entered the gallery and greeted us. We looked at each other, breathing intensely, our bodies still in harmony, our arms wrapped around each other, and we smiled with complicity, on the verge of bursting out laughing, as we were on another planet, proud and totally unfazed at experiencing such a tremendous rush of emotion. Aside from potential clients passing through the ground floor, the large glass doors allowed passers-by to peep in and to guess our sensual ballet, through the steam. As we did not need an audience, though, I led Elizabeth up the steep steps to the stockroom on the first floor, filled with art of all kinds.

Moving upstairs fulfilled a strong urge to isolate ourselves in a place fit exclusively for our pleasure, to hide in a sensual refuge, as the devastating desire for each other was not abating. After a quick look at the artwork surrounding us, and still riveted to her, breathless and close to ecstasy, I kissed Elizabeth's earlobes enthusiastically. I was once again overwhelmed by her hypnotic and glorious scent. Eyes closed, she slid her hand under the collar of my polo shirt, feeling the base of my neck, my chest, and my tense pectoral muscles. Our evanescent bodies and minds were ready to capsize into a spin of lust.

This tango lasted for many more minutes until she asked me, liberating herself slightly from my embrace in a startled consciousness, what the time was. This question brought us abruptly back to reality, gazing at each other and panting. It was close to 6pm and we realized we had spent almost an hour in this jazzy, magnetic, and disconnected realm. She had to pick up Alexander at his school at some point and go to the other gallery's opening. Still holding my hands, she asked me if I wanted to join her. After a slight silence, I stared at her, overcome by the overflow of emotions sanctifying the room and my being. Elizabeth was so desirable, her eyelids half closed, breathing rapidly, her chest moving fast, recovering from the sensual intensity we had just experienced. My mouth was dry and I was gasping for air. After one more moment of hesitation I finally succeeded in saying—with a tone I meant to be witty— that I had to return some videotapes and would, therefore, be unable to join her across the street to see an exhibition I was not overly interested in.

Meeting again later at the other gallery was, though, obviously not about art but a pretext for Elizabeth to finally introduce me to her son. I, of course, had to know and understand this and did not need Elizabeth to be any more explicit or to send me a formal invitation. I damned well had to know it! I shamefully had to know it! Or was I actually so mesmerized by this unbelievable feeling of finally loving someone that I had lost touch with our priorities and had become, unbeknownst

113

to myself, unresponsive and incapable of reacting? Did these transcending and resplendent feelings, which left me in such an ecstatic state of contemplation, take any possible reasoning hostage? Whatever it was, the truth is, submerged by too many emotions exploding in my heart and triggered by the journey I had just shared with Elizabeth in these new and delightful dimensions, I led myself out in space and lost all sense of reality and focus about our relationship.

Having returned to the ground floor, she asked me, hiding well her disappointment, what our plans were for Thursday evening. I told her that I had organized a surprise but that I should maybe slow down my courting, as the more I did, the fewer ideas I might have in the future, and I was worried that she might eventually find me boring.

"No, please don't stop," she replied, smiling. "I love your surprises. I will never have enough."

I accompanied her to the entrance of the gallery and opened the glass door. We kissed, hugged tenderly, and wished each other a good evening. I felt blessed by the unique and sensual time we had just spent together. Dazzled by her magnificence, I watched her slowly climb the stairs of the narrow pedestrian street. She turned around at almost every step, intensely looking me straight in the eyes each time, until she disappeared in the complicit night. I remained motionless for a few minutes, holding the door, stunned by what had happened over the past hour, as if I had just survived being struck by a magnificent thunderbolt. I closed my eyes and for a long moment stayed there, taking in what remained of her exhilarating presence. Was it actually possible that I was no more alone in my inner struggle? That I could now count this incredible woman on my side? The flow of energy holding me against Elizabeth had been so intense that I now felt washed out and needed to sit, rest, and recover. The world suddenly seemed vast, magnificent, and uncomplicated.

BACK IN MY OFFICE, sitting at my desk, my assistants gone for the day, I tried to work a bit. However, my mind was far away in another galaxy, lost in our cosmology, observing a celebration of shooting stars passing through. I hesitated for a long time, trying to decide whether to cross the street and surprise Elizabeth by meeting her and Alexander there. Despite my anticipation and desire to enter her son's life, I have to admit that I let myself be overwhelmed and transported by the supernova of happiness that I had experienced that evening. I recovered my reason only much later.

My mind blinded by the hour of ecstasy spent with Elizabeth, I took my gym bag, looked through the window, and caught sight, across the street, of her with Alexander, soberly dressed in a white school uniform. I walked downstairs, switched the alarm on and the lights off, stepped outside, locked the doors, and walked away toward Hollywood Road and my fitness club.

I spent the rest of the evening at home in an agitated trance, as anyone touched by grace would be. I sent an infatuated text message to Elizabeth, mentioning how blessed I had felt at the gallery with her and how clear and strong my feelings were becoming. It was, perhaps, a somehow extreme message, but I felt liberated and I needed to express my feelings to her. I felt blessed to have such intense and profound moments with this woman. Alas, the emotional black hole was never too far away, a dramatic reminder of my emotional and medical condition.

My nervousness was amplified by the anticipation of the next morning's appointment with Doctor Liu, because I feared the news would be negative. The thought of an unfavorable omen sent an icy sensation down my spine, which forced me to cough, to blink frantically, and to rush to the balcony to get as much fresh air as one could get in Hong Kong, over-polluted as it was. So doomed, and yet so blessed! Why on earth did these dichotomous and intense events have to be linked? Why could I not simply develop this precious relationship with Elizabeth without being perniciously and continuously attacked at the core of my being? Looking at all of these lights surrounding me, and staring at the depth of that November night, I tried to understand.

ON THURSDAY MORNING I woke up a little after 8am, fresh and alert as all the tension, bliss, excitement, and doubts of the day before—plus a late glass of Finlandia vodka on the rocks—had made me sleep like a baby. I went straight to the gym, exercising on the treadmill for forty minutes. Working out in the morning is always an awesome way to start the day fresh and awake, and I was therefore fully ready, and in great shape, to see Doctor Liu. The day was clear and shiny with a sky coming out of one of Sisley's paintings. As I walked through Central, I crawled against the sea of office workers feeding into the surrounding skyscrapers. I had to pass in front of Elizabeth's office building just before reaching Hutchison House, where I had my appointment. I smiled then, remembering the drop off by the Rolls-Royce at that exact spot the week before, the furtive kiss we had shared, and Elizabeth turning around to have a last look at me.

After waiting for a few minutes, Doctor Liu appeared and gave me a solemn look while vigorously shaking my hand, before asking me to follow him. In his office, we sat informally around a red aluminum table and he asked me how I felt. I told him that I could not be better after what had happened the evening before. I did not give him details, but I had already described this remarkable woman to reassure him further that I was looking forward and was not giving up any inch to the alien. He seemed sincerely happy to know that I had met someone like Elizabeth, and without transition picked up the file containing the results of the extra tests he had recommended. As he opened the pastel yellow folder, his face darkened and the room filled with an unusual tension. I suddenly felt like a naughty student before the principal of the high school, ready to be scolded—yet this time I was not showing any defiance. Still, the irremediable verdict had to be announced, and what I feared, essentially the worst-case scenario, came out slowly from the mouth of the man who was in charge of my salvation, "Mister P., the results of the new MRI unfortunately confirm the aggressiveness of the tumor. The initial treatment worked well at first, but alas it could no longer slow down the expansion of the growth into your skull."

From this new diagnosis, the situation was crystal clear: no treatment would restrain the forceful attack of the tumor on my skull and we had, therefore, to set up a date for the critical operation. As the alien was redoubling its efforts to kill me, we could not wait any longer. Given the advance of the growth, the surgery had roughly a thirty-five percent chance of success ... at best! Of course, I had already considered and accepted this possibility, but suddenly I was on the edge of the abyss for real. Although prepared for this outcome, I still could not believe it. I requested again, though—as I had since Doctor Liu first diagnosed the tumor—that we set the operation for the latest possible date. Even though I have always been an irreducible optimist, I wanted to have as much respite as I could—time to reflect and to savor life as much as possible—before a surgery that could potentially toll the death knell for my last days on earth.

Being a fighter, I regained as much composure as possible and handed over the keys of my life to Doctor Liu. I trusted him. Professor P. was also totally confident in his abilities, and I would follow and cooperate fully with his battle plan. The surgery and the recovery period at the Matilda Hospital did not theoretically necessitate more than a week there, so I had already decided that I would have this operation in Hong Kong instead of returning to Switzerland for it. We scheduled a new appointment for the following Monday to organize the timing of the surgery, and I left, feeling groggy and a little dizzy.

Knocked out, I wandered around Central for a while, like a zombie mechanically walking up and down the steep streets, aimless, with my mind running like an out-of-control computer rapidly processing memories, flashbacks and hundreds of other thoughts in my saturated brain, as if I were still looking for reasons and explanations why I had been so unfairly contaminated in the first place. Here I was, again, the lonesome cowboy, facing one more life-and-death duel, a long-distance runner who had to make sure his life would continue to be an exciting and Romanesque marathon. This time, however, the stakes were enormous and the end of the journey potentially near, even though I could not conceive that I would end that way, that young. Yet I had to face the hard cold truth of reality.

Late in the afternoon I called my parents at Valrolz to tell them how severe my state of heath actually was, but nobody was at home then. I called my mother at the University of Geneva, where she was a psychology and education professor, but there, as well, nobody answered. Fighting a sudden feeling of abandonment, I looked for something to cheer me up. By protective reflex, my mind quickly drifted toward the positive things that had happened to me over recent days, and the memory of the last incredible evening imposed itself. I could hang on for hope and light to the magnetic attraction that connected Elizabeth's heart and mind to mine, in the gallery. And that night I would see her again. This prospect filled me with high ardor. Doomed, yet so blessed, indeed!

ELIZABETH CALLED ME AROUND 6pm to learn where we would meet. I indicated the Star Ferry entrance, as this location, filled with sweet memories, was relatively near the Bank of America Tower. We could see each other at 8pm, and then have a ten-minute stroll together, hand in hand, along Victoria Harbor, admiring the myriad of lights emblazing Kowloon, before reaching the restaurant Gaia. I also told her, in case she had thought of dressing up, that I would come straight from the gallery and was dressed casually. I had spent the whole day at my desk, frantically turning the Rubik's Cube of my life in all directions, and I didn't feel like going home to change. This suited her, as she had an engagement extending almost up to our date and would have been unable to go back to her apartment to change either. I actually had thought earlier that day of canceling the restaurant booking and reserving, instead, a suite at the Mandarin Oriental, as a stroll and Gaia did not seem to be original enough. After last evening, my desire for her was also at its paroxysm and I thought it would be exciting to have a candlelit in-room dinner and the rest of the night snuggled against each other sensually, bringing this much-awaited and much-needed dimension to our relationship. However, I stuck to the original plan.

I was also obviously not feeling at my best, as so many contradictory images and thoughts about life and the afterlife kept flashing and clashing in my mind, but I was nevertheless elated to see Elizabeth. Ten minutes before 8pm, I left the gallery and, walking toward my destiny, I felt suddenly quite perky. Once again, I mentally thanked Elizabeth, as the evocation of her presence was decidedly therapeutic. Walking down Graham Street, dressed in washed-out blue jeans, white leather shoes, and an open-necked khaki shirt, I succeeded in slowing down a bit the Big Bang in my head. The closer I got to the Star Ferry pier, the stronger and happier I felt.

I arrived at 8pm sharp and saw Elizabeth appearing from behind a steel pillar, walking decisively toward me. She was gorgeous as usual, despite her legendary subdued style. She was wearing a pair of blue jeans, a kind of black top with laces under a gray tweed blazer, and a pair of brown loafers. She smiled widely when she reached me, and I hugged her. We exchanged a languid kiss. I took her hand and led her toward the waterfront promenade, bathed by the multicolored lights illuminating Victoria Harbor. Indulging in each other's presence and reconnecting slowly with the previous night's memories, we were moving in a unique sphere of benevolence and communion, undisturbed by the hundreds of people surrounding us who were rushing to get their ferries to the Outer Islands after another day of work.

After slightly more than ten minutes of this romantic stroll, we finally reached Gaia. I thought everyone knew about this charming Italian restaurant with its illuminated alfresco space, but for my naiad it was a genuine surprise. We followed a waiter inside the restaurant to check our reservation and after confirmation, I told him that we would like to sit outside. Exiting the restaurant, I lightly touched Elizabeth's back. She turned her head slightly and smiled in an approving manner. I felt comforted in her presence. The waiter showed us a free table near the entrance and I selected instead a place at a little more distance, under a glowing tree, as isolated as possible from the other customers.

AS SOON AS WE were seated, a presentiment swept over me, as it sometimes happens before crucial upheavals in my life. I was looking Elizabeth in the eyes, taking her left hand and landing a delicate kiss in her palm, when an unexpected and almost paranormal phenomenon struck me. In a split second, a powerful outflow of energy left my body all at once, as if a cosmic force had sucked out its core! Suddenly capsizing into an unknown dimension, I felt pounded by a million sledgehammers and I instantly slid into a vegetative state; I was emotionally Tasered! I had never felt anything like this before. My arms collapsed to my body, my composure crumbled, and my brain instantly lost the impulse to articulate words and thoughts. Everything I knew blanked out and I became the Stephen Hawking of seduction in a nanosecond! This amazing energy reversal was in formidable and scary contrast to the powerful and galvanizing jolt we both had felt the previous evening at my gallery.

I was still there physically, but at the same time, my mind was roasting in purgatory, twenty thousand leagues under the ground. Sitting stiffly, I could not think properly and a sense of panic and sickening vertigo overtook me. Even though I should have shouted for help at this sudden imprisonment and communicated this inner and catastrophic collapse to Elizabeth, I failed to do so and thereby deepened my mental torture. I was gone and had been replaced by a pale copy of myself, poised to operate over the next few hours on rusty autopilot. I cannot say how Elizabeth felt as I have only a few recollections of the conversation and emotions—or lack of them—that accompanied this dinner. What I remember precisely, though, is that she brought up a topic to which I did not have the emotional capacity to respond or argue about and that increased tenfold the spinning in my head and the dire sense of totally losing it. In an unsure voice—probably a bit tormented herself—she said, "I think we are in different phases of life."

Being in such a locked-in state, I am not sure I fully grasped the importance of her statement then, even though I obviously instinctively understood the danger that such words revealed and their serious implications for our common future. Did she bring the subject up after the previous day's magnetic evening to confirm where I was standing emotionally? Did she want to be reassured, or did she simply want to share her own doubts or fears with me, so as to be comforted in her feelings about the journey we were sharing? I fully and instinctively understood that this statement was the awaited opportunity to slow the rocket pace by which we were building our relationship, and to clarify any elements that needed to be addressed in order to reassure her. Whatever her purpose, though, there was unfortunately no way I could react properly then to her carefully chosen words, or ask her to elaborate, explain, answer, share, or maybe debate. I was amorphous, trapped in my body, witnessing these unwinding events through a soundproof double glass window, unable to react. Digging into the depths of my distress and confusion, I therefore brushed away her timid claim and said, "I don't think so."

"Maybe not," was her instant reply. The tone of her answer was that of a disappointed and resigned woman, and I guess, because of her own emotionality, she also did not succeed in finding the resources to discuss or develop the topic any further.

The rest of the dinner remained odd, and I would have given anything to go back in time and, instead of it being a disaster, make this date a celebration of the previous evening and the opportunity to clarify any doubt or questions she might have had. To my strong regret, I quickly realized, though profoundly upset and tormented, that the exciting and heartfelt dynamic of our past exchanges was gone and that we had stepped into a new and unknown territory where complicity, gazing, smiles, and sensuality had been replaced by an utterly frustrating status quo. My head felt as if it was exploding as I felt for the second time on that cursed day the darkness that was swallowing me up. Doomed and again doomed! By denial, and because the ball had been dropped by both of us, the automatic pilot continued to fuel the illusion of normality, but the unnecessary and persisting tension underneath our embarrassed smiles highlighted the profound frustration we were both experiencing. Reaching such a standstill a day after that magical time spent in the gallery was utterly heartbreaking.

Moving into neutral territory to give a needed semblance of normalcy that would enable us to reach the dessert safely, we talked a bit about literature. Elizabeth mentioned one of her favorite books, James Joyce's *Ulysses*, and I jumped on the opportunity to flex my erudition, "Talking about another Ulysses, Alessandro Baricco wrote an interesting book called

An Iliad. He vulgarized Homer's masterpiece and made it easily understandable. Have you read it?"

"No, I have never heard of this book or this author, actually."

"He is a compelling Italian storyteller. What is fascinating in his treatment of the *Iliad* is his portrayal of these strong and courageous warriors also as hypersensitive men. They are ready to die bravely to defend their fatherlands, or for a woman. But they also openly express their sorrow at the death of their fallen comrades."

"Yes, it is always moving when men have the courage to express openly their sensitivity and feelings."

"Do you know who Homer considered the noblest of all the heroes in the *Iliad*?" I asked.

"No, I don't know. Odysseus? Or maybe Achilles?"

"Actually Homer's favorite was the greatest champion of Troy. He was peace-loving and brave and was known for his courage, but also for his kind and generous nature. He was thoughtful as well as bold. He was a good son, husband, and father. His name was," I said with an uneasy smile, "Hector."

Smiling gently back, Elizabeth replied, "Of course."

In reflex, I moved an ashtray lying between us to the other side of the table and commented, "I don't think we will use it."

"Not me. You don't smoke either?"

"No. You seem surprised. You never saw me smoking though."

"No, but I thought most Europeans smoked."

"Most Europeans, really?" I was surprised by this comment, as I was not aware of this stereotype and answered, "I am not too sure about that. Maybe twenty years ago, but not anymore." I then added, pertly, "But even though I don't smoke, I don't only have qualities, you know. I also have shortcomings."

"I haven't seen any yet," she replied with a kind smile.

Handicapped as I was, I engulfed myself in these comforting comments and attempted to revive a bit the fire that had animated our senses not so long ago. So as to maybe bring us back to a more intimate and sound path, I opened up a bit.

"You know that I am always thrilled each time I see you. But I wish we could spend longer periods of time together, to have a chance to discover much more about each other. We could, for example, go sometime soon, maybe for a long weekend, to Bali. I know you love this island, and I know it very well."

"Yes, that would be wonderful. I would love that," she answered in a soft and pensive tone.

Continually haunted by the tumor's dire prophecy, the overall malaise I had felt since the beginning of the dinner quickly prevailed and the rest of our conversation returned to an overly neutral and defensive mode. Elizabeth talked about her agoraphobic sister who had visited Hong Kong not long ago, but who shortened her stay and flew back swiftly to her native Oklahoma after a night out in the noisy and overcrowded Lan Kwai Fong bar district.

I could not take it anymore, as faking normality was too painful a torment to bear. Desperate to save this evening, to break the chilly and frightening halo that had engulfed us for too long now, I reached out to Elizabeth, took her hand, leaned over, and, unusually submissive, I told her in an almost imploring tone, "I feel so lucky to be with you."

Seemingly embarrassed, she murmured inaudibly, "No ..."

In need of a diversion, Elizabeth then asked me what my secret was. Maybe she sensed that it was one of the causes and sources of my current stiffness and my occasional lack of effective responsiveness (toward Alexander especially), or maybe she simply needed to have this clarification from the man she had chosen after having been single for so many years. Not knowing the scale and consequences of what I might be hiding was obviously torturing her, especially after the Big Bang mixed with disappointment of the previous night. Alas, it was impossible for me to open up on this crucial and terrible subject, being trapped and in such a state of upheaval as I was then. I was miserable at my inability to reach out and turn this evening around and make it the date of clarification, which might have totally changed the course of our dinner. I had actually planned to disclose my secret later, when giving her the book *The Lady of the Camellias*. But now, destiny had forked the path.

It was obvious that I was the one who could not communicate, as Elizabeth had brought up my secret and had also indirectly proposed talking about her own doubts and fears. I could not, therefore, expect her to bring these subjects up again, since I did not react the first time. If only she knew what was banging and collapsing within me! We were again like two fourteen-year-olds, feeling helpless in the adult roles we pretended to play, looking at each other with an ever-growing malaise, unable to cope with ravaging emotions and, thus, opting for sabotage instead of sublimation.

THIS LAST SUPPER WAS quick by our standard, and the unease did not dissipate in the slightest when I paid the bill a little before 10pm. Elizabeth said she was tired and there was nothing much I wanted to do to prolong this painful and utterly disappointing time, as I felt that already too much frustration had been experienced on both sides. I had been hit hard and was on my knees; my shiny armor was now covered with dust and my head was bent toward the ground in bewilderment. It was therefore wiser to cut our losses now, and talk about it the following day. Yet before setting her free, I still wanted to give her Alexander Dumas fils' book.

We therefore left Gaia confused and climbed the steep Aberdeen Street hand-in-hand toward my apartment. Once there, I opened the door and we were swiftly engulfed in its darkness. The large sofa took so much space that it allowed the main door to open only halfway, and when Elizabeth closed it behind her we ended up face-to-face, up against each other, so close. I moved a hand to her left cheek, raised my lips to hers, and kissed her at length. She finally withdrew, uncomfortable. I moved around the coffee table, switched on the Arco lamp, and presented her with the book *The Lady of the Camellias* and, as a bookmark, a black-and-white photograph of myself, in profile, wearing the famed brown leather jacket. It was a nice photo and the only one I had evoking her foundational act. I had underlined the explanations of my relative's real role in the introduction of Dumas fils' novel and advised her to read this classic and heartfelt story first, and then go through the introduction to understand my special connection with the camellias. We had finally also reached the moment where I had planned, from the morning, to disclose my state of health to Elizabeth, as I could not bear to hide my ordeal and its emotional consequences any longer. Yet the evening had been such a chaos that it did not make sense to divulge my secret now.

This evening should have become a cornerstone in our relationship in which crucial elements that influenced our emotions should have been openly and frankly discussed, to reassure each other about our intentions and commitment. Instead of that and despite the unique attraction we were feeling for each other—dealing with its intensity was certainly one of the issues—we totally failed to express anything coherent. We became childish saboteurs, amateur terrorists of our hearts, attempting to wreck the achievements of the past weeks with our inability to consolidate them further or cope with the hyperintensity of our feelings. Instead of transcendence and celebration, we seemed to have unintentionally opted for pain and desolation. Stendhal seems to have been right when he wrote, "If a particle of passion enters the heart, then there is also a particle of a possible fiasco."

Nevertheless, still navigating without instruments and clinging to as much control as I had left, I said, "Here is a photo to accompany you during your trip, as I will not be able to travel with you to London. With this picture, I will symbolically be with you, more than just in thoughts. It is actually the only image I have while wearing that symbolic leather jacket."

Touched, she looked attentively at the photo, smiled, and replied, "It is so thoughtful, and a very nice picture of you. Thank you."

I had written on the back of the image:

From H. to E. Je t'aime à perpétuité.

She took the book, and slid the photograph inside. There was not much to add; the evening had been over long ago and both of us were mentally exhausted. Back in the street, on Hollywood Road, after spending less than ten minutes in my studio, a quick peck on the lips sealed this sad and disappointing evening, puzzlingly so different from any other time we had previously shared. A taxi stopped beside us and when the automatic door opened, Elizabeth swiftly found refuge in the backseat. I asked her through the wound-down window what day she would be back from London. Her head reappeared from the darkness of the cab, her eyes glowing surprisingly. This was accompanied by an unpleasant and devilish grin that deformed the refined features of her face. She answered sharply, "I will text you that day." The frightening vision of her tense grimace still haunts me today.

SHE WAS GONE AND I was left alone in the gutter, stunned, knocked out, in a silent rage, looking up at the tenebrous sky, damning the tumor, the ravaging doubts, and my incapability of opening up, communicating, or reaching out. I was like the mythical hunter Actaeon, transformed into a stag by the Greek goddess Artemis as a punishment for having dared to watch her bathe naked under a waterfall. He saw her as she truly was, without protection, vulnerable, and, thus, potentially ready to be hurt (again). The lonesome cowboy outfit seemed suddenly too large for me and I wished life would be simpler. I was back in the gumboots of a two-year-old Swiss child from Marseilles, helpless and sad. I felt so angry and miserable to have drifted so low after having almost reached the firmament with Elizabeth just one day before. Once the irrational doubts and emotional invasion had appeared, following the stampede of my vital energy, I had been unable to react or to climb back up.

In the mirror of my bathroom, I did not recognize myself in the livid and shell-shocked man looking back at me. I lay down on the sofa, looking up at the gray ceiling in bewilderment, drowning in mortification and incredulity. Reviewing the film of the evening before falling asleep, I diverted my anger and frustration toward the revolting tumor.

THE NEXT MORNING I woke up early and furious. I had to reach out to Elizabeth to erase the unpleasant taste of the previous night's fiasco, but I did not know where to start, as I felt ashamed, and took full responsibility for not having been equal to myself. I somehow forgot the fact that she had tried to share with me more about her own doubts and fears and that I had not been able to respond to her implicit yet obvious plea.

Being overly critical toward myself and conscious of my own weaknesses and shortcomings in our communication, and of the extreme gusto with which I was courting her, I knew that we would need a reality check at some point. We needed to have some time out, to slow down the relationship Ferrari and readjust our trajectory. I therefore called her to reach out and to apologize. She did not pick up her phone, and—having difficulty getting my composure back, being dreadfully disappointed and feeling awful about myself—I left an uninspired and maybe slightly bleak message on her voicemail.

IN THE EARLY EVENING, I went to Tin Hau with Andy M. to collect the Audi cabriolet. Despite the dreadful previous night, I nevertheless succeeded in feeling excited, imagining driving this mechanical toy soon. The car was parked beside a pink Lamborghini Gallardo and a yellow MINI Cooper decorated like a New York cab, and Chee-Hwa welcomed me with a suspiciously soft handshake. I sat in the black leather driver's seat, proud of my new acquisition, and Andy sat beside me. I turned the key and started the engine. The vroom coming from under the bonnet was music to my ears and reminded me, in an unexpected subliminal flashback, of my weekend drives on the Alpine roads in Switzerland with Stefanie von H., speeding our way to skiing at Crans-Montana. Having brought some music, I inserted the album "Close to the Edge" by Yes into the CD player and pressed the button to automatically retract the roof. No reaction! I pressed again—still nothing. And no sound was coming from the speakers either. I looked angrily at Chee-Hwa, who was watching the scene from the roadside and whose legendary satisfied smile had turned a little forced. I was mad, as his carelessness could mean that I would be unable to bring the car home that evening, despite his promises. We switched places and he tried unsuccessfully to lower the roof canopy himself.

After much discussion and many lame excuses, he finally suggested that we drive to Chai Wan, where his mechanic was stationed, to fix the problems. I was absolutely furious with him. The combined frustration of the preceding night and the current silly situation made me explode with fury, and Andy had to restrain and calm me down so that I did not cross the line. As I did not know the direction of the repair shop, one of Chee-Hwa's staff drove us there, me sitting in the front passenger seat, furious, and Andy in the back.

The workshop was on top of a car park in a shopping mall, fifteen minutes from Tin Hau. The place was dark and strewn with smashed cars of different makes and old tires stacked on top of each other. A mixed aroma of filth and diesel invaded our nostrils, while an ancient radio loudly played old Chinese operas. After inspecting the car, the mechanic in blue overalls whom we met there told us that he would need an hour to fix the electronic system. As we were hungry, we took a lift down to the shopping mall and found a kind of Tex-Mex restaurant. An hour later, refreshed and somewhat calmed down by some jalapeno puddings and tofu tacos followed by a couple of Coronas, we went back to the workshop. The mechanic, however, needed more time to locate the problem. I re-exploded. I could not take it anymore, went ballistic, and called Chee-Hwa to tell him what I thought of him and of his pathetic service. After a long argument, he finally promised to fix the car overnight for good this time, and to deliver it to my gallery on Saturday afternoon. I mentioned that I had a *mechoui* party at a friend's place early that next evening and, wanting to drive there, I needed the car repaired and delivered exactly on time. We took a taxi back to Central and, as I was quite tired mentally, still obsessed with the previous night's *Bloody Thursday*, I skipped the traditional beer chat with Andy and headed straight home instead. Yet, troubled by a multitude of questions, disappointments, and frustrations banging in my brain, I did not fall asleep easily.

THE FOLLOWING DAY I called Valrolz again. I needed to tell my parents about the gravity of the tumor without further delay. After four rings, my mother picked up the phone. She was just back at the estate from a week of conferences in Rome and Paris. As usual, she was glad to hear my voice and her cheerful tone almost brought tears to my eyes, as it seemed that I had nearly forgotten that the lonesome cowboy imagery was pure fantasy and that I actually had unwavering support on the other side of the globe. After some talk about the symposia she had participated in and about art—she and my father had just seen a Calder and Miró exhibition at the Beyeler Foundation that morning—I unveiled, at length this time, the truth about the tumor.

A chilling silence resonated in the handset. My mother was in shock, speechless. My throat was dry and tight as a new acknowledgement of the grim reality submerged me. I strangely had not sensed the extent to which my potential premature end would affect my family. Understanding, through this silence, the horror and shock toward the injustice striking her beloved son, devastated me. I loudly felt the echo of her dismay, which amplified tremendously my own distress. We were in a long-distance communion of sorrows. This time, I explained to her in detail and sometimes in clumsy frankness the truth about the tumor, its current extent, and the unavoidable need for me to undergo risky surgery. Hearing this, she felt the need to take a break and gave the phone to my father.

Unsuspecting, yet absorbed and saddened by my mother's distressed appearance, Alfred greeted me unsteadily. Febrile as well, and only partially understanding the violence of the news, I told him the truth as gently as possible. Even though he usually hides the expression of his emotions as much as possible, I could hear the quavers in his voice. He was brought down by the news, but tried as much as possible not to show it. He asked me many questions about my current mindset, my mood, and how I was seeing the next month coming, and about the treatment, and the surgery. I was by then feeling sad, of course, not to have shared my struggle all along—but I knew that my parents were not thinking about that at all, and their main preoccupation was to be sure I was feeling my best to face this ordeal. I talked further with both of them and could feel, after the first shock, the palpable love of these two people who unconditionally cared about me and were now joining my battle to defeat the alien.

ACTAEONIZED!

It's tough to walk away from something you love, but sometimes
it's the only way

Gladiola Montana, *A Cowgirl's Guide to Life*

On Saturday, late morning, I was still without any news from Elizabeth, but I was quite happy to let some time pass us by to give ourselves some distance from the intensity of our respective reflections and all the disappointments *Bloody Thursday* had brought to us. I was at my desk, sending payment instructions for my commission to a Swiss trustee, settling the successful sale of the Dora Maar Picasso, after the conclusive viewing of the painting in Geneva a few days prior, when my mobile phone rang. It was Elizabeth. Relieved, yet full of remorse and expectation, I answered with a voice as assured and cool as I could muster, "Hi Elizabeth, how are you?"

"I am all right, Hector, thank you, and yourself?" I found her tone surprisingly confident, given our situation.

"I am fine, just chilling out in the gallery. What about you?"

"I am on the train on the way to the airport. My plane for London is leaving in two hours."

"Ah, yes. That's right. You should have told me the time of your flight. I would have accompanied you to the airport."

After a few seconds of silence, she continued, "So how was your Friday?"

"Well, you know, nothing special. I was confronted once again with sheer inefficiency and stupidity. You know, those unpleasant and frustrating situations where someone tells you everything will be set and then nothing is done. So at the end you lose time and your temper."

As I wanted to surprise her with the cabriolet upon her return, I did not want to mention the car purchase, and thus, without a clear subject, my vague diatribe was making no sense at all. I was not feeling well, as I was dying to talk about the disappointing dinner, but at that moment I was incapable of articulating anything meaningful, as I was feeling somehow shameful about failing to turn the situation around at the time it happened. Also, despite her seeming confidence, I perceived a certain coldness and hesitation in Elizabeth's tone and this made me fear the worst. My intuition was right. In an unsteady voice, she eventually dropped her bomb, "Hector, I have thought a lot about us in the past days. I really enjoyed the dates with you, and you are a great man. You are intelligent, charming, witty, gorgeous, and very romantic. But I don't think it will work between us. I am truly sorry."

Even though I was full of apprehension, I had not expected anything of this magnitude. Stunned, I could only reply, in sheer panic, "What? What do you mean, it will not work?" My energy ran away at once. My brain switched off. I could hardly hold onto my phone and had to change hands. My heart stopped for a split second, and I almost choked. My vision became blurred and I began to stumble. My neck was hurting.

Elizabeth continued to talk with a voice filled with regret and determination, "I tried hard, believe me, but I cannot handle all of the facets of my life. It is too difficult for me. I really tried hard, Hector, but my work and Alexander are too overwhelming. You do not know how difficult it has been for me to find time for us over this past month."

Confused, I implored, "But I can give you time, Elizabeth. I will never pressure you on anything; you know that. I told you that your ubiquity would not need to last, as our free time would eventually converge ..."

"I am terribly sorry but I do not think it will work. I really tried. You are the first man I have tried with since my divorce. You have to know that. But I can't. I have to follow my instincts. I am really sorry, Hector."

I could feel how distressed she was, despite her resolute tone. "But I will give you time." I said, unconvinced. "Take all the time you need and think about it in London. We can talk again when you come back. I agree that we need to take some time, and Thursday evening was a mess ..."

Elizabeth's voice suddenly stiffened, "I really don't think it would work. This is not about Thursday. You will find someone else who is right for you, but I am not that person."

I myself did not have the strength to change tone or resonate and could therefore only continue my plea, "We knew we needed to take a step back; we were going too fast. But what we feel for each other is strong. Wednesday was magic, wasn't it? Let's see what happens when you come back from the UK, or let's take a longer break if you need to. Then we can see what will happen. What do you think?"

"Maybe ..."

"I respect your decision, Elizabeth. I understand and agree that we need distance. Thursday was not good, but think about all the other great times we have spent together. You know what I feel for you, and you must know that my door will always be open, no matter what. I do not want to lose you. So, let's talk about all that once you are back ..."

"I have arrived at the airport. I have to go. I am sorry." She paused, then concluded, "Bye, Hector."

"Bye, Elizabeth."

I COULD NOT BELIEVE it! I knew Thursday had been bad, but after all the great and heartfelt times we had had, the extraordinary emotions shared at the gallery and the understanding we had talked about all along, I had thought this distressing evening was just a point of detail in the building of our relationship. I was distressed, even though I had some premonition of this, with her silence of the past few days. Yet the intense emotions we had experienced in the gallery were worth a thousand times more than this little glitch in our common odyssey. And, of course, I could give her time. I never willingly pressured her or complained that I could not see her more often. I sent Elizabeth a text message before her plane took off, imploring her to remember the fantastic times we had together, and what we had felt, and that I hoped and wished we would get over this crisis, once she returned.

My head was spinning and I felt the ground opening up under my feet again, ready to devour me mercilessly. This was becoming an unwelcome habit. We needed time and we needed to talk. I would explain everything to her, the tumor, my burning feelings, and the consequent emotional abyss in which I had recently capsized. This break would actually be beneficial; the reality check we needed. We could move on stronger after this troubling episode, and it could very well strengthen our relationship, as we would prove that we could overcome difficulties, as our feelings were strong. How else could it be?

Left wondering, I went through the details of our dates; I remembered what she had said about steadily building our relationship, I saw her again offering herself on my rooftop and saying she had been looking forward to kissing me. I felt her shuddering when I held her hand for the first time, and I could still hear her agreeing that issues, fears, and lack of communication impair relationships. And what about the amazing experience in the gallery? Wasn't it proof of anything? I did not dream all this up. The magnetism I felt was clearly not unilateral. As I sat alone at my desk, my mind moved in mad ellipses seeking any reason to be reassured, convincing myself that of course everything would be fine after her trip; after all, her fears were understandable following the intensity of that seismic Wednesday. We had been riding at breakneck speed and needed to slow down, give each other some space, and explain and clarify our actions and reactions—or the lack of them. That was what could and should happen, as there was no reason for Elizabeth to just cut herself off from me. We could indeed pause, and then continue at a steadier, calmer, and more confident pace. Several flashes of optimism countered my distress, giving me some balance. Doomed and so doubly doomed? Or finally blessed and so doubly blessed? I knew what I wanted and I was ready to fight for my emotions, as I dearly cherished this woman. Her sudden rigidity could not change that.

CHEE-HWA'S MECHANICS ARRIVED AT a little before 4pm, parked the convertible on the street just below the gallery, and handed over the keys. A few minutes later Werner K. showed up, dressed in faded blue jeans, a gray polo shirt, and his usual hiking boots. I had invited him to a *mechoui* party to meet some of the bankers who would attend this roasted lamb feast, as he was always looking for more contacts within the financial scene. Werner considered himself an existentialist and abhorred any form of luxury, more because he did not know how to appreciate it than by real moral conviction, it often seemed. This ascetic friend therefore refused to get into my car to go to Lantau Island, using his highly personal ethical standard against a supposedly flashy Audi as an excuse instead of admitting that he was concerned being in a car that I would be driving for the first time. I therefore closed the gallery and we walked together through Hong Kong's mean streets toward the pier to catch the 5:10pm ferry to Mui Wo.

WAKING UP ON SUNDAY, despite having spent an enjoyable evening the day before, I was still furious and frustrated. As soon as I opened my eyes, the film of our past dates played in my head. Each time, different details and reflections appeared, giving me hints and potential reasons for the sudden break-up and for the reconciliation talk that I hoped would come. I needed to share my distress, to find some reassurance among friends that this crisis was only transient. I therefore called my friends Patrick and Evelyn to invite them to drive in my new toy to the seaside, and have brunch near the scenic Sai Kung Country Park. I thought that this couple was perfect to share my situation with, as they had been married for more than four years now but had prior to that been through a few crises, including Evelyn running away a few weeks before their wedding day, panicked by the implications of this commitment.

The day was hazy and cool but pleasant enough to take full advantage of the convertible. The electronic system was now working properly and, except for driving too close to the left side of the road, I recovered my driving skills and reflexes quite swiftly. Most of the conversation we had during the ride was about driving directions, maps, and about other subjects related to the car and to the depressing forest of tall, monotone and uniform apartment towers composing most of Hong Kong's suburban areas, through which we had to cut to reach the shores. I did not mention Elizabeth then, because I was awaiting a calm and static location in which to have a serious conversation about my situation and hopefully to receive insights that would comfort me, in the hopes that everything would get back on a positive track.

Pondering the pros and cons again, I was optimistic about a reconciliation, as the fabulous moments we had shared were strong proof of her genuine emotional involvement. I also understood that, paradoxically, the intensity of what she felt could be the cause of her sudden escape. She might, therefore, reach out to me when, with time, she will come to her senses.

A few kilometers before reaching the town of Sai Kung, I parked the car in front of the Deck Chairs restaurant. We sat on the second-floor terrace and after some consultation, I ordered for all of us a grilled salmon in Bois Baudran sauce and saffron polenta, a rock shrimp ragoût with feta cheese, and a Fattoush salad together with a bottle of white Mâcon-Chaintré. The sun had difficulty piercing through the haze and I was not hungry, an unsurprising knot twisting my stomach. I actually did not really know how to talk about Elizabeth's reaction, as I had kept my friends informed about the progress of the relationship all along, so they knew how important I considered this woman.

Yet the previous day's phone call would not easily fit into the cheerful story I had depicted over the past weeks. I was somehow embarrassed to fall into such a situation, especially after having been so enraptured about Wednesday's magnetism.

Also, it had just happened a few days before, and even though I was stunned and shattered, I was also convinced that Elizabeth would think further, react, and reach out, once she came back from London. I think my unease was also because I never shared about my tumor—or my inner doubts—with Patrick and Evelyn, or indeed with any other people, except my parents and my doctors. It was therefore actually difficult to bring a clear perspective to the conversation. The most important thing for me, though, was not to be alone that day, to get the anguish and pain out of my system, and to stop thinking in circles all by myself. I therefore briefly mentioned Elizabeth's phone call and, despite my state of shock, I brandished my optimism like a standard, as Thursday's glitch was surely just a pause in our journey, provoked by fears and doubts, and nothing more.

ON MONDAY, NOVEMBER 19, I had an appointment with Doctor Liu in the early afternoon and I decided to call Devorah beforehand, at 11am. Aside from Werner K., she was actually the only acquaintance I had who also knew Elizabeth. As Devorah was her close friend, I guessed that they had been talking about me and about the evolution of the relationship all along. She should therefore have some insight on Elizabeth's state of mind, and might even know the real reasons behind her sudden decision. I hoped she would act as Prudence in The Lady of the Camellias and become a much-needed link between the shattered lovebirds. After two rings, a woman picked up the phone.

"Hello?"

"Hello, is this Devorah?"

"Speaking."

"Hi, Devorah, it's Hector. How are you?"

After a brief silence, she hesitantly answered, "Hi, I am fine, and you?" Her voice was filled with embarrassment. I felt that she might have apprehensively waited for my call and might not know how to position herself without betraying her friend, especially since she actually hardly knew me.

I continued, unfazed by her reserve, "Well, it could be better. I don't know if you know, but I am going through a kind of a crisis with Elizabeth."

"Yes. Lizzy told me that she called you before leaving for the UK. She was feeling sad and I thought it was really nice of you to tell her that your door would always be open."

"Well, that's because I do not want this story to end. I honestly do not understand what happened and what prompted her sudden decision. But I know that she probably misunderstood some of my intentions. Even though I do not think I did anything wrong or anything that hurt her, there are definitely issues that need to be explained and clarified."

"What would you want to tell her and clarify?" she cautiously asked.

"Well," I paused. "These are personal things. I need to speak to her directly, as there is really no reason to be in this situation. Did she actually tell you anything about us?"

"You know Hector, I don't want to talk for her, but Lizzy is under extreme pressure. She may not have told you about it but she has ongoing problems with her ex-husband. He tries to make her life miserable, and that creates a lot of pressure."

I tried to fully understand what Devorah was getting at, as she seemed to be eager to talk. She continued, "So when you picked her up at the airport and you drank Champagne when she had to work that also pressured her ..."

I took this blow right in the guts, especially since we did not drink Champagne then. Elizabeth herself brought a bottle to the rooftop, but I had only served us Bellini in the Rolls-Royce.

And reducing this romantic journey from the airport to a burden was a sucker punch. Devorah kept talking, "Also, have you ever wondered why Lizzy is always seen alone in Hong Kong?"

Was she implying that Elizabeth might have a boyfriend overseas? Even though I could understand that because of the trauma caused by a divorce, having a relationship with a man living abroad would be much easier, commitment-wise, I was positive, praising her intelligence and integrity that she had been fully into our relationship when we were seeing each other. I did not want to take Devorah's veiled suggestion—as the way that she revealed it did not match with the reality of what I had experienced with Elizabeth—as a reason to funnel anger and start smearing and diminishing her. I did not want to fall into this easy trap. Devorah then continued to astonish me by saying that Elizabeth had very few interests in life, that her world was quite monochromatic and narrow and that I was, by contrast, much more eclectic, living a more exciting life and that I would easily find someone more colorful than her to share it with. The way that she trashed her own friend reminded me of how the ancient Tibetans disguised their children with unflattering names to keep away the evil spirits. I was somehow touched by this attempt, even though, at first, it was surprising to hear her running down her own friend. Her odd comments made me automatically wonder, though, if Devorah was also playing this confusing game with Elizabeth, denigrating me, and thus encouraging and comforting her in the decision to break up. As if she had been reading my mind, she suddenly changed her tune and said, "You know Hector that I am slightly older than you both." (I think that she was forty-five.) "Before I got married, I had many relationships, and I have always valued dialogue and communication, whenever I had issues with my boyfriends. Even now, with my husband Lazlo, we argue all the time. But we talk and we always solve our problems through conversation."

I could not agree with her more, even though I smiled when

she brought to mind the image of the "more experienced woman" with whom she was identifying herself. In reality, she was objectively not really the most graceful person, and therefore did not fit the full profile of a woman who collects men. Furthermore, even though Elizabeth and I had been acting like two infatuated teenagers, we were also not born yesterday and had, thus, our own experiences. Anyhow, I was not there to argue and therefore replied, "I totally agree with you about the need to communicate, clarify, and explain. But after her last phone call, I don't think Elizabeth will want me to call her soon, or even send her letters or e-mails. Her voice at the end was so cold that I did not think she would want to read anything coming from me."

"Of course she would," replied Devorah spontaneously. Her sympathetic tone suddenly offered a little ray of hope, and was an indication that Elizabeth cared something about me after all. She then added, "Send her a short e-mail asking her to meet for coffee when she comes back. I am sure she will accept."

Her voice was once again encouraging, and the possible prospect of meeting Elizabeth and talking about our situation was obviously what I wanted. It was what two reasonable and intelligent people like us should indeed do in such a difficult situation. Thanking Devorah for her mixed and sometimes contradictory insights, I hung up, somehow reassured, and I immediately sent an e-mail to my naiad:

"Dear Elizabeth,

I hope everything is going well for you in London. You know that I respect what you said when you called, even though I think it is truly unfortunate and your decision saddened and hurt me immensely. I think, though, that we deserve to have a conversation, whenever you feel ready for it, face-to-face— without Rolls-Royces, Champagne, or red sails—as we certainly have to talk through the misunderstandings, confusion, and differences in perceptions ... and probably many other things as well. There are always solutions to crisis, but the key is communication and understanding. Give us this chance. To cut and run is never the solution.

I hope you will not take this wrongly as overwhelming or as pressure, but I would like to quote Sidney Orr, Paul Auster's main character in *Oracle Night*, "As long as you are dreaming there is always a way out."

I wish you a smooth flight back and hope London is a great success.

Take care,

Hector"

I felt a sense of relief, sending this proactive message, as I was not blaming her or putting any pressure on her. I had indeed grasped from the conversation I had with Devorah that the need to free herself from the extra strains provoked by building up our relationship might have been one decisive factor in her escape. At about 1:30pm I walked from the gallery to Hutchison House, having of course some bittersweet thoughts as I passed by the Bank of America Tower, but I was still full of hope—for us, and also for the other great battle I was fighting.

DOCTOR LIU WAS, AS usual, fifteen minutes late, but what are a few minutes lost in comparison to gaining eternity? He was looking fresh, as he had just spent the weekend playing golf in Shenzhen, and he tried to share as much of his confidence in the surgery as he could, despite its limited chances of success. As he had stressed the Thursday before, we had to do it, there were no alternatives, and I needed to have full trust in him, and in my life, now more than ever before. We therefore scheduled the *all or nothing* operation for January 22, at the Matilda Hospital, with an option to do it earlier, in case of emergency.

I later called my parents to give them the date of the surgery. Over the weekend, they had made the decision to come to Hong Kong at the time of the operation to be with me during this critical time. I felt relieved and thankful. Having their incommensurable support was indispensable, as I had not yet announced the news to many other people. I saw again suddenly, in my damnation, a small window of blessing in having such parents. They had as expected, informed my sister about my situation a few days before, and she phoned me to get the details and to give me her full moral support. It was good to feel her on my side as well, and now the four of us were united in this confrontation with the Grim Reaper.

I received an e-mail from Elizabeth two days later:

"Dear Hector,

Thank you for your message, but I am afraid I don't feel the same way as you do. I don't think it is a matter of misunderstandings, mistakes, missed opportunities, whatever. For me, I simply realized that we are in different phases of life and the relationship was not going to work in the long term. I think you're great, charming, handsome, romantic, and many other wonderful things, but that doesn't make you right for me—or me right for you. A lot of things have to be right for a relationship to work. I thought we had many of those things, but it seems, not enough of them.

I wish you all the very best, and I thank you for the times that we shared.

Elizabeth"

The lack of empathy, the clinical tone of this message, and its irremediable implications were extremely puzzling to me. "Different phases of life"—this was what she had tried to bring up before, during the *Bloody Thursday* dinner at Gaia, and when I had evasively said "No," she had answered "Maybe not." I know we were both not at our best—far from it, obviously—and I was not going to take her subdued answer for more than an admission of her frustration in the face of my disintegration and inability to communicate. Yet what perception of *my* phase of life did she get? What did she know about it, or mean by that? I was dying, that was my phase—but what else? And what was hers, then?

Elizabeth had also written that we had many things in common but not enough for the success of a long-term relationship. Yet there were indeed explanations and clarifications to make, and her statement was therefore biased, as her perception of me could surely not be totally correct, when an emotional black hole of doubts had perversely started to swallow me bit by bit. I was revolted, because a conversation was obviously required. How could she just slam the door of our future like that, and not give the strong emotions we felt for each other a chance to blossom and glow? Did she truly believe that what we had experienced together in the past weeks and during that magical Wednesday could have such an abrupt ending, such an unfair conclusion, conveyed by a quick phone call and a cold message?

MY MIND WAS BOILING and my head was ready to explode. I had been living in a dichotomous world, mixing death and rare emotions, since I had come back from Europe and started seeing Elizabeth, but it seemed now that I was colliding with another kind of reality—a reality that I did not, and could not, relate to or understand. I therefore sent her a new e-mail, giving her hints and trying to clarify certain behavior she could not understand without my own insights. Yet I still could not mention the tumor, as it would have been inappropriate, would have added even more pressure, and would also have looked like a desperate attempt,

147

almost blackmail, to be granted the audience I wished for. I opened up as much as I could in this missive, answering those doubts and questions that I thought she had and speculating on her reasons for behaving so unilaterally. Being as sympathetic as a hurt and shattered man can ever be, I tried my best to be correct and, thus, not blame her or put any pressure on her.

The e-mail I sent tried therefore to explain why, putting aside any implications about my health issue, when submerged with emotions—and she was obviously a source of strong ones—I could sometimes become overwhelmed and thus unresponsive and disappointing (to myself at least). I also wrote that I had no agenda and could wait as long as it would take for her to be ready, if she felt too pressed by such an intense relationship at the present time.

Devorah had mentioned pressures exerted by her ex-husband without clearly naming what was going on, yet I could sense that this was a key element in Elizabeth's current state of mind. It was therefore crucial to stress that I could be understanding and willing to give her—to give us—as much space as needed, on top of my full support. I also could not help claiming, as it was what I felt at the time, that we were exceptional people, smart people and that what we had tried to build was not a relationship like any other. I strongly believed that we had a special bond, a unique attraction, which had peaked when we collided like magnets in my gallery. I believed that we were like the two missing pieces of a puzzle, alike in our qualities and flaws, perfectly crafted for each other. Despite the biased and enhanced perceptions the tumor had likely provoked, I knew that we had shared an exceptional emotional moment.

I could also probably not readily cope with the incomprehension of being hit by this lethal tumor in the first place, and therefore needed to find reason in Elizabeth's decision and attitude, as I could not or did not want to understand at that time that the pressure she was experiencing could also trigger irrational behavior. Surprisingly, I also totally ignored the fact that I was myself in an irrational condition and that my actions and reactions were influenced significantly by my unfortunate state of health. My world was collapsing under my feet and I needed, for sanity's sake, to hold on to some good old classic and subjective Cartesian behavior. I simply could not understand how someone like her would act and react that way, or why this had happened to me.

I did not receive an answer to my e-mail. Her silence and my sudden and total exclusion from her life was driving me insane. I actually was not so much heartbroken, but rather brain-broken. I went back in time, going step-by-step over the "crime" scene and beyond, trying to remember every sign, every sentence, every word, every whisper, every gaze, every kiss, every scent, every look, every move, every caress, every smile, every touch, every call, and every text message. Yet I could not come up with a single reason for her to dismiss and write off in a snap and without explanation all the exceptional times we had shared. Her extreme reaction seemed so disproportionate. What was criminal in her behavior was that it forced me to doubt everything that I was. She forced me to strip myself bare, to carry a painful and lonely introspection to the depth of my being and to the abyss of my soul, as the only way to find out what had been the trigger to her unequivocal and firm decision. Forcing me to become an abstraction only linked to my humanity by ravaging, universal, and primal doubts was a violent, extreme, and painful experience that brought me to the boundaries of sanity.

Why would a woman, especially a woman like her, do this, be so cruel? My need for rationality—in my own irrationality— was forbidding me to accept this unfortunate lack of realism. If I did, I felt that some gigantic creature emerging from the center of the earth might as well gulp me down. Giving myself up to a Kafkaesque realm was unthinkable, as I had to be anchored in reality to fight the tumor, which, in a paradoxical twist, was continually blurring my perception of my so-called reality. I could accept that Elizabeth had issues that were triggering primal fears (and actual fear of commitment), but why not have the courage to talk about them, instead of counting me in the number of the victims of her unresolved pathos? What could she not tell me?

Her beacon was irremediably off, and I was left spending sleepless nights seeking answers, drifting by myself in the ocean of our sweet memories. As my doomed condition was unbearable, I sent her another e-mail, on December 8, to again seek her mercy.

"Dear Elizabeth,

After opening up to you in my last e-mail, I went again and again through the memories of our dates and your text messages (the only tangible traces I have) to try to understand what happened and to explain how it is that I am forced to suffer from your unequivocal and devastating decision. You will understand that I can't readily accept it without pleading for clarification and explanation, as things are simply not adding up. Everything seemed fine until Wednesday evening at the gallery. I believe that something happened after you left that evening, or on Thursday, that made me become a pariah to you. I still have the image of you turning around, while walking up the stairs when leaving the gallery. What we felt at that time was so amazingly powerful! What equally strong phenomenon could therefore have come about to counterbalance such intensity, to make you want to run fast and furiously away from this beautiful nascent story? Could Thursday's disappointing dinner actually be the cause of your irrevocable decision? I can't seriously believe that.

I may obviously be utterly wrong, as I am totally blind, left to guess alone in the darkness of your incommunicability, but I also believe that your distance and decision to end our relationship is likely to have been increased—or maybe even triggered—by the sheer intensity of our feelings. Indeed, when one feels what we felt, then a fear of losing control, a sense of extreme emotional vulnerability emerges, and the subsequent fear of potentially being hurt (again) can provoke a high panic and the urge to "get out of it!"

I do not know everything, of course, but I think I understand that you are under a lot of pressure on different fronts, and my adding another source of stress is simply unmanageable, especially when our relationship is supposed to bring happiness, support, and love, instead of additional strain.

If I am totally off the mark, though, then it would only be fair—after what we felt, and still feel, on my side, for you—to tell me. Yet what saddens and hurts me the most is that our relationship is being sacrificed on the altar of our respective fears and pathos! Not us, Elizabeth! Not our relationship! We are bigger than that! Much bigger! I wish you could have more trust in our common story, trust in yourself, and trust in me.

I have so much faith in you. You have the keys to this relationship; you know the real reason for this overnight relationshipus-interruptus, and if I am right about my conclusion, then IT'S OKAY, as these emotions and fears are actually a clear proof of the intense feelings we still have for each other.

So please, let's communicate, let's be rational, let's be strong, and let's get over this together. This crisis is not about our feelings, but it is about our pathos and about our hypersensitive souls. Overcoming this challenging time together will make us, and our relationship, stronger.

If you can get some distance, hear this message, and then have trust in me, in my feelings, this will be an easy thing to do. It would not add pressure on you; to the contrary, our relationship would give you so much relief, so much hope, and so many positive emotions and energy that this would help you to be stronger in facing your personal struggles ... and I would be at your side, supporting you, whenever you needed it.

If all of this makes any kind of sense to you, then please Elizabeth, give me a sign showing me that you still believe in us.

Take Care,

Hector"

ON DECEMBER 12, I received an answer from Elizabeth. Being able to finally have a dialogue brought a lot of hope. Yet I opened it with an uncomfortable mix of expectation and apprehension:

"Dear Hector,

I am really sorry that you are in pain. I know what that is like, having been there before, and I'm sorry that you are going through that.

Yet I must say you are thinking way too much. I simply decided I didn't think a relationship with you would work. I wanted it too, and, like you, I tried ... until I decided that Thursday night that I just didn't want to try it anymore—that we are not right for each other. You didn't do anything wrong, nothing happened, it just wasn't working for me.

You also said you have become a pariah to me. I don't know why you feel that way. I have never said anything like that, and I don't have any negative thoughts about you. I just don't see the point of continuing to talk closely about everything, when we obviously have two totally different viewpoints. If you are going to think a lot about something, I suggest you think about why you would have strong feelings for so long for someone and yet not express them.

I wish you all the very best, and always will, as I think so highly of you.

Elizabeth"

The radical tone of her message and her ongoing refusal to give me any explanation about her overnight radical U-turn, leaving me helpless in the dark and tortured by doubts, were overly disturbing. Her indifference was upsetting, as it contrasted so much with the charming and affectionate Elizabeth I had held in my arms only a short time before. Saying she was sorry to know I was suffering and that she knew what it was like, as she had been through that as well meant what? That she thought it was normal and okay to cut loose suddenly, without any explanation, because she had experienced that before? How could she think I would accept her reaction without even batting an eyelid? What type of a person would do this, and who would consent to it? Should I have accepted her sudden and incomprehensible decision as a mark of her gender—as some sexist friends suggested—and forgotten her for good?

I categorically refused to become a *Sex and the City* character, turning the pages of one relationship after another, unfazed, unattached, unmoved. I hated being cornered into such recurring and clichéd roles. Or maybe, instead, she was thinking that I was a teenager, who had just experienced his first serious breakup? This kind of condescension enraged me. It was the way she had suddenly ended this nascent relationship that was intolerable to me, more than the breakup itself, as it seemed it could be simply a glitch prompted by fear and doubts.

I also considered her supposedly compassionate reassurance that she did not consider me a pariah as an insult to our intelligence, as in fact I had indeed become for her an Untouchable; I was banned from seeing her, from meeting her, from talking to her, and these e-mails—our only open link now—were like a thin bone cruelly given to a dog following weeks of delicious victuals.

I effectively became, without further explanation, one of the few men on earth whom she forbade to see, talk to, or call her ever again. This sad predicament resonated with one of Marcel Proust's novels, somehow reassuring me that my situation and struggle were not an anomaly and that love was, indeed, for many humans on this planet a paramount feeling that was worth all sacrifices and sufferings, "And Swan was nevertheless happy to feel that, if of all mortals he was the only one forbidden to see Odette, it was because he was someone different from all others—her love. This restriction to the universal right of free movement was only a form of this slavery, of this love that was so dear to him."

Elizabeth was also probably wondering why I had told her that I needed to be in the right emotional and professional mindset to start a relationship with her, when she had seen me before with Olivia and Su-yeon. Maybe she thought I was inconsistent—or even worse, a liar—and that could have triggered some more doubts. Yet, the answer was simple. The relationship with Olivia was *light* and until I met Su-yeon, I did not think I was ready for a steady relationship. When I started dating her, I had not seen Elizabeth for a long time and I therefore had no opportunity to contact her. It was at Yoshitaka Amano's party at the Kee Club that I had a clear and decisive revelation about Elizabeth, feeling an unequivocal attraction, which is very different from having "strong feelings" for someone.

Yet, despite perceiving where some of her doubts might come from, I could hardly comprehend that she would not be willing to meet with me, knowing that I was now able and keen to communicate. I honestly could not understand why she chose to abruptly smash into a million pieces the crystal trophy of our nascent love story, reducing to nil and sheer irrelevance everything we had said, withdrawing from any kind thoughts she had ever had for me, and denying the real emotions she must have felt! How was I supposed to observe this shattering without overreacting, especially when also battling on another front an invading alien killer? How could anyone have accepted her reaction without being revolted? There was something clearly rotten in the state of Oklahoma! No dialogue, no explanation, no reasoning was possible anymore with her. Even after writing "I think so highly of you," Elizabeth would not grant me a few minutes to talk.

Fantastical and anachronistic images were further coloring my confused dwelling. I suddenly transposed my painful reflections to the American Midwest, to the tall and impassable Fort Gibson, where I imagined my unforgiving Artemis hiding in its darkness after having punished the hunter Actaeon for the sin of finding her wonderful. Yet, despite the thickness of the walls, her fearful and shivering heartbeat could be perceived far away in the prairies where the lilacs grew. Her stubbornness and lack of explanation were too suspect not to believe that something else was urging her to act in that way. The image of a fragile and young Elizabeth came spontaneously to mind, replacing the evocation of the strong yet suddenly vulnerable Greek goddess. Through the prism of this scared little girl, I intuitively felt that she was overprotecting herself mentally and had developed, probably from a most tender age, reassuring and protective reflexes against the life traumas she or her family had experienced. I did not want to speculate on the reasons for this psychological construction and the urge to take refuge behind reinforced walls when fear occurred but I felt strongly her anguish, inside her protective fort. I also remembered the dramatic story of her ancestors that Elizabeth had spoken about during our first date, and my friend Harold's description of his wife and her reaction after they divorced. Both of these women came from families of survivors. This common heritage undoubtedly influenced their personal reactions toward adversity. Elizabeth's pragmatic view of love and relationships was therefore certainly extremely different from that of a privileged European Romanesque man blinded by his nineteenth-century references to romance and the dramatic love story of his parents.

SINCE I HAD DIVULGED the extent of the tumor to my parents, they had been calling me every two days. They were obviously concerned about the success of the surgery and wanted to reassure me and to make me feel surrounded and loved while going through this critical period of my life. As a breach with our unspoken tradition, I had mentioned that I was going through a crazy story with a woman, but I had not given any details— and, in their reserved way, they did not ask for any. Yet they could probably feel that, behind my self-motivated optimistic stance, I was not totally there. They could understand, though, that it was quite normal to not be fully in the present, as to be potentially scythed by death at thirty-six years old was not an easy situation to experience, and I could be forgiven for some level of detachment. I was now, indeed, feeling mentally tired. After going through an ecstatic phase in the first months—when the presence of the alien provoked a kind of hyperexaltation, as if the apocalypse was near and I could blissfully savor my last days on Earth—that same excitement was no longer anywhere in sight. Even though I was not resigned, but in full fighting spirit, the bitter taste of the past weeks had created a strange biosphere to navigate, in which only a few solid references remained.

Understanding that there was not much I could do to convince Elizabeth of anything, as she was lying low, motionless, and indifferent, in the dampness of her fort, I wrote an incredulous e-mail to Devorah, hoping to maybe provoke a ricochet reaction from Elizabeth:

"Dear Devorah,

I am writing you this e-mail as I am still totally bewildered by

Elizabeth's attitude. I wrote to her two long messages to explain many things, with the hope of solving our misunderstandings and misperceptions. I believe these messages were crucial for our relationship, as they were sensitive, open, and sincere, and I honestly thought that anyone in our situation would have been willing to open a dialogue after that. Unfortunately, that did not happen. To make things worse, I actually still do not understand why Elizabeth suddenly cut me out of her life. I still do not understand what happened that is so totally irrevocable, or why she cannot keep a small door of hope open. Why this extreme and sudden reaction? Indeed, after analyzing so many options and opening ways for solutions, the only "explanations" I got from her were that "she follows her instincts" and that "she decided that she did not want to try anymore." I obviously can't take that as an "explanation."

What hurts me the most is that this incomprehensible behavior comes from Elizabeth, an intelligent woman, not only with whom I was falling in love, but also of whom I genuinely think very highly. She is therefore the last person I would have expected to have such a definite and irreversible reaction. Anyone but Elizabeth! And yet she is the one who did it! The toughest thing for me is truly to be in total bewilderment, confronted by a Kafkaesque situation. I simply cannot comprehend this, as it is not making any sense. But it is actually also because it is a woman like Elizabeth who is behaving like this that I still have some hope, as I have tremendous faith in her, and in her capacity to eventually come to her senses, after the depth of what we felt for each other. I may look like a blind fool, but I can only believe that reason will eventually prevail.

Kind regards,

Hector"

Yet neither of them answered this missive or sent any smoke signals in my direction. I was still moving in mental circles, sharing with friends the revolting silliness of the situation in which I was enmeshed. Every minute I had spent with her was still fresh in my memory and I spent sleepless nights dwelling upon this undignified story. If the emotions, the energy, and the magnetism felt during Elizabeth's gallery visit that mythical Wednesday had not happened and if she had not been responding to my advances and even, often, anticipating and initiating them, I would not have considered this breakup as unacceptable as I was then viewing it.

As only she held the keys to her precipitous reactions, I had to keep contacting her, not only in search for answers but also in an attempt to blow sparks in her direction with the desperate hope of regenerating a fire. Christmas was approaching fast, and I took this opportunity to move my king across the chessboard toward my now ex-queen.

WHEN I HAD TALKED with Philippe G. a few weeks previously about the story of the Comte de P., my relative spitefully depicted in *The Lady of the Camellias*, he had mentioned with his usual bonhomie that he had gone some time ago to the Mongkok Flower Market and had seen camellias. Having mentioned the flowers to Elizabeth without explaining their particular meaning, and having offered Dumas' book to my merciless Artemis, I thought that bestowing her with this symbol would make for an original, memorable, and lasting Christmas gift. Aside from the flowers, I wanted to add a thoughtful sign showing that I had actually (despite my lack of responsiveness) always listened to her and understood her interests and priorities.

The French equestrian company Zingaro was going to plant its big top in Hong Kong in February for some exceptional performances and I knew that she would enjoy the show, being an eager equestrian. I was obviously hoping to have vanquished the tumor by February, and hoping that enough distance and perspective would have passed to allow Elizabeth to accept my invitation to this performance. I offered her two seats for adults and one for a child—obviously with Alexander in mind. I included in the envelope a card, on which I expressed again—given that Christmas was a time for reflection and understanding—my sadness, regret, and hope that she would now have enough distance to reach out and fight for a revival of the strong feelings we had felt for one another, and I wished her a heartfelt and merry Christmas.

On Friday, December 21, I took a cab with Kenix and we drove with the Zingaro tickets and the beautiful red *Camellias Hongkongesis* in a transparent wrapping, laid on my knees, to the Bank of America Tower. As the Silver Spirit Rolls-Royce had done before, the taxi stopped right in front of her office building. Holding the gifts, my assistant walked up to the entrance and took a lift to the twelfth floor while I waited in the car, my mind, and body boiling.

ON CHRISTMAS EVE MY parents and my sister called me from Valrolz, perpetuating our family tradition of being together that day, to get some general news and to be reassured that everything, my health especially, was going as well as might be hoped. I thanked them dearly for that, and for their continual support and kind thoughts, which were natural and yet still deeply moving. My parents had already made their plane reservations, and would be arriving in Hong Kong three days before the surgery. They thus asked me to book for them a conveniently located hotel. I genuinely felt blessed to be surrounded by so much love and consideration, and it was enough to bring me close to tears. I smiled at this sudden rush of emotion, almost nervously laughing out of happiness, as this call brought me out of the melancholy provoked by the disillusions I had been experiencing on different emotional fronts.

THAT EVENING I HAD accepted an invitation by Jean-Loup A. to dine with several of his friends at his atypical apartment—a kind of small loft, in a former printing shop filled with Burmese Buddhas—located in a dark lane near the Sun Yat-sen Museum. I was the first to arrive; the melody of Bach's Goldberg Variations by Glenn Gould was agreeably floating in the air. Jean-Loup greeted me and we sat around a Balinese coffee table on which was casually dumped a 500gr open can of Russian Sevruga on a bed of ice. The chilled Muscadet wine that accompanied the caviar helped to improve my mood substantially, until I felt almost ecstatic. I obviously badly needed to escape, for one night at least, the stranglehold in which my tortured mind was trapped.

I had bumped into Jean-Loup after my first evening with Elizabeth but had not informed him since of the evolution of the relationship. Having said then, carried away by the fulfillment of that delightful first date, that I had found the love of my life, I know he was now surprised and sincerely saddened to hear of the unfortunate outcome. Yet even though the sky had lately fallen on my head, the phone conversation with my parents earlier that day had actually made me so pleased that I was, surprisingly, in remarkably good spirits. I could feel that Jean-Loup was a bit puzzled and intrigued by my contradictory behavior, as he was himself coping with his recent divorce with a lot of hidden confusion.

The other guests arrived soon after I did, most of them couples, except for two single French women, Nathalie and Sophie. I had met both of them a few times in the past through other common friends. Sophie was a twenty-six-year-old tall and pretty brunette, a dance teacher and performer. Her slender figure and her cute nose above a wide and enthusiastic smile were major turn-ons. As we knew each other already, we started talking as soon as she walked into the open living room. Half an hour later we sat together around the long glass dinner table, nicely lit by numerous white candles, and continued our lively conversation throughout the luscious banquet. Our host had prepared imaginative starters aplenty that included creamed crawfish bisque, foie gras samosas with black raspberry coulis, swordfish carpaccio with orange, ricotta and pine nuts, and small brioches stuffed with chanterelles and caviar. Four large lobsters Thermidor, cardoon gratin, and morels and truffles in puff pastry, also prepared by Jean-Loup, followed these exquisite entrees. These gargantuan dishes were absolutely delectable and no drink could have contented us better than the Champagne flowing seemingly endlessly that evening.

The atmosphere was joyful and the conversation was varied, sometimes intense and provocative, funny and witty, and our ongoing laughter made me almost totally forget my inner state of distress. The presence of Sophie by my side, giggling, was also extremely appreciated, as I needed to feel again the cheerful and seductive presence of a woman beside me, having been invaded by so many existential doubts.

The alcohol and the pleasant and comforting atmosphere brought us into a state of euphoric inebriation. At about 1am, after dessert, our symphonic troupe agreed, at the suggestion of our host, to move to Drop, a small nightclub situated under the Central Escalator, just below Hollywood Road.

My need for affection, Sophie's charming smile, and flirting eyes, and her elegant shiny black suit and low-cut satin tank top lightly covering her beautiful body were variables likely to lead to a sinful, yet delicious, outcome. It was almost 1:30am, I think, when we cut through the party-pack stamping their feet outside Drop. We entered the smoky and cramped club while the DJ was playing "Hey Boy Hey Girl" by The Chemical Brothers and we installed ourselves comfortably on the orange and white vinyl sofas reserved by Jean-Loup.

Sophie sat sensually beside me and the Champagne served at once and with cheers gave us the anticipated opportunity to share a first kiss. Our group split quickly, as the blissful and friendly atmosphere of the dinner had been replaced by loud electro beats. Some couples left quite early, others were boogying madly, and Jean-Loup and Nathalie were soon unaccounted for. Feeling tired after a few dances, I took Sophie's hand and led her outside. There I pushed her gently against a wall on a shady corner and we kissed, hidden, yet only meters away from the entrance of the club and the noisy and frustrated ravers queuing up there.

WE EMERGED SLOWLY FROM our diaphanous sleep around noon, opening our eyes uncertainly, still in a tight embrace. The pillows of the huge sofa and our clothes were scattered around my studio and the reminder of our common tousled nudity under the duvet made us giggle after noticing that the blinds of the bay window were not closed and that we had therefore been potentially exposed to thousands of eyes all along. After remedying this omission, we reveled again into lust, as Sophie devilishly offered to my morning ardor her silky and toned body.

During the dinner at Jean-Loup's, I did not go into detail about my story with Elizabeth, as I am not the whining type, seeking consolation. But I did mention to Sophie, though, that I was currently coping with the aftermath of a *crazy story*. She understood, without my having to spell things out, where I stood emotionally, and she therefore already knew that I was not free mentally to become seriously involved with a new woman, especially as I still hoped for a turnaround with Elizabeth. She actually understood my situation well, as she had separated from her former boyfriend only four months previously and did not feel ready to dive into a new romance quite yet either. Meeting each other at this similar emotional level probably brought us closer that night—like two castaways realizing that they were actually not alone on their island. After a copious brunch on my balcony, I accompanied my French dancer back to her apartment on Bowen Road.

The following afternoon, December 26, I picked her up at her place and we drove to Deepwater Bay, from which we took a sampan to the Yacht Club on Middle Island. It was a sunny day, with a rare unpolluted sky, and so we sat on the terrace, a privileged perch hidden among the luscious Bauhinia trees, overlooking the charming coast and the variety of sailboats far out to sea.

This time I could not avoid talking at length about my story, again not to be solaced, but instead to gain from my companion some potential insight that would highlight some new angle of reflection, as I was obviously still compulsively dwelling on the overall situation. I certainly had succeeded in feeling light and relaxed during the Christmas dinner, but the knot in my stomach—and the hammers continuously pounding in my head—were relentless reminders of the inner distress that I was experiencing.

Sophie was compassionate, and an excellent listener. She carefully pondered the events and conversations I was revealing without trying to judge someone she did not know. She was, however, quite bewildered by Elizabeth's inflexible attitude. I disclosed my state of health just after ordering for a snack a mahi-mahi with ginger and Sophie some baby soft-shell crabs with grape jelly. She was truly touched by the hardship I was going through with the tumor and she encouraged me to hang on and fight. I, of course, never had the intention of giving up— even an inch—to the murderous vermin, but it was moving nonetheless to receive such spontaneous, genuine, and heartfelt support. She kept any opinion she may have formed about

Elizabeth to herself, out of respect for the strong feelings I still had for my ex-naiad and maybe also out of a certain solidarity with a fellow woman she sensed was probably not in full control of her emotions or reactions.

Nevertheless, Sophie could not totally comprehend Elizabeth's sudden and irrevocable stance. Trying to peep under the surface of her attitude, she speculated that Elizabeth maybe had another man somewhere who had resurfaced, or had perhaps been in the background all along. I could obviously not concur with this speculation, as I still had too much respect for Elizabeth's moral standards to accept that such dishonest and fake behavior could be the source of our breakup, especially remembering the dedicated, genuine, fond, and sensitive woman of the beginning of our relationship. Sophie also surmised that Elizabeth might have felt threatened by the overflow of emotions during our dates, and especially during her visit to my gallery and that she had decided to run away as quickly and as far as possible. The fear of losing control because of this relationship, becoming overly vulnerable to feelings, and thus to potentially being hurt, might have been too overwhelming for her, especially with the double responsibilities of her busy life and Alexander. Obviously, as I was the source of this threat, she had to cut loose from me, almost in a panic escape. Sophie also speculated, as carefully as she could, for fear of hurting my pride, that my own emotional overflow, provoked by the tumor and my infatuation with Elizabeth, together with my seeming lack of response toward her son had made me potentially look too soft to support and protect her and Alexander. Sophie added, quite convincingly, that it was a natural and subconscious reflex for a woman, and especially for a mother, to look for these specific aspects in a man. I know that she probably touched here another key factor in the imbroglio.

Yet, I told Sophie I still could not understand why Elizabeth had not left, in her escape, some thoughtful little signs, white pebbles maybe, or some light through a half open door. I needed to understand this fundamental mystery for my own peace of mind. Yet maybe, as my friend Laure had stressed during one of the numerous discussions we had about this situation, I actually could not understand this rebuttal, as I had fantasized about a woman who was maybe far from the person that Elizabeth really was. I could understand this view, even though I refuted it, as for me, the unique and strong metaphysical attraction I felt for Elizabeth, the enthusiastic responses I had received all along in our time together, and her fervor and willingness to move the relationship forward, were real and not fantasized. Furthermore, even though the tumor was affecting my perception of reality, the incredible Wednesday evening at the gallery was not an illusion. What we both felt was so powerful that I was committed to fighting dearly for this cause.

Sophie took my hand in support and gave me a kind smile, as she could feel how agitated I was. I returned her kind gesture with a kiss on her cheek. Thirty minutes after finishing eating my exotic fish, I left this sensitive woman lying on a long chair on a smaller terrace below, reading Sissy Hankshaw's adventures in Tom Robbins' *Even Cowgirls Get the Blues*, and went paddling for an hour and a half on my outrigger canoe.

LATE THAT AFTERNOON, PHYSICALLY and mentally drained by this solitary exercise in the sea, I drove Sophie back to the big apartment beside Lovers' Rock that she was sharing with a girlfriend, and I went to the gallery to follow up on several new deals.

I was especially interested in and motivated by the demand of a Swiss collector based in New York to find her a cubist Harlequin painting by Picasso. What fascinated me the most with this subject was the idea—expressed by the artist to Jean Cocteau—that if an army wanted to be invisible at a distance, they only had to dress their men in harlequins! What Picasso meant was that the concept of camouflage, deconstructing patterns and colors of nature, actually came from cubism. And the harlequin was one of Picasso's trademark characters. I had talked about this concept a few years before to this collector while she was visiting Hong Kong, and she had recently decided to dedicate part of her collection to artworks depicting or inspired by camouflage. She had already purchased, through me, a camouflage self-portrait by Andy Warhol, a painting by Takashi Murakami (using actually one of Yoshitaka Amano's Time Bokan characters together with reference to Warhol), a few large photographs printed on canvas by AES+F (*The Last Riot 2* series), and an edition by Thomas Ruff (the *Substrat* series).

A Harlequin by Picasso was next on her list, as the initiator and main reference of the collection. Given the potential limitation of finding art that she actually liked with military camouflage patterns (or explicit references to them), we had also been talking about potentially stretching the collection concept to the idea of camouflage within the artworks themselves. This would deviate substantially from the core cubist reference and would take a more literal approach to the word itself, yet it would also open the scope of the collection to more diverse art trends; it could incorporate, for example, abstractionism (especially artists using monochromatic patterns, like Malevich, Yves Klein, Soulage, Robert Ryman, Damian Hirst or Dale Frank) or artists creating "shapes" in their art that could be associated with camouflage patterns, such as the abstract expressionists (Pollock or de Kooning). I also suggested that she incorporate, in a full-circle type of move, paintings that would represent nature itself (the "home" and goal of camouflage) in a kind of abstract way—thus becoming a camouflage. This would allow her to potentially incorporate, later, works by naturalist Georgia O'Keefe or some Nympheas by Claude Monet.

Arriving at my gallery, I noticed under its main entry door

the mail of the past few days, scattered on the floor. Among the bills and greetings cards, a small red envelope stood out from the rest. I picked it up. Inside, on a red card, the following note was handwritten:

"Dear Hector,

Thank you for the very thoughtful gift, but I don't think it is right to accept. I don't know how to return the camellia, but allow me to return the tickets.

Regarding your last message, I am sorry but I just don't feel the same way as you do. Not even close.

That's why I can simply cut off a relationship that wasn't right for me. You are making it much more complicated than it is. I just decided, after a few dates and a few weeks, that this wasn't going to work for me. That's all. I am sorry to be so blunt, but perhaps you can't understand it because you do not want to hear it.

I hope you have a merry Christmas and I wish you all the best in the New Year.

Elizabeth"

Once again, her message did not content me, but this time her choice of words was truly uncalled for. I also could not understand how anyone could be so rude as to send back a Christmas gift, especially to a nonpariah and someone of whom she "thought so highly." I could grasp, however, that my insistence on receiving answers from her was now pushing Elizabeth into a corner and that this had started to annoy and irritate her.

Throughout our written exchanges, I had tried not to blame or to accuse her of anything. I stayed as proper as I could the whole time, even though I understand now that my frustration and perseverance in the quest to receive answers was probably enhancing her frustration. Yet the unfortunate "not even close" was now strongly clashing, inscribed in dripping red letters, on the battle flag of our exchanges.

Having these thoughts, I was standing by the belief—not shared, though, by most of the friends and acquaintances to whom I had told my story—that Elizabeth was not simply a vile person. This too-easy conclusion would obviously account for any unanswered questions, and yet I could not then, and still today cannot, believe that this was true. I therefore preferred to masochistically torture myself further, even to think stupidly and blindly that we might still have some chance together in the future, once she had enough distance to reflect on her reaction and to reach out. How else could it be? Yet the rudeness of this message forced me to acknowledge at least a temporary defeat, as there was not much I could do to go on from there, despite my utter state of distress, frustration, and subsequent rage. Of course, she had the right to smash in the firmament of our fading cosmology what we had felt for each other and the delicious experiences we had lived together, into a thousand pieces. Yet I did not have to accept the massacre of our memories without reacting and without being revolted. I tried to keep as much dignity and respect for her as I could in our exchanges, but her full denial and consequent bad faith was unnecessary, harmful, and beneath what I had expected of the woman I thought I was seeing in Elizabeth.

The only possible action was to send her a last message squaring things off, yet showing her that despite her provocation I would always remain polite—while also demonstrating how biased her last message had been.

"Dear Elizabeth,

What an unfortunate tone and use of words in your note with the returned gifts. Despite your ongoing attempts to force me to think differently about you, I still want to remember the kindhearted and caring Elizabeth that I once was falling for, instead of the insensitive woman I have been confronted with since that *Bloody Thursday*. I prefer to keep in my memory the soulful Elizabeth that I was once so close to, and who shared her sincere tenderness with me through the following text messages, which contrast incomprehensibly with the coldness of her later e-mails:

November 14 (the Wednesday at the gallery)

Hi! I am excited to see you too! Would it be ok if I came by myself at five for a private tour? I'll need to leave around six to pick Alexander up to go to the opening with him.

November 13

I'm just back, exhausted and looking forward to seeing you tomorrow! Xoxo.

November 12

Morning! How about we get together on Thursday at 8:30pm? Friday I can't, I am with kiddo. Besides, I want to see you as soon as possible. Plane taking off ... must go.

November 5

Hi from Beijing! It is sunset here, but not terribly romantic, unlike the Peak, with you. Hope you had a great weekend.

October 29

It was delightful to be with you last night! I will miss you while I'm in Tianjin, but I will be in work-hard mode then. Let's play when I come back on Thursday 8. E

October 26

Hi! I had a great time last night. I'm looking forward to seeing you Sunday, and I just saw that my flight lands at 7:20pm. Sorry it's a bit late! I'll call you from the airport after I land and we can sort out where to meet. Have a terrific weekend. E.

October 25

Hi! I had a fantastic time with you last night. Thank you again for a wonderful evening. By chance, will you be at the SportAsia party at 1/5 later? It would be great to see you. I will be there around 9:30pm. Can you? Elizabeth.

Beside my vivid memories, these short messages are for me eternal proof and evidence of what we truly felt for each other, of the strong emotions that we shared and that, for some reason known only to yourself, you have decided to deny and to shatter into a million fragments now.

Be assured, though, that despite my profound disappointment and the strong regrets about your unbending stance and about being in this inexplicable situation, the intense feelings I have for you remain and I will never have any resentment against you.

Take care,

Hector"

Writing this last e-mail was exceedingly painful, as going through each text message, I could feel again as objectively as I could that we were indeed on the same sentimental journey until the end—and that I had not fantasized all of these shared and warm emotions. These recollections flooded my heart with new suffering, as I truly liked and missed the woman who had written all of these short missives. So what had happened? Why had this cruel Mrs. Hyde suddenly appeared and bulldozed the foundations we were building? I was hurt, and hoped that by rereading her own messages she would realize how insensitive and unnecessarily hurtful she was now being toward someone whose only crime had been to fall for her, with the sole purpose of cherishing her and making her happy.

THE FOLLOWING FRIDAY, DECEMBER 28, I had an early dinner at Zuma with Laure and her English friend Neil. They often hung out together, almost acting like brother and sister—to the great displeasure of Neil, who had been seriously in love with his French companion all along. For more than a year now, he had been patiently and platonically waiting by her side until the wee hours, partying at the Kee Club, Drop, or Home Base, for her to finally succumb, one day hopefully, to his British charm. At about 10:30pm, after finishing our second round of assorted sushi and yakitori and a bottle of sake that followed some imaginative martinis, we decided to continue the evening at the Kee Club. Living nearby, Neil wanted to drop off his gym bag at his apartment before continuing this well-started evening, and I therefore let them go to his place and decided to wait for them at the club. The temperature having dropped lately, I was wearing that evening my foundational act brown leather jacket with a white shirt, a pair of dark blue jeans, and black leather ankle-boots. Arriving at Kee, I directed myself swiftly to the bar upstairs and ordered a Corona without lime.

This trendy place was almost totally empty, except for a few people ending their dinner at the restaurant opposite the bar I was now leaning on. Quite tipsy, lost in nebulous and varied thoughts, I suddenly caught sight of a tall and blonde woman who, emerging from behind one of the club's pillars, was walking around the balustrade toward the ladies' room—Elizabeth!

What a coincidence! I knew she sometimes frequented this place, having seen her there twice in the past, and that she liked the Kee's restaurant a lot. However, the last time we had met here was more than a year before, so why again tonight? Destiny had struck again, and was bringing me this golden opportunity to talk to her. She did not acknowledge me while walking past the stairs, yet from her table she could not have missed my arrival several minutes before. After a while, she came out and headed directly toward me, stunning as usual. She was wearing a light white blouse tucked into a pair of tight black jeans, and she sported a half-smile that was rather uneasily hiding her nervousness. I was myself beyond flustered at the sight of her; my head was exploding with a myriad of contradictory thoughts and ideas that banged in my skull like electrons in a particle accelerator.

The emotions I felt when seeing her again after a month of insensitive, harsh, and unfruitful virtual exchanges were so intense that I was dying to trespass the now-forbidden limits of her body. I wanted to hug her with passion, kiss her delicate lips, and smell again her exhilarating scent. She was my drug, my muse, my everything! The alcohol in my system hardly helped to calm down my fever, and I tried to keep as much composure as possible while facing this woman who, I had to admit, I masochistically adored that night, despite all the sufferings she had inflicted on me with her cruel behavior. Elizabeth spoke first, her voice clear yet slightly unsteady, "Hi, Hector, how nice to see you."

"Hi, Elizabeth, what a coincidence," I answered, agitated. "You know, I am not stalking you. It is a very big surprise to see you here. I am waiting for some friends and ..."

As my pause was getting a bit long, she interrupted the silence and said, "You know I just received and read your last e-mail and ..."

And ... I should have let her speak. Instead, missing her so much, suffering in my flesh so much and therefore, in total desperation and incomprehension, having so many things to clarify, so many details and explanations to glean from her, having an atomic centrifuge instead of a brain and having drunk too many chocolate martinis, sake, and Coronas, I could simply not let her speak when I know I should have. She was maybe going to mention the text messages, to talk about her unfortunate "Not even close," maybe even show me that the Elizabeth I had fallen in love with was still alive and had not been replaced by an icy monolith.

Rubbing off her tense yet kind initial smile, she looked at me like a rabbit trapped in a car's lights, eyes wide open in bewilderment, she looked at my nervous gesticulations and listened to my babbling incoherent phrases. The third world war had just been declared in my head, with nuclear missiles dropping and exploding all around. I could not stop mumbling questions, and I pleaded for Elizabeth to change her course, her mind, to give us time, to explain clearly her reasons, to stop standing her incomprehensible ground, and to open her door for reconciliation. I was mentally exhausted!

Thinking back about this tragic scene in which I showed myself totally bare, utterly vulnerable, and broken by the throes of love in front of a woman I once adored—and still did—I now believe that Elizabeth was also feverish and emotional when she walked toward me. Yet she seemed to have long before this learned to cover herself with titanium scales, to stand firm or to duck internally when an overwhelming Dust Bowl of emotions was likely to submerge her. Mesmerized by my feverish pantomime, unable to help and tell me to calm down and listen to her, she could only stand there, muted and cold, witnessing my auto-annihilation. Yet, during an inadvertent split second, the pain of seeing this once valiant knight in dire torment and wounded at heart may have touched her, unaware, behind her protective lines. She confessed, to a sharp question asked intelligibly, despite my distress, that the overflow of electric emotions I had felt during the magnetic time at the gallery was indeed shared, "Yes Hector, the strong emotions and feelings felt at the gallery were reciprocal."

Despite this unexpected overture, however, I could feel that my ongoing mumble of unintelligible thoughts was frustrating Elizabeth. Yet the confusion in which I was navigating forbade me from pausing and reacting adequately to this unexpected admission. After seeming to indicate a readiness to talk to me following the emotional crack in her cuirass—such an amazing confession after weeks of denial—she quickly huddled back into her iron shell. Maybe understanding that no clear dialogue with me was possible that night, given my state of inebriation, agitation, and confusion, she walked back to her table with an unpleasant look meaning "but what do you want after all?"

Destiny had improvised a summit meeting and my hypersensitivity had blown it big time! Yet her welcome admission was a relief, a sweet that I could savor with delectation even though, entrenched in her now trademark stiffness, it was not followed by an awaited reconciliation. Could it be possible that she had so little trust in love?

A few minutes later Elizabeth walked down the stairs, followed by an old Indian man with whom she had been having dinner. As she looked straight in front of her, her inexpressive face was uncompromisingly closed. Laure and Neil luckily appeared at that very moment, passing her walking up, right on time to collect the thousand pieces of my shattered soul, heart, and ego strewn on the floor. Once again, I had been left agonizing in the gutter of my incorrigible infatuation for this woman. Knocked out, Patrick Bateman's closure statement chillingly emerged in my mind: "But even after admitting this, there is no catharsis, my punishment continues to elude me and I gain no deeper knowledge about myself. No new knowledge can be extracted from my telling. This confession has meant nothing."

YEAR ZERO

Existence can be rearranged. A man can be many things.
I am special and free.
And the world is round round round.

Tom Robbins, *Jitterbug Perfume*

Waking up in the New Year was like having a hangover and not knowing when I would recover from it. The calendar change did not succeed in magically repelling the thoughts that had been torturing me up to New Year's Eve, and the wishes made the previous night under the mistletoe did not seem to work either. I was still clearly obsessed with the need to find rational answers and reasons for the situation in which I was trapped. Being confronted by an unequivocally closed iron gate in the face of my pleas frustrated me greatly. Yet I also had an ultimate fight ahead of me, against the Grim Reaper. I was not going to let these tormenting thoughts lower my guard and weaken me. I could not stop thinking of our silly situation, and somehow I did not want to. Therefore, continuously looking for answers among people I knew and new people I met, I was also physically and mentally preparing myself for the ultimate showdown with the alien, scheduled for January 22 at 3pm.

I had kept this secret for a long time, but now, so close to the date, I had the need to share my experience, my story, and the changes I was experiencing. This need to frantically talk about the tumor so close to the ominous day of my surgery, after a full news blackout on the subject, was definitely a cathartic way to reassure me—to feel that the lonesome cowboy was not alone this time—in my potential last duel with fate. The sudden need to inform the whole world about my situation gave me the impression of gathering an army against which the neoplasm would tremble and find no alternative but to capitulate and run away as far and as fast as it could. It was my life, my battle, but this time I needed all the external resources I could get on my side, as I would have no second chance.

Like Sylvester Stallone in *Rocky*, I spent the following twenty-one days sharpening myself; I followed an intense training regimen with kickboxing world champion James K. and literally put myself into the mind and body of a martial arts fighter. James was merciless with me and took his role very seriously, as he sympathetically understood right away what was at stake. I would therefore start each day, before going to the gallery, with ninety minutes of stretching, cardio exercises, and weightlifting, to get quickly into optimum physical condition. In the afternoon, at 5:30pm sharp, I would bandage my fists, don my yellow gloves, and perfect and drill the techniques of hit and dodge. While sparring, James would push me to the limits by throwing combinations of punches and kicks. I therefore soon became physically sharper and mentally stronger, in the optimum spirit to confront my destiny.

Imagining the battle, like a tai chi shadow fighter would do, was crucial because, in reality, the tumor was obviously out of my reach and Doctor Liu was the one to soon face my enemy with his surgical instruments, not me. Yet this was the preservation of my future we were talking about, and I needed thus to be totally part of this fight, in my own dimension. Imagining this coming collaborative fight, the two of us strategically and symbolically circled the alien and gave it no option but surrender. This allowed me to feel fully responsible for the hoped-for positive outcome, although I still constantly remembered that the odds were favoring the tumor against me on the betting board of life.

THROUGHOUT THE COUNTDOWN OF these critical weeks, aside from toughening myself up, I had the increasing balancing urge to be surrounded by feminine presences, to soothe the overall atmosphere of violence of the upcoming battle. I also had the growing need to feel seductive, emotionally diverted, and positively fulfilled—to dive back into erotic exchanges after having been clubbed and left agonizing in the cloudy underbrush by the *Artemis of Oklahoma*.

Feeling alive in the arms of women I could count on, and letting myself dive into a world of sensuality and desire—far away from the deception, pain, and hardship I had faced lately—

seemed crucial to lead me back into sanity. During this pivotal period, aside from the time I was spending with Sophie, I had renewed more constant contacts with two former conquests, Kirsten and Isabella.

I had met the charming athletic and brunette Australian criminal lawyer Kirsten almost four years before, during the exhibition opening of Fabien Verschaere at my gallery, and had maintained a casual relationship since then; we saw each other regularly for concerts, plays, or lengthy dinners—usually followed by some carnal indulgences at her apartment overlooking the beach in Repulse Bay. Meeting too early in my Hong Kong endeavors for me to be ready to get into a steady relationship—and feeling anyhow, despite our mental and physical connections, that we were probably not fully compatible—caused us to opt, from the beginning, for a sporadic relationship, without pressure or commitments that suited both of us perfectly.

It had been a week before spring the year before when I had seen the blonde Isabella for the first time, during the after party of a Gucci fashion show at the Convention Centre. She was married to the secretly gay Asia-Pacific CEO of a European bank, and was what she herself called with a mix of resignation and sorrow a *trophy wife*; alluring, smart, well-mannered, and entertaining, she was the perfect asset for her ambitious husband in climbing the financial establishment's ladder. Yet, after fifteen years of this game, her heartfelt altruism had finally reached the far limits of the self-denial of which she was capable. One year before she had finally proclaimed her own right to independence, yet by some sense of duty and because her husband was after all a fatherly figure whom she did not want to lose, they continued to live together and to put on the public face they had been presenting since they had met at Oxford University long before. As Lermontov wrote, "She respects him as a father! And she will cheat on him like a husband!"

My rituals with Isabella were slightly different from those

with Kirsten. On any given Saturday or Sunday, I would either pick her up somewhere in Central before noon, or she would playfully bring me some croissants and hot chocolate at my place in the morning. Later we would drive to some discreet restaurant on the Southside beaches or to Sai Kung for lengthy and bracing brunches. We reveled in each other's company and in our passionate debates before going back to my apartment to cook inventive dinners as a prelude to some more desirable and soothing desserts.

I obviously did not have any physical interactions with these diligent and mischievous women during the period when I was dating Elizabeth, and had only recontacted them after Christmas, when I was craving some affection and care. They enthusiastically obliged without asking questions, even though I knew they sensed that something solemn had veiled the soul of their lover. The renewed presence of these sensual friends, as well as the daily strengthening exercises, was making me feel both mentally and physically strong.

WHEN MY PARENTS ARRIVED on January 18, four days before my appointment with destiny on the operating table, they could hardly believe I was actually potentially living my last days on Earth. I welcomed them at the airport, fit and smiling, touched and blessed to have their vigilant presence during this most crucial episode of my adult life. As usual, my father was holding back tears of emotion, and I could feel how confused my mother was; I witnessed for the first time this independent woman literally falling apart, as she almost collapsed when I kissed and hugged her at the arrival hall. The journey to the city in my cabriolet was bathed by a halo of benevolence. Answering at length their thoughtfully inquisitive questions, I tried not to be any more alarming than absolutely necessary, keeping my head as high as I could. Not faking my defiance toward the tumor—because my spirits were genuinely high—I did not want my parents to fall into an overly compassionate mode that could topple my confidence. Nevertheless, having them beside me and feeling their love and concern were extremely valuable, as the lonesome cowboy imagery had evolved and developed into the one of a boxer surrounded by his team, ready for the fight of his life!

MESSAGES OF SUPPORT COMING from friends in Hong Kong and abroad were also of considerable comfort to me, but one person was missing on that list. No matter what, maybe naively and foolishly, I still felt the need to reach out one more time to Elizabeth. Having her support ahead of the surgery was important for me. I therefore sent her an e-mail one day before the operation date, on January 21:

"Dear Elizabeth,

I have finally woken up from the delirium I brought both of us into, and I would like to apologize for it. I now see things more clearly and I understand that you did not "cut me off" but, instead, needed to "get out of it." I still have immense regrets, but this time for having "screwed up" our expectations and the time we spent together. I really feel foolish to have acted as I did, unable to control my exultation, putting so much pressure on myself and then on you. So again, please accept my apologies. Then forgive me also for sharing only now my "secret" with you—I never mentioned it to you before this, because I did not want to pressure you further or to cloud the time we spent together. Later on, I did not want it to generate a "pity factor." As these days I have the need to talk openly about it to my friends— and to the whole world—and as I believe that concealing it then markedly influenced the way I behaved with you as it ran all along, parallel, in the shadow of the time we spent together, I

181

really need to disclose it also to you—to put the record straight, and to have total peace of mind before a related surgery takes place tomorrow.

I was diagnosed in September with a tumor in my middle ear. The cyst spread so fast that it now threatens to attack my facial nerves and my brain. I therefore have to undergo surgery to try to sanitize and cure the infected area and thus, hopefully, avoid any dramatic or irreversible damage. Tomorrow is the day.

I honestly do not know where I stand now with you Elizabeth ... if I am just a total abstraction from the past, or if I belong anywhere in the present, but to know that some of your supportive thoughts will be with me tomorrow would definitely contribute to cheering me up.

Life is indeed complicated. ... Bummer!

Hector"

I received her answer that same day:

"Dear Hector,

I'm so sorry you have to go through this! This is indeed a big surprise. It sounds scary. I am sure you are in the best of hands and that the outcome will bring a big relief, to have the tumor taken out and yourself taken care of.

I will check with Werner K. about the surgery tomorrow to hear how you are doing, and I'll be sending good thoughts your way. Get well soon!

Elizabeth"

I was once again disappointed by her continuing insensitivity. Yet, in my emotional blindness, I gave her the benefit of the doubt in thinking that she might not have perceived the lethal nature of the tumor or the fatal consequences if the surgeon failed. I did not want in my message to mention my potential end, so as not to sound dreadfully fatalistic or doomed, and yet to contact Werner K. instead of writing or calling me represented once again an incomprehensibly cold and soulless act.

HOWEVER, FOR THE TIME being I put all of my disappointments and regrets aside and enjoyed a last supper before the operation with my parents at my favorite Italian restaurant, Domani, outside Pacific Place. The atmosphere at this dinner was surprisingly lighthearted, as I guess we all needed to let the pressure off a bit. In an ironic twist, probably premeditated by my parents to create some diversion and in an attempt maybe to curse the darkness somewhat, they brought up the subject of their will. It was a heartfelt move from them, almost, in a way, an invitation to the Grim Reaper to spare their son and take them instead. I was extremely touched by this symbolic act, but I nevertheless asked them to postpone this conversation until my fate was clear. I then realized that in my excessive optimism, I had not, myself, thought of putting down any instructions regarding my belongings (including my art collection), my bank accounts, or the way to deal with my gallery and the art stock.

They then asked me how the crazy story I had mentioned before was evolving. I told them that the situation was blocked and blurred. I explained my frustration over the fact that it was already difficult enough to develop a relationship when there were real problems or serious issues between the protagonists, but when the reasons for a breakup might be, instead, that emotions were too strong, then it was discouragingly silly! Yet I will always believe that the apparition of love in a relationship should be the beginning of a magnificent realm, rather than its end. Fighting for this transcendent dimension is the most noble of all causes.

Domani's cutting-edge interpretation of classic Italian dishes was delicious and provided a great boost to this lovely evening. I thought then that there were definitely too many good things on Earth that I still wanted to experience to allow myself to depart too early. Anthony S., one of the best jockeys racing in Hong Kong, appeared with his new girlfriend and sat at a table beside ours. Being a client of mine and an enthusiastic collector of Yoshitaka Amano and Troels Wörsel, he greeted us. Feeling compassionately sorry, his facial expression changed when I told him about the following day's surgery and then introduced him to my parents. Sincerely concerned, he said that he would pray for me. It was genuinely touching to sense these sincere emotions.

At about 11:30pm we left Domani, and our taxi dropped us at the bottom of D'Aguilar Street a few minutes later. From there I accompanied my parents through the steep Lan Kwai Fong to the LKF Hotel, where they would be staying until January 25. This slow walk was refreshing, and even though we did not speak much, I still felt their love and concern all over me.

Kissing each other goodnight in the lobby of the hotel, we decided to meet there again the next morning and take a taxi together to the hospital on the Peak. Walking back on Wyndham Street toward my apartment, not really tired, I suddenly stopped in the middle of the walkway and felt overwhelmed by a flow of uncertain emotions. It was not hysteria, not a breakdown, but a puzzlingly powerful flow of energy, almost like the Holy Spirit, passing through my entire body. Shivering and yet not quite knowing if this sensation was a sign of despondency or, instead, a reaction of defiance or encouragement, I did not feel like going back home right away, to think seriously again, and at length, about the operation. I therefore decided to stay in the open for a while, and entered the almost deserted Goccia bar.

I sat on a high orange stool near the bay window and ordered a carrot juice with ginger, while looking at the few smiling and laughing night revelers passing by. I pulled my mobile phone out of my back pocket and switched it back on, as I had disconnected it while dining with my parents. Five voicemails and eight text messages had been left since the beginning of the evening—all from different friends showing their heartfelt support for the next day's ordeal. These signs of caring touched me and I lost myself in abstract and nebulous thoughts while looking out at the dark and cold night enveloping the city.

AFTER A SURPRISING SERENE sleep and a slow stretching session at the gym with James—relaxing my body and lightening up my spirit to feel fully ready for the upcoming battle—I met my parents at their hotel and we took a taxi to the Peak. The surgery was going to take place at 3pm, but we had to be at the Matilda Hospital by noon. Their emotions were once again palpable and their pale and tired faces were indicative of the distress they couldn't hide, and of how short their night must have been. The lighthearted spirit we had shared the evening before was now gone, and the leaden silence reigning during the eleven-minute ride in the cab would have made even Pol Pot uncomfortable. I did not let this gloomy cloud affect my own mood, which was, maybe by pure protective denial, stronger and more positive than it had been for a very long while. Nothing could prevent me from going into the pit, twisting the neck of this scummy tumor, and then waking up victorious, after the surgery, holding my trophy high for everyone to see.

I was feeling a healthy aggressiveness mounting and spreading through my veins, in a rush of awakening adrenaline. I guess it was also understandable to be in such a hyped-up mood, as after all I had trained, motivated, and conditioned myself since the beginning of the year to be in this optimum shape for D-Day. It was an ultimate duel I had to win, and the first requirement for success in this, as in any serious endeavor, was to have an uncompromising will and a titanium spirit.

As good Swiss, we arrived at the Matilda Hospital promptly at 11:59am and Doctor Liu warmly welcomed us on the front steps and led us into his office to discuss in detail the modalities and the different procedures that he and I would have to follow in the operating room. In sharp contrast with his Hutchison House practice, which was filled with colorful designer furniture and pseudo-artworks, the room here was unusually cold and cramped, and painted in a pristine and almost blinding white. The only noticeable decorative item among the aluminum furniture was a small painting, probably made in Shenzhen, of Van Gogh's self-portrait with bandaged ear. What an ironic provocation!

My parents were asking Doctor Liu a few questions about the risks involved in such an operation when a nurse knocked on the door and asked the doctor for permission to take me to my room to change, make the required preparations, and meet the anesthesiologist. The doctor seemed supremely confident and reassured my parents about his mastery of such an operation, despite being open and honest about the risks involved when working on someone's head.

At 2:45pm, two male nurses entered my room and with care directed me through a long and dark corridor leading to the operating theatre, followed by my parents. It is during this short walk that I realized, mortified, and disappointed, that during this ultimate and ferocious fight for my life, I would be wearing an unflattering turquoise hospital gown, instead of a shining metal armor! Bravely mustering up as much assurance as possible, my parents held my hands, kissed me, and wished me a successful operation. I smiled with confidence. Yet, facing this ineluctable reality, I started to feel butterflies in my stomach and I closed my eyes.

When I reopened them, I was already laying on the operating

room table with Doctor Liu by my side. Despite his mask, I could guess a soft smile behind it, and his dark piercing eyes, through his glasses, were full of reassurance and confidence. I smiled back to my teammate, nodded, and told him that I was fully ready to rumble and was looking forward to finally getting on with it! He explained swiftly, yet in detail, again, how he was going to proceed through an incision in the back of my right ear right up to the skull and showed me one-by-one the instruments he was soon going to poke in my head. He then gave some instructions in Cantonese to the green-gowned staff surrounding my bed and without further ado—and after being asked to take a few deep breaths by the anesthesiologist—the intravenous serum mixing with my blood soon induced me into a profound sleep. I just had time to hear the bell ringing the first round!

I emerged from my lethargy several hours later, mumbling words in a language I could not identify. As soon as the nurse guarding the recovery room heard my incoherent jeremiad, she put the tabloid she was reading aside and came to my bed to calm me down and to accompany and assist my reawakening. Soon after that, I was transported back to my room and I noticed then, through the wide window overlooking some faraway twinkling islands, that it was already dawn outside. Still in a mental mist and unaware of the pink bandages wrapping my head, I was just conscious for long enough before succumbing again to Morpheus to be greeted with love by my parents, who had returned to the hospital one hour earlier.

THE FOLLOWING MORNING, SURROUNDED by my parents and Doctor Liu, I felt well. Despite some pain and itching in my skull and the inside of my right ear, I was not drowsy; my mind was clear, and my battling energy was back—it had apparently prevailed throughout the entire operation. The doctor was satisfied by the surgery and, almost cocky, he reckoned that his part of the fight actually had gone more smoothly than he had anticipated, as he had succeeded in reaching all of the infected areas with ease, as if the tumor had actually somehow capitulated, resigned to losing its battle, and had surrendered to his instruments. I was not surprised, as I honestly believed that, unconsciously, I had directed all of my combativeness to the lair of the alien and, with the help of the surgeon, forced it to abandon the strongholds of my skull and to accept defeat.

My parents were relieved. Tears fell from their eyes as they thanked Doctor Liu and embraced and kissed me at length. I was myself ecstatic; a smile lit up my face, so wide that it hurt my healing head. I stretched my arms and, pointing my fists to the ceiling and beyond in victory; I shouted, "Yes!" I felt light and euphoric after so much suffering and doubt; an enormous weight had been lifted off my chest.

Doctor Liu did not want to spoil our celebration but he had to insist, gravely now, that I had to rest and stay under close observation for several days, as, despite the success of the operation, there was still a high risk of post-surgery complications, potentially involving brain swelling or facial paralysis, both with dire consequences. After these warnings, he smiled, greeted my parents, and, again, congratulated me. Shaking my hand before leaving the room, he asked me to make an appointment for the following week at his practice. Holding his hand warmly in mine, I sincerely thanked him for having saved, so far, my precious life. I told him that I would never forget the spiritual teamwork of the day before, as what he had done was not just a job, but was allowing me to continue building my dreams, and for that I would always be his debtor.

Once he humbly disappeared behind the door, a nurse gave me a bag containing some art and lifestyle magazines and a DVD box with a selection of movies that Su-yeon had brought to the hospital the previous evening. I was extremely touched by these thoughtful presents, and the small handwritten note she had left with them made me smile.

Three days after the operation, as I was preparing to leave the hospital as planned, the same nurse arrived to explain how to take care of my bandaged head. It was then that I learned that I would have to wear these colored bands for more than a month.

The healing and the surgery aftershock went well and without complications. Even though I would have to be on close watch for most of the year, I could finally start to savor uncompromisingly, and with a new zest, this second chance.

TWO WEEKS LATER, AFTER early toasts of fresh watermelon juices on the terrace of Sevva with Laure   I had stopped drinking alcohol for a while before and after the operation—followed by some spicy Chinese dishes at the Yellow Door Kitchen on Cochrane Street, we went for some late night Shirley Temples and Virgin Coladas at the Kee Club. The air was still cold, and I was wearing my black cashmere coat and sporting a dark blue Detroit Tigers baseball cap on top of my pink medical turban.

I was in great shape, displaying a super strong survivor spirit; I was ready to save the world ... and myself! The conversation with Laure was light, yet interesting, as usual, when she suddenly announced, timidly, that she had finally succumbed to more than a year of discreet yet persistent courting from Neil, her English sailboat salesman friend. She had been scouting for the right man for a long time and had not realized until just recently that her soul mate had actually been beside her all along. Sitting opposite the bar, by the balustrade overlooking the stairs, while celebrating this exciting news, my attention was suddenly caught by a blonde woman in a black top walking up the stairs. Her silhouette and gait were familiar. She turned around at the top of the steps and walked in my direction, stopping in front of me. Elizabeth! I was taken off guard and, despite the fighting spirit I was in, the emotional whirl that this woman had the power to provoke instantly destabilized me. She was Artemis, my Achilles heel; I was her chronic Actaeon! Feeling a violent rage, equally mixed with strong masochistic and repressed feelings of infatuation, I smiled and, as I stood up, suddenly remembered the pink bandages covering my head. Sporting a seemingly embarrassed smile, she greeted me, "Hi, Hector, it is very nice to see you."

"Hi Elizabeth ..."

Nodding toward Laure, who was looking at her with a disdainful and killer gaze, she continued, "I do not want to disturb you ..."

"No, you know you never do ..."

Trying to relax her smile, she then asked, "How are you doing? How are you feeling after the surgery?"

"I am very well actually." I pointed to my head. "I won this deadly battle, you know. Surviving the tumor changed the way I look at life now." I was holding my fist close to my chest to look as convincing and strong as an emotionally shattered man could be.

"It gave you a new perspective on life I guess." she added.

"Right ..." I replied, without enthusiasm.

There was apparently not much else we were ready to share that evening. She walked away slowly, with a resigned face, around the balustrade and toward the stairs, and I resumed my seat in front of Laure. Walking down the steps, Elizabeth turned toward me for a fleeting last glance; I continued with my conversation without acknowledging this uninterpretable sign, as there was obviously nothing more I could do. Having not shown any sincere sign of compassion and, according to Laure, who knew too well what I had gone through and what Elizabeth had meant to me, "having greeted me as if I were only an acquaintance she barely knew," she slid further into her inexplicable and now legendary indifference.

AT THE BEGINNING OF June, while installing the exhibition of the French artist Pascal Lièvre at the gallery—giant canvas reinterpreting with glitter paint iconic works by abstract artists such as James Motherwell, Franz Kline or Joan Mitchell—I received a call from Werner K., who had been at the Hong Kong Club the evening before when Devorah, Lazlo, and Elizabeth had sat at his table for a casual chat. Apparently in need of confiding in him, she briefly opened up to my fellow countryman, "You know, Werner, I reacted with Hector the way I did because when we started seeing each other I was under extreme pressure from Robert (her ex-husband). He was planning to relocate with his new wife to Bangkok and he wanted to take Alexander with him. I had to fight to keep my son beside me and could not handle at that same time all of these tensions, in addition to a new relationship."

Even though I had not known the full details of the mental suffering and legal battles she was going through to retain joint custody of her son, I had perceived all along—thanks to Devorah's hint—that her torments had indeed been one of the main reasons for her unequivocal attitude toward me. Yet I felt upset, as her clarifications did not explain the harsh and insensitive reactions or her incapacity to reach out, until now. I also did not understand why she felt the need to express this to Werner K. then, especially without accompanying this brief confession with a message for me. However, foolishly and genuinely caring about her and her son's well-being, I enquired, "But where is she, then, in her legal battle to keep Alexander?"

With his characteristic Swiss-German accent, Werner K. gave me the little information he had, "I am not sure, but I think she is still in the middle of the procedure. She looked quite sad and desperate at the Hong Kong Club, as she still doesn't know if she will be able to keep her son or if Robert will take him to Thailand. She fears that she may lose him, as Robert remarried with a Thai maid one year ago and already has another child with her."

Feeling angry about this late admittance, and incapable of understanding the motivation behind her pseudoconfession, yet unable to avoid feelings of compassion for a woman I had felt strongly for, and about whom I still thought, I contacted my lawyer, Jerry P., to get a recommendation for the best family law attorneys in Hong Kong. He gave me the name of two female lawyers with the highest reputations and I passed them to Werner K., asking him to discretely transmit these contacts to Elizabeth without of course mentioning who was behind the gesture. Talking to my friend, I realized suddenly a new paradox about my feelings for Elizabeth. Loving this woman had not been a choice; it simply had been. Yet I couldn't say that I had not loved her freely.

FOR A WHILE AFTER this conversation with Werner K. I had the relieved impression that the specter of this crazy story had finally disappeared—time, as usual, gently erasing sorrow and grief—yet in August an unexpected resurgent flow of memories leading to a renewed need to understand manifested itself strongly.

To my astonishment, I started again to almost daily dwell frantically upon such remembrances, before going to bed, and I was soon suffering from short and agitated nights. I had thought I had seen the last of this unfortunate and intense story, but I then realized that it had actually covertly darkened and weighed down my spirits all along, while my attention was focused elsewhere. One of the most unfortunate consequences of this reminiscence was its effect on my relationships with Sophie, Isabella, and Kirsten. Earlier that year, and until recently, I had been a bulimic of carnal love and I had so much affection to give and receive that my gang of hedonistic women were feeling fulfilled, having my full attention and ardor when we were together. Now a profound wave of melancholy was emerging, coming from the innermost depths of my mind. My loyal mistresses began to feel that I was being distant, cold, and unmotivated in our usually fun, playful, and bracing physical mingling.

My affliction was also affecting them. When asked about this sudden lack of involvement, I was unable to answer, as I did not then understand myself how severe the damage inside me really was, or why I was suddenly stricken again by the Elizabeth fever.

Apart from spotting her silhouette walking through the Hong Kong Art Fair with Alexander in the middle of May—her beauty and my frustrated infatuation and desire to hold her in my arms hit me right in the guts then—I had not formally seen Elizabeth since the post-operation encounter at the Kee Club more than six months before. Yet this ephemeral vision, despite what had happened between us, was a painful reminder of my ongoing attraction to this woman and my ban from her life. Trying to brush away the clouds of hyper-emotion that this surprise resurgence brought back, I realized that I was still frustrated by the impossibility of having any direct dialogue with (or any true explanation) from Elizabeth. My Cartesian mind prevented me from understanding why such a woman had reacted so incoherently and disconcertingly, and this was what I worried myself sick about, as her attitude was so foreign to me, so far from my perception of reality. I therefore decided to send her a letter by post, to free my heart from this heavy weight, in a desperate attempt to bring this crazy story into a realm to which I could relate—and hopefully finally initiate closure:

"Dear Elizabeth,

You may be quite surprised to receive a letter from me after all of these months and you can well imagine that it is not an obvious thing to write for me. Indeed, you worked so much to blur your image that I do not honestly know who you are anymore or what

I think of you (as the episodic recollections of us bring a mix of equally strong emotions).

But don't worry, as I am not writing this as a plea for anything. I am actually writing this letter more for myself than for any other reason, I suppose, as I obviously do not know what you are now feeling or thinking. The purpose of this missive is the need to bring, at last, our common episode into a rational place, to restore its link with reality and with who we really are.

I should obviously not even dare writing to you, as there is technically no existing space for it—or for any further communication between us, for that matter—as you closed any possible ways. Yet rules exist to be bent, and I therefore break them here, shamelessly and with courage—as it takes courage to make a fool of oneself—because I cannot accept the role in which I have been cornered. I therefore need to bring as much sense of reality back into, and to free myself from, a situation to which I do not relate. I actually secretly wish you would tell the same to yourself.

What happened is part of us, and I will never deny what I felt for you when you came to the gallery. This was beyond words. I can also now look back at the total distress that followed without trying to close my eyes on it. This is part of me, of us. You understand that freeing myself does not mean that I am trying to forget anything. It would actually be impossible, as your name regularly reappears, sometime in the most unexpected ways. The last time was actually one month ago; I was taking some rest in Bali and had brought a few books with me. Among them was one that my sister gave me—Jane Austen's *Pride and Prejudice*. I have absolutely no idea why she chose and offered me this book. Nevertheless, I started reading it and then, after few pages, a smile shone on my face; on page six, the second of Mrs. Bennet's daughters was formally introduced—Elizabeth ...

One of my mottos is to go through life with a certain ethic; hence this letter. The only element I try to somehow rewrite here is the epilogue, bringing our common episode, and us, into rationality. Writing this letter is therefore an important step—the only one I can take, actually, as blind and as totally alone in this endeavor as I am, I have not much leeway—toward saving it from its current Kafkaesque dimension and toward symbolically restoring some soul and sense of reality to our common record.

I wish you well and so I take my leave.

Hector"

What an incredible and ironic surprise it had indeed been when I discovered Elizabeth's name in Jane Austen's book while spending one of my regular long weekends with Kirsten in her contemporary eco-house situated on the crest of a narrow hill, near Ubud. These soothing times together were fulfilling, with my favorite criminal lawyer exciting herself by continually feeling frisky in the most unlikely locations throughout the island—or surprising me by spreading out naked on the side of the pool over the rice paddies, a few times even playfully sprinkling her bare body with sushi.

After witnessing a vibrant and blinding sunset overlooking the hills, I was reading Austen's novel by the poolside when suddenly my heart stopped and I almost choked, sipping a chilly Bintang beer. I like it when Destiny manifests such irony, and I turned to Kirsten beside me, smiled, and mentioned this totally improbable coincidence to her. She was surprised as well, yet much less amused than me, I must say, by that other woman's symbolic incursion into our holiday, but she obviously fully understood the incredible unlikelihood of this name's retro-reference and she gave me a sweet kiss to brush away any potential malaise.

Needless to say, I sadly did not receive any answer, comment, or complaint from Elizabeth following my last missive.

Within our context, *Pride and Prejudice* actually contained many ironic elements. Besides the name similarity, the attraction felt by Elizabeth Bennet and Mister Darcy was also paved with actions leading to misunderstandings and confusions, impromptu encounters, and attempts by the main male character to please and reach out to give their future relationship a chance, whatever the difficulties. And, as Darcy confessed, I also, "Had never been so bewitched by any woman as I have been by Elizabeth and I am not ashamed to have felt in love with Elizabeth Bennet."

Maybe this novel also held clues to my obsessive questioning. Elizabeth Bennet from Oklahoma was actually the fictional character Elizabeth Bennet from Longbourn, intelligent, attractive, and witty, but also prone to judge too quickly and be a little selective of the pieces of evidences upon which she based her judgments (perhaps as a form of self-protection). I also recognized her pragmatic Midwestern spirit in the shadow of the admittance of this nineteenth-century English heroine, "There is a stubbornness about me that never can bear to be frightened at the will of others." Yet, in Austen's book, Elizabeth eventually overcame the differences, doubts, and issues that separated her from Darcy and they ended up together.

THE REGULAR CHECKUPS AT Doctor Liu's practice fortunately did not show any complications, and the autumn months went smoothly, with an almost sold-out exhibition of Yoshitaka Amano's Deva Loka anime paintings series that depict imaginary mythological creatures battling in a Buddhist-referenced equivalent of the original chaos. Unsurprisingly, these huge, colorful, and glossy pieces on aluminum met a strong and positive response from collectors and art critics alike.

During that time, a Japanese collector had also agreed to sell a lovely cubist Harlequin by Picasso to my Swiss client, and I also found her an exceptional four-color Rothko that consolidated and moved further forward her broadened Camouflage collection. Several other modern art deals to different overseas collectors, including the sale of an exquisite Matisse—a charming erotic Odalisque—and a small, typical, yet rare Mondrian, helped make that year a milestone in the life of my gallery. The extreme conditions I had gone through when establishing this art dealing and artist-representation business in this cultural desert of a city four years before had finally paid off. I could now contemplate having again a comfortable and luxurious standard of living—at pre-Hong Kong levels—and I moved to a new apartment with a large terrace overlooking Victoria Harbor.

THE AUGUST LETTER HAD a cathartic effect and served somehow as a kind of closure for me—even though Elizabeth's permanently locked iron gate was still objectively highly disturbing. I was therefore savoring my success during an economic transition year that was already starting to confirm my concerns, openly expressed almost a year before during Elizabeth's speech at the American Club, about a coming profound recession. Yet I could look through the eye of this upcoming cyclone with defiance, and I was looking forward to laying down the strategy to get through this worldwide economic commotion as well as possible, and even stronger, in fact—much stronger! I had also begun once again to look for the right woman for me, and I was excited in anticipation of someone new entering my life. Epicurus said that love—like art, I would add—is a natural but unnecessary pleasure. We indeed do not fundamentally need love (or art) to live; we can eat and breathe without it. Yet I believe that once we are stricken by this uplifting and ravaging feeling, our perception of reality changes and we enter a wonderful, almost mystical new world full of magnified colors and feelings, worth every effort taken to reach it.

AT THE BEGINNING OF the second week of November, Sharada, an Indian economist working for my former company, invited me and four other people to dinner on the Saturday of the following week, at her place. I did not know her from my past life as a banker, as she was not working for my firm yet when I left, but my friend On-Sang C., with whom she occasionally played tennis at the Ladies Recreation Club, had introduced us. She therefore sent an invitation by e-mail to me, On-Sang C., Kumar N., Courtney R., and ... Elizabeth! Destiny had struck again in the most improbable way! Hong Kong is a small place, but reducing the seven million inhabitants down to six, and then to two, is a bit hard to swallow—and hard to take as a pure coincidence!

Sharada had never mentioned Elizabeth's name before, and she did not know that she was the woman hiding behind my Artemis, as I had mentioned my *crazy story* to her before but without naming anyone specifically. Given the naïve and unsuspecting nature of this Indian friend, she had never connected the anyway vague dots. Yet having Elizabeth's name unexpectedly pop up on the screen of my computer took me aback totally, jolted me, and provoked such a tsunami of exultation that it surprised and puzzled me. I sometimes still thought of her but, resigned, as there was nothing I could do further about this frustrating and revolting status quo, I had been looking in other directions, and my fire for her had been dormant since August.

My first reaction after receiving the virtual missive was to explain to Sharada the irony of her short guest list and to understandably suggest that I did not join the dinner, as Elizabeth might feel uncomfortable in my presence. I must also say that I furthermore did not know in advance how I would behave. Our hostess told me, though, that Elizabeth could not come, as she had already planned a long weekend with Alexander and the case was therefore closed. I could, however, not possibly let such a coincidence vanish without jumping at the opportunity. The e-mail had woken dormant emotions within me, and having a new potential link was undreamed-of. I therefore had to take full advantage of this twist of fate.

Interestingly, time and the excitement that I was suddenly experiencing had lifted a veil from my eyes and I could now understand that someone can act irrationally when pressured by extreme circumstances; this was an enormous acknowledgement, as all along, throughout my first lengthy e-mails and even in my last letter, I was trying to bring Elizabeth back into rationality, when I was actually, myself, acting fairly irrationally!

My mind also suddenly became clear on an issue that was certainly part of her unequivocal reaction. Mentioning during our romantic cruise on the harbor that I had a secret might have actually planted the poisonous seeds of her self-withdrawal. Elizabeth would likely have gone through tense and traumatic times in the last years of her marriage, during her divorce, and now with the legal fight to keep her son beside her. Developing a relationship at that time with someone holding a secret might have seemed just too complicated and too risky, when what she was actually seeking was peace of mind, relief, and a stable man she could rely on and who would embrace her as well as Alexander. Genuinely falling for me, yet being unable to make me disclose what I was withholding from her, probably brought so many speculations and doubts into her mind that she could not bear not to know the truth. The stakes of stepping into another complicated and traumatic story were simply too high. Understanding this brought some relief, as—if this was true— what she had felt for me was actually as strong as what I had felt for her. However, Elizabeth was a Midwestern divorcee, the mother of a young boy, and she simply did not have the luxury to throw her whole life out for love. Her personal situation forced her to hold on to the pragmatism and hardness of her roots, as she not only had to take care of herself, but also of Alexander.

Yet a halo of sadness quickly surrounded my being, as I

realized that I simply had no choice. Explaining to her from the beginning my preoccupying state of heath would have surely prevented Elizabeth from giving herself emotionally to me. Yet telling her nothing and perhaps dying in January would obviously have been abominably cruel. Mentioning that I had a secret, without disclosing it, forced her to increasingly wonder what was lying behind this man, making her suffer, even as her feelings for me were increasing. The alien had been defeated in my head, yet it could claim one victory; it had been instrumental in the sabotage of my relationship with Elizabeth.

These thoughts were like a thunderbolt, shining clarity on the obsessive darkness of my questionings. Yet, despite these acknowledgements, the current stance of my ex-naiad was still a total enigma to me, as I could not objectively understand her refusal to leave a door ajar for me, maybe for later. However, the dinner invitation was such a coincidence that I had to embrace the opportunity to reach out again, as I realized that despite all the anger, suffering, confusion, distress, and revolt, the negative and mean-spirited emotions I had once felt had evaporated. My consuming infatuation for this difficult woman had masochistically persisted throughout this ordeal, similar to the Stockholm syndrome, and I felt the need to proclaim it to her.

Therefore, during an intense lunch with Sharada at the China Tea Club on Friday a few days later, I asked her—almost in a trance, so electrified was I to see this new light timidly flashing in the thick mist of this *crazy story*—to talk to Elizabeth, to help bring forward my plea for reconciliation. I had gladly learned a few months back that she had won her legal battle and succeeded in retaining joint custody of Alexander. As my own struggle with death had ended in a victory and our separate sources of intense stress and pressure were by then well behind us, I hoped that we could finally forgive all of these unnecessary harms and perhaps find mutual redemption.

Love is too valuable, within my conception of life, to neglect any chance to live an amazing and fulfilling story, as this ravaging and uplifting feeling is the only salvation from our human and terrestrial condition. I therefore would never miss an opportunity to live such a marvelous *loventure*, just because of some misunderstanding, temporary lack of responsiveness, or cultural or background differences. I am not a stalker, but I will always reach out as much as possible when opportunities arise as I would rather look foolishly insistent or just plain naïve and silly, than regret all my life that I had not expressed fully and sincerely what I felt. Tumors kill; passionate blindness does not.

Sharada seemed to take seriously her mission to plead my case to the ex-empress of my trussed heart. She was the only known chance I had to try this one last time to provoke, in Elizabeth's soul, the long-awaited flicker of resurrection.

They met at Elizabeth's apartment the following day, and I waited the entire weekend for her feedback and hopefully a positive answer.

ON SUNDAY, IN THE early evening, having just come back from a day sailing off Sai Kung with Sophie and a few Australian and Italian friends, not having received the awaited call from Sharada, I phoned her. Embarrassed, she told me that Elizabeth had refused to receive any overtures from me. As I was not willing to go into detail over the phone—still disliking this means of communication—I invited her for lunch the following day, to learn more about what had been discussed. I was, of course, utterly disappointed, yet Elizabeth's reaction was to be realistically expected; though I had myself kept the door open all along, it would have required a miracle to breech the hardened titanium gates behind which she had been hiding for a year now. My excitement therefore abated quite quickly, as behind the self-hype, I probably did not have too many rosy illusions about the outcome of the talk between my Artemis and Sharada. Yet I had needed to try my fate one more time, because I totally refused to end this story like a bad movie.

Monday's lunch with Sharada at Spices in Repulse Bay did not bring too much clarification. The insight I could glean, though, while wondering about the tone and real content of their conversation, was that I was roughly right about the overwhelming state of mind that had inhabited Elizabeth when we started seeing each other while she was at that same time fighting for the custody of her son. The combined stress and pressure were too intense for her and she had to run away from one of the sources of too many emotions. She also said that my lack of responsiveness (especially toward Alexander, I guessed) had hurt her. She had not succeeded in talking about it with me and therefore had to run away, given her state of high emotional vulnerability. Understanding all the reasons she was giving to justify her quick, sharp, and definite decision, I could still not comprehend their inability to be remedied and my irrevocable *ad eternam* ban and total disqualification from her life.

Sharada then disclosed a compelling new element that shed light on this last shadow. Elizabeth seemed to have convinced herself that what she had felt for me was unimportant after all and that it was therefore fine to treat me as a pawn and a pariah. She essentially said that of course she had emotions for me, but these were part of what one normally feels when dating. Nothing more. Nothing less. She seemed to have persuaded herself that our story was indeed insignificant, because of the short timeframe within which it took place—even though time is obviously of no importance when it comes to passion and love—and to the high emotional states we both were in at that time that blurred our senses of reality. She also blamed me for idealizing her into a woman that she was not. I then guessed that my visible lack of readiness to understand who she truly was had made me, therefore, more of a romantic lunatic than someone with whom she could fall in love. In considering me out of touch with reality, in characterizing me as someone living in a fantasy world, she was actually discrediting everything she could have ever felt for me. Such a conclusion allowed her to absolve herself of any unpleasant feelings she might have had about her unequivocal and irremediable reactions.

What saddened me the most in Sharada's account was the realization of the mental and emotional efforts that Elizabeth had forced herself into for the past year; when a wound is open, by self-preservation, one is tempted by denial. When I was, on my side, trying by all means to keep a salutary link between us, she was instead—through a desensitization process—working hard to find justifications for accepting her own actions and burying our story for good.

A few days later, following the one-way deaf letter tradition established the year before, I sent Elizabeth a final missive:

"Dear Elizabeth,

I would like to thank you for having been willing to see my emissary, Sharada, last Saturday. Even though the outcome of your talk was obviously not what I was hoping for, I totally understand that, after more than a year, you did not want to go back there and that you had already moved on (which obviously seems much more difficult for me to do).

As I mentioned once long ago, I have immense regrets that it did not work out between us, since it started so well. I also have immense regrets about the way I acted and melodramatically reacted, as if I were lost, in your presence and while thinking of you, in an emotional black hole into which I was freefalling and yet from which I could not extirpate myself (the tumor is an obvious—easy—explanation but I really still wonder what took place and how I lost myself that much and so deeply). The fact that this happened with you makes this acknowledgement and my questioning all the more painful. There are obviously a lot more things in my mind that I wish I could share with you, but instead, to stop here is, I guess, one step toward the needed and compulsory moving on, whatever the frustration I feel at it. So, Elizabeth, as my heart has no more anger but contains only devastating and intense emotions that I cannot share anymore, I would like to sincerely wish you a fantastic future.

Hector"

One week later, without answer from Elizabeth, as expected, I felt that I had written the letter too quickly and had the impression that I should have taken more time and composed it differently. I had no illusion though that another version would have succeeded any better in finally cracking her concrete heart. I would have however found it wiser to say, instead:

In my last missive Eliza

I invited you to return

To a land where our combats

Haunted us with dire concerns.

Shining in my healing heart, Eliza

I propose you now an adventure

To a new Kingdom called Futura

Bathed in peace and loving azure

I should have opened the prospect of a *now*, of a *today*, or even of a future, instead of trying to revive our suffering past. Ignoring all the unnecessary harm done, and starting again from where we had stopped, was not well thought out, as none of us really wanted to go back in time through this painful journey. Yet a *today* in which she had proudly emerged victorious from her struggle to retain joint custody of Alexander and where I myself had exultantly survived my duel with death indeed potentially existed. The causes of our irrationality and unresponsiveness being behind us, I would have liked it if Elizabeth had the courage and courtesy to finally reach out to me, as I still believed in our capacity for common resilience. Overcoming adversity often becomes the strong foundation of the most wonderful of relationships. As a true Romanesque, I love beautiful stories, and our life is a true and amazing tale that we are tirelessly writing and editing with passion and hope. Alas, Elizabeth opted to unconditionally split with my sense of reality and to remain in her silence, eventually dehumanizing herself to truly become the eponymous character from Jane Austen's 1813 novel and from the one I was soon to write.

DURING THESE LAST WEEKS, my eyes had opened, and a heavy weight had been lifted from my heart. I had spent the past year with a mix of burning rage and passion consuming my soul—all of which was making the anticipation of potentially bumping into Elizabeth around town intensely painful, as I was like a volcano ready to erupt. I would have hated to lose control again in front of her, as I had too many emotional conflicts banging within my being. Yet, lately, this pressure had evaporated. No longer in need of having direct answers to the fundamental questions surrounding the breakup and the way she behaved afterward, I had accepted, at last and to a certain extent, the irrationality in my own reality. Only the myriad of positive emotions and the masochistic Pavlovian attraction I felt for this woman remained in my soul. "The heart has its reasons which reason knows nothing of," as Blaise Pascal said.

I finally felt at peace, for the first time in a year. This recovered serenity, without the loss of my natural intensity, reassured me tremendously, and yet I felt by instinct that I still needed to work on my resilience. This story, intimately relating love and death, was too traumatic and revolting, and had affected me too deeply, to just file it away.

The idea of writing a book about a drama—without making it into a drama—eventually imposed itself. Boris Cyrulnik said, "Writing the tragedy that I underwent, I transform my sufferings into a beautiful thing. In making you smile, I take control over my own suffering and I transform my destiny into a story. Here we are. It happened to me. I have been wounded. But I do not want to continue my life with it; to be subject to my past." Sigmund Freud also wrote, "Smiling in the middle of tears allows keeping grief at a distance. It is the painful and sharp memory of the trauma, its representation that becomes less painful when the novel, the art, works to build a new sense of self." And Nietzsche concluded, "One must still have chaos in oneself, to give birth to a dancing star."

When the idea of writing a book became a certainty, I naturally understood the pertinence and the power of these concepts. I needed to express the unspeakable through a novel, to finally extract this trauma from my core being. I thus decided to use this hapless sentimental experience as a base for a novel, instead of keeping it rotting in me as a reality imposed by someone else, and in which I did not recognize myself.

Even though Elizabeth left in me a salient wound colliding with persistent strong feelings, this intense and unfortunate experience is part of my life and it contributed to testing and further shaping the man I am today. Instead of nurturing this trauma in my depths, of letting it remain a shapeless abstraction, I decided to transpose and transform it into a universal object—a book—to share this sentimental journey in the open, with you and with many others as witnesses. This novel is therefore an ultimate act of catharsis, an ultimate act of survival to enable me to recover myself fully, to re-enter the world, after having been expelled from my humanity.

EPILOGUE

Do you ever think of us, Kate?
About what might have happened?

Nicholas Cage to Tea Leoni in *The Family Man*

On Friday, December 19, almost two years to the day after I started writing my book, I received a call from my friend Mary Edith R., who was passing by Tokyo and wanted to see me for a drink. Many things had happened since I wrote the last letter to Elizabeth, among which was my relocation to Japan. I did not leave Hong Kong entirely, as I still had a gallery in the city, but I opened a branch in Tokyo and had moved there six months before. I was also contemplating the idea of opening another space in Los Angeles fairly soon. I was feeling the need to reconnect with the West after so many years in Asia. Driven by a regenerating energy and a sense of urgency triggered by surviving death and coming out of Elizabeth's story a new and stronger man, I became more focused and dedicated. It took me two years to truly assimilate the fundamental teachings and understandings brought about by the tumor. In that time an urge and a thirst to maximize my potential appeared and matured, and the world I was living in lost most of its time and place constrains. I felt I could do anything, anywhere, anytime. During these past two years I therefore had brought my art dealing and gallery projects to previously unknown heights and had decided to expand regionally first, then intercontinentally. I finished writing my novel just before moving to Tokyo, and I therefore felt a strong and fulfilling sense of accomplishment.

Mary Edith was a friend I had known for about three years now, having met her when she was working in Hong Kong for a local publishing house. She had moved back to New York recently and was now the managing editor of the Sebrof Literary Review magazine. Because she was a friend and one of the few professionals working in the book industry who I knew, I had sent her some time before the unedited version of my manuscript. She was therefore thrilled when I told her that I had found a publisher and that my novel was currently being edited. Mary Edith took the opportunity of traveling to Tokyo to meet the Japanese writer Haruki Murakami for a cover story to see me as well and talk about my book with the idea of reviewing it, once published. I suggested meeting her at 5pm at the 1970s-style cocktail lounge Montoak, on Omotesando Dori.

THE WEATHER HAD CHANGED dramatically since the early morning, and a dark and gloomy veil had now clouded the Nippon sky and was steadily enveloping the city, confirming the risk of unseasonal tropical rain coming later in the day. It was already raining gently when I stepped out of my gallery in Jingumae, fourteen minutes before our appointment, and I took an umbrella with me. There was a massive demonstration on Meiji Dori, with people of all ages asking for radical changes in the gerontocracy governing them following the mishandling of the nuclear disaster of Fukushima. Led by influential intellectuals and inspired by the Arab Spring, the Japanese took the opportunity of the dramatic consequences of the Tohoku earthquake to finally try to get rid of a morally corrupt and objectively incompetent politician caste. In a nationwide movement of resilience after the traumas of Nagasaki and Hiroshima and the defeat of WWII, the Japanese had brought their country, as the phoenix, from ashes to economic glory. It even was, for a time, the second largest economy in the world. Yet for the past twenty years or so, this dynamic had worn down. Since then Japan had been drifting away in its own dull ocean while the rest of Asia, galvanized by a roaring China, was becoming the new economic powerhouse of the world. The leaders of the demonstration were hoping that the traumatic chain reaction earthquake-tsunami-nuclear disaster would provoke a new sense of common resilience that would save their country from self-suffocation and bring it back to life and to the world one more time.

This part of the city was therefore almost totally overrun with determined demonstrators. After waiting unsuccessfully six minutes for a taxi on Killer Dori, I finally decided that the best option was to walk through the maze of three-story design houses and fashion boutiques, as the rain was more a light liquid mist than the presaged tempest. I was also, after all, only eight minutes away from Montoak. The light dripping stopped just as I was crossing Omotesando Dori. Arriving by the large glass-window entrance of the bar, I saw twenty meters away, at the level of the ice-cream store Baskin-Robbins, Mary Edith coming toward me. We smiled at each other, kissed, and entered the bar together.

Built in a multilevel glass cube, Montoak looked quite bright from the outside. Yet, because of retro black furniture, dim lighting, and the tense weather and early nightfall this time of the year in Tokyo, the place was actually quite dark. We followed a server dressed in a brown tunic up the stairs to the mezzanine floor. The only other people there seemed to be two young fashionistas in their twenties watching attentively a loud disco-beat stage performance by local electropunk goddesses Trippple Nippples on a giant plasma screen. As we needed a quiet spot to talk, we sat in a corner slightly disconnected from the rest of the upper floor, yet near the staircase, overlooking the entrance.

Mary Edith ordered Jasmine tea and I a Campari Tonic. After catching up for a while, as we had not seen each other for a long time, she brought up the topic of my book, "I have to tell you first of all, Hector, that I really enjoyed reading your novel."

"Thank you. I am very happy to hear that."

"Yes. Your novel is genuine and universal. I actually read it twice, as the first time I was a bit shaken at the end."

"Shaken? Why?" I was actually glad to have provoked such a strong reaction and, thus, interested to know more.

"Well," she continued, "the intensity of your feelings for Elizabeth, the emotions you succeeded in transcribing regarding the doubts and questioning your tumor was bringing, falling in love with her, and your experience as a hurt man after the breakup, brought back personal reminiscences. Your story really moved me."

I did not want to be indiscrete and inquire about her own sentimental experiences. I therefore asked some more questions about the content of the novel, "What do you think of the pertinence of the background analysis of Elizabeth, compared to the one of Hector? Did you find their differences interesting? I mean, as an American, did it sound right?"

"Definitely. You know, I am from upstate New York. But my father comes from Beaver City, Nebraska and ..."

I interrupted her, smiling, "Really? Beaver City, huh?"

"Don't laugh please." She smiled back.

"I won't." My grin increased. "Go ahead."

"Well, what I mean is that I think you were right in your perception of people from the Great Plains. My father always had difficulty expressing his emotions with my mother, but also with me and with my sister. That's the way they are. Also, having lived many years in France and Italy, I could relate to the emotional differences between Midwestern Americans and ... how would you say it?" She paused. "Classic Europeans? In other words, I would say that Elizabeth might have been more used to cowboys like John Wayne, square and straight in their boots and mind. And Hector was more like a d'Artagnan or an Edmond Dantès coming out of one of Alexander Dumas' novels. I don't know if your courting scared her as such, but expressing your feelings as you did, trying again and again to get an explanation once she ran away, imploring her to give you a second chance and to brandish love and passion over all may have been unusual for her. I mean, not letting go and turning around for good, as she did herself, was probably surprising to her."

Agreeing with her and pleased that she had read my novel thoroughly, I asked her what her view was on the main question mark in the book.

"Frankly Hector, I think that Elizabeth was, at first,

genuinely falling for you. I think that she believed she was finally ready to start a relationship. But she obviously was not. And I don't think you actually were, either. You were weakened by the tumor playing tricks with your emotions while you were falling in love. But besides this unfortunate timing, I think that the turning point in your relationship was when you did not cross the street from your gallery to see her and her son." I was listening attentively to her pertinent observation. Mary Edith continued to develop her view, "She may not have been able to say it to you, but I think she felt betrayed then. As a mother myself, I would have felt hurt. You wrote in the book that you saw her and her son through your window. If you see, then you can be seen. She may have seen you too and taken your no-show as a stabbing in the heart. I am sorry to be so blunt."

"No, it's okay," I replied, quite impressed by her perspicacity. "I actually believe the same. I don't think that she saw me looking at her, but you are probably right. She likely saw the lights in my gallery being switched off. Maybe for a few minutes she was hoping that I would join her and Alexander. But I never came. I must say that I didn't realize, at that time and for a long time afterward, that this would have such consequences. That it may have been *the* break point in our story; the supreme pretext that Elizabeth grasped to get out of it. I admit, I was overly focused on the analysis of the conflicting emotions triggered by the tumor and by my feelings for Elizabeth. I could not have any perspective on anything. Do you know what Kierkegaard actually said about this?" I took a sip of Campari Tonic.

"No. I don't know. What did he say?"

"He believed, 'Passionate people are always absent of themselves, never present in themselves.' I was like that. I also know that I have never been openly receptive to her expectations toward her son. Yet there was nothing I could have done differently at that time either. I am still mad at myself for not having expressed my own interest and expectations toward

Alexander. But again, I was falling down in an emotional spiral from which I could not extirpate myself. It is not an excuse but a fact. So, you are right, the twenty meters of street separating us that night probably became our Rubicon. Our Berezina!"

"Uh-huh," Mary Edith's tone was sympathetic. "She likely took the decision to stop the relationship that evening, despite obviously having strong feelings for you. These overwhelming emotions probably made her feel vulnerable and scared her. So I think that she needed a pretext to escape despite what she felt for you." She paused briefly, then, smiling pertly, added, "I told you, I can relate to your story on many levels. Talking about it actually brings back intense memories, I must say. So I need now to order a stronger drink."

She ordered a Pimm's spritz and we talked for a while about my writing style and about more structural aspects of the novel. At some point during our conversation, I perceived some unusual movements behind me, coming from a hidden corner of the mezzanine. I instinctively turned around to see what was happening and caught sight of a tall blonde woman, elegantly dressed with a long gray shawl nonchalantly thrown over one shoulder. She was walking out of the darkness in my direction, heading back to the staircase. My eyes focused on this silhouette and I thought it was a mirage. Elizabeth! Unbelievable! It was Elizabeth! In Tokyo! In Montoak! What were the odds? I had not seen this woman for almost a year and there she was, by an extraordinary and astonishing coincidence. Like in Greek mythology, one of the playful Gods had once again brought us together in the most unexpected way. The surprise and split-second emotional jolt triggered an uplifting chain reaction in my entire body. Seeing her for real here, now, so close, unlocked waves of frustrated ecstasy that washed over my soul. Unbeknownst to her, this woman could boast about being the sole creature on earth to have the power to rock my balance with one single gaze! Despite years of cathartic dwelling and reasoning and writing the novel, I have to confess that the spell I had been struck with a few years previously was still tremendously real.

Yet, despite destiny drawing us together in Tokyo, Elizabeth had long ago set up her own rules toward me. There was, therefore, not much to make out of this encounter, as unbelievable and transcendent as it was. My book was the sanctuary of everything I had to tell her, and I had sent her an unedited copy a month before. Looking at her, I therefore simply held the tornado of emotions together and expressed a genuine yet controlled surprise to see her there, "Hey! Hi, Elizabeth." I then turned my attention right back to Mary Edith and continued our conversation.

As surprised as I was and looking uneasy, Elizabeth had just time to say, "Hi, Hector, it's very nice to see you," before continuing her hesitant stroll toward the stairs.

Here we were, two supposedly intelligent individuals, but in an undignified and uncomfortable predicament. Having kept my overall capacity for indignation, I was of course revolted to be forced to act that way, as this situation was appalling, yet this encounter was a perfect illustration of our past years of living through oblivion. It was the very reality that Elizabeth had decided to impose on us both, and I was not going to argue about it or try to change her position anymore, despite the enormous frustration I felt.

I had moved on and was already on another journey, yet, no matter what, I was saddened, as this situation was utterly silly. I secretly hoped that she felt that way as well, even if she needed to dig deep behind the walls of her seemingly impregnable fort, into the chasm of her soul, for that. Mary Edith felt how shaken and confused I was by this apparition. Unintentionally bursting the bubble of thoughts I had drifted into, she asked, "Hector, are you all right?"

"Sure," I smiled, "But you will never believe who that woman was."

"Who?"

Mute, I held her gaze.

"No!"

"Yes!"

"No way!" She turned around to see if Elizabeth was still on the stairs.

"Yes. It was her. It was Elizabeth!"

"You are kidding me!" She was almost shouting. "This is crazy! This is unbelievable! Are you serious?! Did you know she was in Tokyo?"

"Absolutely not. I have no idea what she is doing here. I have had no direct contact with her for two years and we have seen each other only a few times, during some events in Hong Kong."

The intrusion of this fictional character into our reality surprised and puzzled Mary Edith as much as the unlikelihood of the situation. "This is absolutely unreal. We were just talking about her. How do you feel about that?"

"Frankly, I am now living most of the time out of Hong Kong, and she cut and run more than two years ago without allowing me to have any contact. So, I can't miss her, as we have two totally different lives now. Yet each time I see her or we bump into each other, the instant seismic emotions I feel are as intense as they were the first time! I can't deny it. I admit that I am totally transcended each time I see her. What can I say? It's like that. I know it sounds crazy, but that's what I explained in the novel when I talked about the metaphysical attraction."

"I can definitely feel how emotional you are about her. I feel your intensity now. It actually puts your book further into perspective, I must say. Maybe after tonight she will actually contact you. Don't you think?"

"I really doubt it. She didn't react to the manuscript I sent her a while ago, and I would think that its content is denser than what just happened."

"Did you actually hope that she would comment on your novel? And maybe even reach out?"

"Sure. Of course, I hoped that she would read it. On the other hand, she may think it is a vindictive book with the sole purpose of hurting her, which is obviously not the case."

"No, it's definitely not."

"My book is actually a hymn. It is a celebration of love and life. And resilience is obviously the opposite of vengeance."

Eleven minutes after destiny struck and after having given a few more details about some of the multiple aspects of the book to Mary Edith, we left Montoak. Outside, the sky had opted for a dark gray mantle and it was clear that it was looking for an excuse to burst into thick tears soon, maybe stunned and revolted by the pitiful moment that had just taken place in the bar. Surprisingly, Elizabeth was still there, outside, in the queue waiting for a taxi on Omotesando Dori, a few meters from us— looking just as tense as the weather. I kissed Mary Edith goodbye, while she affectionately pressed my arm. I wished her a fantastic upcoming Christmas with her family, and she slid away toward the compact crowd of demonstrators still congesting Meiji Dori.

Feeling in my flesh the high tension in the air, I opened my umbrella by protective intuition and had started walking in the opposite direction, toward Aoyama Dori, when, in a loud and violent cry, the sky ripped open and ejected a cascade of thick rain at once. Although I felt unconcerned and unfazed by the vocal complaints and cursing coming from the people waiting for their taxis, pounded, and soaked by the cloudburst, I recognized among them the chant of Artemis, under her waterfall.

The Actaeon that I once was smiled at the biased playfulness that destiny had manifested once more in this Japanese grand finale. I then simply continued my stroll—dry, amused, yet ...

ACKNOWLEDGEMENTS

Even though a vital urge prompted me to produce my first novel, the decision to write it in English—in a foreign language to me — was an uneasy one. This difficulty, together with the attempt to analyze and understand how certain women and men react to given emotional circumstances, incited me to seek the assistance of people who gave me priceless information, advice and help. I am especially thankful for the insights and encouragements received by Michele D., Anna S., Sandy B., Susannah H., Maud P., and to Myriam P., Paul S. and Sandra J. for their hard work and for the lengthy hours spent correcting my writing, my mistakes and the numerous redundancies. I also dearly thank the editing and publishing team at Bronco Publishing for having believed in my book all along and for having showed a lot of patience and understanding in dealing with this author.

I finally would like to give all my appreciation and love to Christiane and Berthier for having given me the essence to pursue this journey through humanity and to develop a taste for intensity.